MURDER ON THE MENU

I didn't bring up my new case until we were nibbling away on the fortune cookies. But all the while I was telling my niece Ellen about Evelyn Corwin and her poor little granddaughter Catherine, I was steeling myself for her reaction.

"I don't *believe* you, Aunt Dez!" she screeched, the normal upper range of her voice extended by two octaves, at least. "You took on two murder cases before this, remember? And you came *that close* to getting yourself killed both times! Don't you ever *learn?*"

"But this isn't really a murder case," I protested. "I'm just trying to prove to my client that her granddaughter died of asthma or this congenital lung condition she had."

"Oh, sure. And the last time all you were going to do was establish the identities of the victims, remember?"

"But that just . . ."

"You almost got yourself wasted!"

"Look, Ellen, believe me, the odds are one in a million that Catherine's death will turn out to be murder."

"I'll take that bet," she retorted soberly.

And with Ellen's words came the first twinge of doubt about just what it was I was getting myself into.

MURDER CAN STUNT YOUR GROWTH

A DESIREE SHAPIRO MYSTERY

Selma Eichler

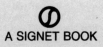

A SIGNET BOOK

SIGNET
Published by the Penguin Group
Penguin Books USA Inc., 375 Hudson Street,
New York, New York 10014, U.S.A.
Penguin Books Ltd, 27 Wrights Lane,
London W8 5TZ, England
Penguin Books Australia Ltd, Ringwood,
Victoria, Australia
Penguin Books Canada Ltd, 10 Alcorn Avenue,
Toronto, Ontario, Canada M4V 3B2
Penguin Books (N.Z.) Ltd, 182–190 Wairau Road,
Auckland 10, New Zealand

Penguin Books Ltd, Registered Offices:
Harmondsworth, Middlesex, England

First published by Signet, an imprint of Dutton Signet,
a division of Penguin Books USA Inc.

First Printing, January, 1996
10 9 8 7 6 5 4

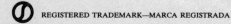 REGISTERED TRADEMARK—MARCA REGISTRADA

Printed in the United States of America

PUBLISHER'S NOTE
This is a work of fiction. Names, characters, places, and incidents either are
the product of the author's imagination or are used fictitiously, and any resemblance to actual persons, living or dead, events, or locales is entirely
coincidental.

For Anton

Acknowledgments

I couldn't have written this book without the help of Harold Eichler, M.D., and Martin Turkish, M.D., both of whom provided information essential to the development of the plot.

My thanks to Abraham Nagel of Parkside Memorial Chapel for supplying some necessary facts—and clearing up some of my misconceptions.

Others who were extremely helpful were Police Officer Merri Pearsall of the Office of the Deputy Commissioner of Public Information, NYPD; Cesar Marzan of New York City Emergency Medical Services; and the Office of the Chief Medical Examiner, New York City.

I thank Nikki and Julian Scott, who assisted in so many ways.

My thanks, too, to Ida Sitron for her special efforts.

I am grateful to my wonderful agent, Luna Carne-Ross, who does more than anyone could expect an agent to do—and then does even more than that. I am also grateful to my editor, Danielle Perez, for her help and encouragement.

And I'd be remiss if I didn't acknowledge the following for their contributions: Nancy Alloggiamento, Ilene Betman, Vivian Chasin, Claire Chiaravalloti, Joyce Gordon, Zelda Gruber, Margery Hyman, Corinne Kay, Gloria and Sid Kay, Michelle Komarek, Amanda Krigsman, Helen Krigsman, Dorothy Lam, Selma Levy, Kally Loizides, Karen Ramsey, Judy and Joseph Todaro, Dr. Marion Turkish, and Rudy Valentini.

And, finally, a thank-you as always to my husband, Lloyd, for reasons too numerous to mention.

Chapter 1

I've never really been sure what a private investigator is supposed to look like. I mean, I realize that when most people think of a P.I., they picture some seedy character in a trench coat with a cigarette dangling from his mouth. Still, even when someone comes into my office *knowing* they'll be meeting with a woman, for some reason they never expect the woman to look like me.

It might have something to do with my lack of stature, since I never made it past the five-foot two-inch mark on my mother's kitchen wall. Or maybe they're thrown by the glorious red hair (a product of Egyptian henna). Then again, it could be my weight that's getting me those open-mouthed stares. I have to admit to being just the other side of pleasingly plump (all right; *way* the other side). But what that—or any of these things—has to do with my being a bona fide, practicing member of my profession completely escapes me.

At any rate, as soon as my eleven A.M. appointment walked in that Thursday, she developed the same slack jaw I've been encountering since I first took out my investigator's license more than twenty years ago—when I was practically still teething, of course.

My elderly visitor was tiny—I doubt if she was even five feet tall—and elegantly turned out. Her salt-and-pepper hair was pulled back into a beautifully groomed chignon, and her carefully made up olive skin was almost devoid of lines. But what really struck me were her eyes; the woman had maybe the brightest blue eyes I'd ever seen. The one discordant note was that she had to rely on a cane—although a fairly decorative one—to make it the few feet from the doorway to my desk.

It was almost impossible to get a real fix on the wom-

an's age. Taking a stab at it, though, I'd have put her at
close to seventy, in spite of her youthful appearance. But
that was mostly because of the cane and the fact that
her hair had quite a bit more salt than pepper in it—
neither of which, of course, really proves a thing. Anyway, I found out later, to my complete astonishment,
that she was well over eighty.

I stood up quickly as she hooked the cane to the back
of my desk, and then I hurried over to greet her.

"Mrs. Shapiro?" she asked tentatively, looking like
she'd feel a lot more comfortable if I responded in the
negative.

"Call me Desiree," I told her, extending my hand.

If she was disappointed, I had to give the woman
credit; she hid it well. "Mrs. Corwin, Desiree; Mrs. Evelyn Corwin," she said softly, briefly grasping my outstretched hand with her own. Her icy touch jarred me.

"Let me have your coat," I offered.

As she undid the buttons of her expensive-looking
navy cashmere reefer, I saw that her fingers were
trembling badly.

I disposed of the coat on a hanger behind the door.
Then I resumed my seat as she took the chair alongside
my desk—the only other seating accommodation in the
cigar box of an office I rent from this law firm. I noted
that she was restricting herself to the very edge of the
chair, as though poised for flight.

"What was it you wanted to see me about?" I asked
gently as she sat there nervously, hands fidgeting in the
lap of her smart navy and green tweed suit. But even
after an audible intake of breath and a few flicks of the
tongue over her lower lip, the woman didn't seem able
to find the words. I waited a minute or so before quietly
prodding her again. "How can I help you, Mrs.
Corwin?"

"I ... uh ... it's about my granddaughter, who ..."
That was as much as she managed before choking up,
the bright blue eyes overflowing with tears.

Now, after so many years of dealing with the anguish
generated by philandering husbands, runaway kids, and
missing cats and dogs (and even an errant pet boa con-
strictor one Christmas Eve)—to say nothing of the grief

I'd encountered on my more recent forays into murder—
you would think I'd know how to handle that sort of
thing, wouldn't you? Well, as it happens, I don't. And
by this time I have to assume there's very little hope I
ever will. "Uh, can I get you something?" I ventured
awkwardly as my elderly visitor, tears streaming down
her cheeks, rummaged around in her handbag, finally
extracting a delicate lace handkerchief that she immediately pressed into service. "Uh, a glass of water?"

"Please," she whispered without lifting her head.

I hurried out of the office and down the hall to the
water fountain, grateful for the opportunity—however
short-lived—to leave the woman's unhappiness behind
me. When I returned, she was dabbing at her eyes. She
all but grabbed for the paper cup I handed her, quickly
disposing of its contents.

"Thank you," she said when I held out my hand again
for the empty cup. "I'm sorry. I was hoping I could get
through this without losing control, but ..." She broke
off, embarrassed.

"It's okay; please don't apologize. Just take your
time."

"I'm all right now."

"Just take your time," I repeated.

She looked at me gratefully. Then, flicking her tongue
over her lower lip again, she said softly, "Mark Valentine advised me to talk to you; he thinks you might be
able to help me."

Well, how do you like that! Valentine was an attorney
I'd done a little work for on a child-custody case years
back. I was surprised he even remembered me, much
less sent me a client. But you never know, do you? Of
course, it really wasn't that long ago that I'd been involved with those two murder cases of mine, the first of
which made all the papers here in New York. (My picture even showed up on the third page of the *Post.*)
Maybe those fifteen minutes of semi-fame were what
had brought me to mind.

"I lost my granddaughter just over a month ago," Evelyn Corwin was telling me now in this hushed, faltering
voice. "She died exactly a week before ... before her
tenth birthday."

"I'm so sorry," I murmured. I mean, what can you say in the face of a tragedy like that?

"Yes, well, I guess that ... that losing Catherine will get easier eventually. Anyhow, that's what they tell me. But the thing I can't live with is knowing that Catherine didn't just *die,* she was murdered. And I—"

"Murdered?" I blurted out before I could stop myself.

"It's true," Mrs. Corwin responded angrily. "And what's particularly terrible is that no one believes me. But while I'm still around, I'm going to prove it. To all of them!" Her mouth began to quiver, and it looked very much as if she was about to have herself another cry.

"You've talked to the police, I suppose," I put in quickly.

"And talked. And talked some more. But according to them, Catherine's death was due to respiratory failure. *Acute* respiratory failure, they said it was. She had a bad case of asthma, you see, along with a congenital lung problem that I'd never even heard of until ... until my poor Catherine had the misfortune to be born with it."

I looked at her questioningly.

"Something called alpha-1-antitrypsin deficiency."

I shook my head to convey that I'd never heard of it, either. (And if I had, I probably wouldn't have been able to say it.) "There was an autopsy?" I inquired as gently as I knew how—this is not the kind of thing you like to ask a grieving grandmother.

"The results just came in. But they messed up somewhere; they missed what *really* killed her. Listen, Desiree, it's a known fact that my granddaughter's health wasn't the best, so I doubt if they looked too hard." Then, straightening herself in her chair and locking my eyes with her own, she added in this suddenly matter-of-fact tone, "Sick people get murdered, too, you know."

She did have a point there. But then again ... I had a little trouble putting my next question to her, too, tripping over my tongue before I finally managed to get it all out. "Uh, Catherine ... she wasn't ... her condition wasn't ... her illness, that is—I gather it wasn't considered terminal?"

There was a long pause before Mrs. Corwin replied, and when she did, she seemed to be choosing her words with care. "The doctors said that Catherine's life expectancy wasn't a long one. But, of course, she might still have had *years* ahead of her. And someone robbed her of those years. Besides"—and she sounded almost belligerent now—"with all that medical science can accomplish these days, they might even have been able to cure her eventually." I didn't respond immediately, so she challenged with: "Well, you never know, do you?"

I admitted that, no, you never did. Then I said, "I assume, though, that in light of her prognosis, you have a pretty good reason for believing Catherine's death wasn't the result of her illness."

Once again Mrs. Corwin appeared to have difficulty speaking. She looked down at her hands, which for the past few minutes had been more or less stationary in her lap. I followed her gaze. She was now viciously digging the beautifully manicured nails of her right hand into the soft, tender palm of her left. "I have a very good reason," she said finally, without raising her eyes. "It was the *second* attempt on Catherine's life. She herself told me just two weeks before her death that someone had deliberately tried to run her over. I didn't believe her then, just as no one believes *me* now. What is it they say: 'What goes around comes around'? At any rate, I kept insisting to her that the car must have been out of control—after all, who could possibly want to do something like that deliberately?—but Catherine was sure the driver was aiming straight at her." Evelyn Corwin shook her head slowly from side to side. "God! If only I'd listened. If only . . ."

This thought produced a fresh supply of tears and, hard-boiled P.I. that I am, I could feel my own eyes begin to sting. I warned myself I would kill me if I didn't manage to get a grip on my emotions.

"Would you like some more water? Or how about some coffee?" I suggested, feeling totally useless.

Unable to reply, the woman rejected both offers with a wave of her hand. It must have been at least three minutes before the final trickle of tears was wiped away.

"Do you feel up to continuing?" I asked then.

"I'd better be," she answered with a game attempt at a smile.

"Good. Mrs. Corwin, can you think of any reason at all that someone might have wanted to harm your granddaughter?"

"It's completely beyond me," she admitted. Then she looked me full in the face, and her voice took on an authority that hadn't been there before. "But, the fact is, someone did harm her, didn't they?"

"And you have no idea who it was."

"None at all," she confirmed.

"And Catherine? She didn't get a look at the person who almost ran her over?"

She shook her head. "It all happened so fast."

"What can you tell me about it?"

Mrs. Corwin sat back in her chair, evidently making up her mind at last that she'd be staying awhile. "It was a Saturday morning, about eleven-thirty," she began. "Catherine and Terry—she was my granddaughter's nanny—were walking over to Central Park, which is only a few blocks from the house. They didn't get very far. As soon as they came to the corner—it happened." She shivered almost imperceptibly before going on. "Catherine had hold of Terry's hand; the light was in their favor, and they were just about to cross the street. Catherine stepped off the curb first, and suddenly this car came barreling around the corner, heading straight for her. Terry just froze. But my granddaughter saved her *own* life; she jumped back just in time." There was a momentary look of pride on Evelyn Corwin's face. Then it was gone, and the face was blank. "The car kept right on going," she finished bitterly.

"Was your granddaughter able to tell you the make of the car? Or the color?"

"I'm afraid not. Catherine doesn't—didn't—really know anything about cars. All she said was that it was a dark color—black, she thought—and that it was big. But I have no idea what she would have considered big. And I didn't bother to press her at the time because I was so sure she was mistaken—about the thing being deliberate, I mean."

"How about the nanny?"

"Terry? She wasn't able to tell us any more than Catherine did. She just kept repeating over and over that a car almost ran Catherine down, and that she—Terry, that is—didn't even react. She was very hard on herself about that."

"But Terry didn't get the idea that it was on purpose?"

"Oh, no! She thought maybe the driver was drunk or on drugs or something. It never occurred to her that it might have been anything intentional." And then, sighing: "It never occurred to any of us. Donna attributed Catherine's version of what happened to the fact that she spent so much time watching all those crime programs on television."

"Donna is ... ?"

"My daughter-in-law. Catherine's mother. Silly of me. I should have mentioned that, shouldn't I?"

"And your son—what did he think?"

"My son died of a heart attack six months ago," Mrs. Corwin answered evenly. *Well, this woman has certainly had her share!* I opened my mouth to commiserate, but before I had a chance, she murmured, "I keep wondering if things would have been different if Clark were still with us. Maybe *he* wouldn't have doubted her. Maybe he ... Oh, I don't know."

"Did anyone report the incident to the police?"

Mrs. Corwin shook her head slowly. Then, in a voice thick with regret: "I wish we had. I did consider it at the time. But there was really no harm done, you see, so I ... so *we* just decided to forget it."

"Let me ask you this. How many people were aware that Catherine would be going to the park that day?"

"Everybody who knew her well, I suppose. She and Terry always walked over to Central Park on Saturday when the weather was nice. If Catherine was feeling up to it, that is. And then they'd go and have lunch somewhere like Rumpelmayer's. Catherine *loved* Rumpelmayer's."

I smiled. What kid didn't love Rumpelmayer's? (And some of us older kids don't exactly have an aversion to those sinful ice cream concoctions of theirs, either.)

"Unfortunately," Mrs. Corwin said then, "the day

Catherine died, it was nasty out. The weather report predicted rain—incorrectly, of course—but, anyway, Donna thought it would be best if Catherine stayed at home. Particularly since she'd had a little upset stomach the night before."

"Tell me about that day. What exactly happened?"

"The housekeeper found my granddaughter dead on the library floor; *that's* what happened."

"This was two weeks after the incident with the car?"

"Exactly two weeks."

"I'd like you to fill me in on what took place before the housekeeper discovered your granddaughter's—before the housekeeper discovered your granddaughter. Whatever you can tell me."

The dark, artfully penciled eyebrows shot up, wrinkling the smooth forehead. "Let's see . . . Catherine had been in her room all morning, reading or maybe watching some television. Then, at a little after twelve, she came downstairs. Luisa—she's the housekeeper—was just about to start cleaning the library when Catherine told her she was hungry. Well, Luisa was so happy to hear it, she went right into the kitchen to prepare lunch. My granddaughter was not the world's best eater," the old woman explained with a poignant smile.

"Catherine didn't go to the kitchen with the housekeeper?"

"No. She went into the library to read."

"What happened then?"

"Well, as soon as Luisa opened up the refrigerator, she saw that, since breakfast, someone had finished up the last of the milk. So she had to run out to the store to pick up another carton. She was back in fifteen or twenty minutes, and then as soon as she had lunch on the table, she went to call Catherine into the kitchen. She found her on the library floor, and it was . . . and she was—" Mrs. Corwin stopped and took a deep breath. A moment later she resumed her narrative in a surprisingly level voice. (I noticed, though, that her nails were digging into her palm again.) "Luisa dialed 911, and the emergency people were there within minutes. But it was too late. It was probably already too late when she . . . when she found the body."

"And the police say your granddaughter died of acute respiratory failure; is that right?"

"That's what they *say*."

"Let me ask you this. Aside from that business about the car, do you have any other reason for insisting that Catherine was murdered?"

"I certainly do. For one thing, one of the chairs in the library was overturned. And a lamp was broken, too. It certainly looked as if a struggle had taken place in that room."

"What did the police have to say about that?"

"They believe that Catherine had this asthma attack, and they think the furniture must have been knocked over when she was trying to get to the telephone to summon help. There's a phone on one of the tables in the room; it has a buzzer system that connects to various parts of the house." A shake of the head. "They *believe;* they *think*," Evelyn Corwin reiterated with disgust. "Very scientific, isn't it?" She looked at me piercingly. "All right. Now, tell me. What do *you* think?"

I tried hard to be diplomatic. "Look, Mrs. Corwin," I said, "I can see why, because of that near miss with the car, you might have come to the conclusion that there was something sinister about your granddaughter's death. And I can understand your feeling guilty about having doubted her. But, honestly, from what you've told me, this whole thing was just a terrible coincidence. There's absolutely no reason to believe Catherine died of anything but her illness."

"Oh yes there is," Evelyn Corwin insisted, her small chin jutting out stubbornly, the bright blue eyes glaring at me defiantly.

"I really don't—"

"Catherine kept *saying* that someone tried to kill her, and two weeks later she was dead. I wouldn't call that a coincidence." She leaned toward me, and the words came out slowly, emphatically:

"I'd call it *murder."*

Chapter 2

I spent another five minutes or so trying to persuade Evelyn Corwin that she really had no need of my services since there was nothing to suggest that a crime had been committed. Which I thought was pretty damned noble of me, considering that business was so lousy lately I was even cutting down on my dinners out. (Not on my food, you understand; just on where it was consumed.) At any rate, my arguments got me nowhere, so in the end I finally agreed to look into things. Mostly because it seemed like the only way to convince the poor woman to put the tragedy behind her and get on with her life.

"I'd like to have a talk with the housekeeper. Suppose I come over—say tomorrow night, if that's okay," I suggested.

"Of course it's okay," Evelyn told me decisively. "You just tell me what it is you want—whatever it is—and I'll *make* it okay."

A few minutes later, I walked her to the reception area, where a tall man of about fifty wearing a chauffeur's uniform was sitting and waiting, cap in hand.

As the chauffeur rose and took her arm, my new client turned toward me. "I can't tell you how relieved I am that you've agreed to help me," she said, misty-eyed.

With that—and her obvious wealth notwithstanding—Evelyn Corwin made me feel ten times worse about taking her money. I quickly reminded myself of my loftiness of purpose.

It was my niece Ellen's day off, and I was having dinner at her place that night. I didn't have to tax my mind speculating about the type of cuisine she'd be serving; Ellen's specialty is Chinese takeout. Which is just fine with me, since I happen to love Chinese food. Besides, the only meal Ellen is able to prepare with any degree of success is breakfast. And pancakes and sausages are not always my menu of choice once the sun goes down.

But, anyway, I'd like to tell you about Ellen.

To begin with, she isn't actually *my* niece at all; I mean, she isn't my blood niece. Her mother and my late husband, Ed Shapiro, were sister and brother. Which is how come a nice (although non-practicing) Catholic lady such as myself wound up with a niece who has a mezuzah on her front door. But blood relation or not, Ellen and I are very close. She even does double duty as a sounding board, particularly when I'm working on a difficult case.

Now, people who don't know her very well might wonder about that. You see, in some ways Ellen's incredibly childlike. In fact, at times she's so naive it's almost like she's a twelve-year-old kid who sneaked into someone else's not-that-far-from-thirty-year-old body. But then at other times she can be so wise, so remarkably perceptive, that more than once—for a few minutes, anyhow—I've found myself resenting her for doing my job better than I did.

But back to that Tuesday . . .

On the way to Ellen's apartment after work, I stopped off at a Häagen-Dazs for a pint of Belgian Chocolate, her favorite flavor, and a pint of Macadamia Brittle, which could very well be my favorite thing on the entire planet. The store was a lot more crowded than an ice cream store has any right to be on an end-of-September evening that felt more like middle-of-December, plus the two kids behind the counter were unbelievably slow. And then, to make matters worse, the traffic heading downtown that evening was unusually heavy. So I got to Ellen's about a half hour late. She greeted me like I'd returned from the dead.

"Aunt Dez!"

"I'm sorry I'm late, but I—"

"I was so *worried*!" exclaimed my worry-wart niece. "What *happened* to you?"

Well, I wasn't as late as *all that.* "I'll tell you, Ellen. I got abducted by these little gray men with no ears who schlepped me aboard their spaceship to perform God-knows-what-kind-of-experiments on my person. But thanks to my strange hypnotic powers, I was able to zap them into unconsciousness and make my escape."

Ellen didn't laugh. "Think you're pretty funny, don't you?" she muttered. Then she added defensively, "There were two muggings on this street alone last week, to say nothing about what's going on all over the city. And I think if you—"

"All right, all right. I'm sorry. I didn't mean to upset you. The cab got caught in traffic. And before that I was held up at Häagen-Dazs. And I do not mean that literally," I put in quickly.

With that, Ellen giggled—as only Ellen can giggle. And I knew all was forgiven.

After a two-second discussion—we didn't even have to bother looking at the menu; it's indelibly etched in both our brains—Ellen called our order in to Mandarin Joy. I could hardly wait for her to hang up so I could ask about Mike.

And that's another thing I should probably clue you in on. . . .

Mike was the darling young doctor I'd met during the course of my last murder case. And almost from the minute I set eyes on him, I had visions of Ellen and Mike eating out of the same Chinese food cartons for the next fifty years or so.

Of course, I realized I might be in trouble with my sister-in-law Margot, Ellen's mother, for getting the two of them together if it turned out that Mike wasn't Jewish (which I later found out he wasn't). Then I figured his being a doctor would more than compensate for just about anything she didn't normally approve of. But at any rate, it wasn't easy for me to get either the prospective bride or bridegroom to take a chance on a blind date. In fact, I did everything but threaten to throw myself in front of a speeding train before they both agreed to give it a shot. And damned if they weren't practically engaged now! Well, maybe not practically *engaged,* but they'd been dating for months, and that had to mean something, didn't it?

When Ellen finally finished relaying our order and exchanging pleasantries with the old woman who always answered the phone at Mandarin Joy (after supplying my niece with so many dinners, the woman probably regarded her as a member of her own family by now), she was at last available for interrogation. I didn't lose any time in asking about her date with Mike the previous evening.

"It was great," she told me, beaming.

"Where did you go?"

"Just out for pizza. Mike had to get up early."

"Has he *said* anything yet?"

"Oh, Aunt Dez!" Ellen admonished.

And that was all I got out of her. I was prepared to be very hurt if I found out later that the answer should have been yes and that she hadn't seen fit to confide in me.

My plans for this possible future pique, however, did not spoil my appetite in the least. We had quite a feast, too: dim sum, egg roll, and spare ribs, for starters. Then a segue into a delectable shrimp dish with black bean sauce and a tasty chicken creation with honeyed walnuts. And, finally, all that Häagen Dazs—with which we gorged ourselves practically into oblivion.

I didn't bring up my new case until we were nibbling away on the fortune cookies, which, a couple of minutes earlier, I would have sworn up and down we'd never have room for. But all the while I was telling Ellen about Evelyn Corwin and her poor little Catherine, I was steeling myself for her reaction. And when I wound down, she came through with flying colors.

"I don't *believe* you, Aunt Dez!" she screeched, the normal upper range of her voice extended by two octaves, at least. "You took on two murder cases before this, remember? And you came *that close* to getting yourself killed both times! Don't you ever learn?"

"But this isn't really a murder case," I protested. "I'm just trying to prove to my client that her granddaughter died of asthma or this congenital lung condition she had, so that poor, heartbroken old lady can stop feeling so guilty about having doubted the little girl."

"Oh, sure. And the last time all you were going to do was establish the identities of the victims, remember?"

"But that just—"

"You almost got yourself wasted!" It's a real kick hearing Ellen use police terms. I mean, they sound so weird coming from her.

"Look, Ellen, believe me, the odds are one in a million that Catherine's death will turn out to be murder."

"I'll take that bet," she retorted soberly.

And with Ellen's words came the first twinge of doubt about just what it was I was getting myself into.

Chapter 3

Ellen's prediction didn't have much staying power.

By the next day I was certain once again that, although terribly sad, there was nothing criminal about little Catherine Corwin's death.

I got to my office at ten and spent most of the morning trying to decide which bills to pay and which ones could wait until next month without anything important in my life being shut down, hauled away, or canceled.

Around twelve-thirty I went out to lunch with Jackie, who is both my friend and secretary—the best secretary in New York, really—and whose invaluable services I am able to afford only because of this arrangement I have with the law firm I rent office space from—Gilbert and Sullivan, it's called (honest!).

That day the weather was so absolutely perfect— sunny and mild with just a hint of a breeze—that after we scoffed down matching greasy burgers, soggy French fries, and flat Cokes, Jackie was actually able to persuade me to put aside my natural prejudice against exercise in any form, and we went for a short walk. Evidently, just about everyone else in midtown Manhattan was also seduced by the temperature, and more than once we had to battle for sidewalk rights. It was almost two o'clock when we got back to the office, and for want of something better to do (I told you business had been slow), I spent close to an hour filing my nails, repairing my makeup, and spraying my hair. After that I managed to make enough personal phone calls and move enough papers around the desk to waste what was left of the afternoon.

On the way home from work, I stopped at the D'Agostino's near my building, where I had no trouble at all spending a nice chunk of the retainer I'd received from Evelyn Corwin the day before. When I finished loading up on juice, milk, salad fixings, chicken breasts, and lean ground round—along with such indispensable items as frozen pizza, kosher franks, Sara Lee cheesecake and, of course, Häagen-Dazs Macadamia Brittle—I headed for my apartment. I prepared a quick bite, did a little more fussing with the makeup and a lot more fussing with the hair, and then headed for Park Avenue and Sixty-eighth Street.

The door of the rather drab-looking town house was opened by a woman of medium height with curly light brown hair sprinkled here and there with a few strands of gray. She was wearing a plain tan dress, sensible brown shoes, and an expression of concern. I guessed her to be somewhere in her late forties. "Mrs. Corwin is waiting for you," she told me after I'd introduced myself. Her voice was low and pleasant, and there was a trace of a European accent I couldn't exactly pinpoint. "Please come with me," she instructed.

As the woman led the way down the wide central hall, I quickly revised my idea about the house being unimpressive. The ceilings were high enough to qualify for the term *soaring*. The wood floors were a handsome herringbone pattern and so highly polished that even in this dimly lit corridor you could almost see your reflection in them. And the corridor itself—the walls of which were liberally covered with beautifully framed artwork—seemed to go on forever. We walked past I don't know how many darkened doorways before we approached a section of the hall that was splashed with light. Here the woman stopped before an open door and, stepping aside, gestured for me to precede her into the brightly illuminated room beyond.

I found myself in what I soon learned was referred to as the sitting room, but which was about the size of a small barn. Nevertheless, it had a comfortable feel to it. The walls were a soft cream color, with one of them dominated by a fireplace in which a small fire, obviously on its last leg, was sputtering weakly. Decorating the remaining three walls was an eclectic collection of more handsomely framed paintings. The upholstered pieces, most of them Queen Anne, I think—and I wouldn't have been surprised to learn they were genuine antiques, either—were all covered in either a cream velvet or a nubby black wool. But what really caught my eye was a stunning red, black and bone Oriental rug that defined the parameters of the furniture grouping nearest the door. In fact, I was so taken with the rug that it was a moment or two before I noticed Evelyn Corwin sitting there, her back to the fire, her tiny frame dwarfed by the large black armchair in which she'd settled herself.

"Hello, Desiree. How are you tonight? Please. Take a seat wherever you like." Then as I sank—and sank—into the plush, down-filled sofa, she turned to the woman still standing only a foot or two from the threshold. "Come in, come in, Luisa," she directed, her tone managing to stay just a fraction short of testy. "You *know* Mrs. Shapiro would like to have a talk with you." And to me: "I assume Luisa's introduced herself?" There was no time to answer. "I imagine it would be best if I left you two alone," she went on, beckoning the housekeeper. Then handing her the book she'd been reading, the old woman retrieved the cane that was hanging on the back of the chair and attempted to stand. It was an obvious struggle, and Luisa took her arm to help her to her feet. "I don't know why I find this chair so hard to resist," Mrs. Corwin muttered with disgust, mostly to herself. "I can never get out of the stupid thing."

As she began making her slow, and apparently difficult, exit, she spoke to me over her shoulder. "Join me in the living room when you've finished talking with Luisa. Oh, and Luisa, see if Mrs. Shapiro would like some refreshment, will you?"

"Why don't I walk over with you first," the other woman suggested quickly.

"Don't be silly. If I can't make it as far as the living room on my own, you may as well put me in a box and nail down the lid." It was said lightly, but the housekeeper apparently felt she'd been reprimanded (which, in a way, she had), and her cheeks turned crimson.

Then Evelyn Corwin, chin held high, hobbled out, shutting the door firmly behind her.

* * *

"May I get you a cup of coffee? Or a cold drink of some kind? A glass of wine, perhaps?"

I declined with thanks, and Luisa took a seat in one of the black wool slipper chairs facing the sofa. She straightened her skirt for a moment, then looked at me expectantly.

"How long have you been with the family, Luisa?" I asked.

"Almost eleven years."

"You discovered the little girl's body, I understand."

"Yes." The word was barely audible.

"I know this must be very difficult for you, but I'd like you to tell me all about the day that Catherine died—anything you can remember, no matter how trivial. Why don't you start with when you first saw her that morning."

Deep furrows appeared between the housekeeper's eyes as she struggled now to recall the details she had no doubt been trying for weeks to forget. She spoke thoughtfully in a well-modulated, educated voice, the slight accent giving the words an agreeable lilt in spite of the unpleasantness of the topic. "Well, I prepared Catherine's breakfast around eight as I do—did—most Saturdays and Sundays," she began. "And then Mrs. Corwin—Catherine's mother, that is—joined her in the breakfast room. By that time Catherine was finishing up, so she and her mother didn't chat for very long. They just spoke about it not being a good day for Catherine to go to the park as she usually did on Saturday mornings." The narrative took a slight detour here as Luisa elaborated on this point. "Catherine's nanny was off for the weekend, you see, and Mrs. Corwin had been planning to take her herself, but, well, because the weather was a bit raw, they decided against it."

"I understand Catherine hadn't been feeling too well."

The furrows became more pronounced. "Not that I . . . Wait. She did have a slight upset stomach the night before, but it was really nothing much. Is that what you're referring to?"

"Well, her grandmother mentioned something about it. But go on. Please."

"Now, where was I?" A momentary pause. "Oh, yes. Mrs. Corwin said that since they wouldn't be going to the park, she could use the time to do some shopping, and she asked if Catherine would mind if she went out by herself for a while. And Catherine said of course not. Then Mrs. Corwin mentioned that Catherine's grandmother would be coming over some time after lunch to visit with her. Catherine was very pleased about that. She just adored her grandmother."

"That's her *other* grandmother you're talking about?"

"Other grandmother?" the housekeeper echoed, looking confused. "I didn't know Catherine *had* another grandmother. One that was still alive, I mean."

Now *I* was confused. "But you said she was *coming over* after lunch. Doesn't Mrs. Corwin—Mrs. Evelyn Corwin, I mean—live here?"

"Oh, no. She has an apartment four blocks away. She says there are enough people living in this house as it is and that at her age she needs her peace and quiet."

"I guess I jumped to the wrong conclusion." (A frequent occurrence with me and one that can be very unfortunate for a P.I. and, worse yet, after so many repetitions, one that I can only attribute to a malfunction in my brain.) "Okay, what were you going to say before I so rudely interrupted *this* time?" I asked disgustedly.

"Let me think ..." The housekeeper sat silent for a minute, pressing her lips together, her head tilted back, her eyes heavenward. It was almost as if she were expecting some divine help.

I did my best to fill in. "I believe you were saying something about Mrs. Corwin letting Catherine know her grandmother would be coming over," I prompted.

She shot me an appreciative glance. "Yes. And then Catherine told her mother she would be going up to her room to read; she was quite the little reader."

"What happened next?"

"Catherine went upstairs, and Mrs. Corwin had another cup of coffee."

"Can you tell me what time Mrs. Corwin left the house that morning?"

The reply came without hesitation. "Ten twenty-five.

I was doing the second floor at the time, and I saw her going downstairs with her coat on."

"You happened to notice the time?"

Luisa smiled. "I couldn't help noticing it. There's a big grandfather clock in the upstairs hall, and I was dusting it when Mrs. Corwin passed me."

"I guess that would do it, all right," I told her, returning the smile. "Okay, now let's get back to the kitchen. What did you do after Mrs. Corwin and Catherine finished eating?"

"I fixed breakfast for Ms. Lundquist, her son, Todd—he's twelve—and this friend of Ms. Lundquist's who—"

"Hold it a sec. Now, who is Mrs. Lundquist?"

"Catherine's half sister—Mr. Corwin's daughter by his first marriage." She seemed to be waiting for some sort of acknowledgment, so I nodded; then she went on. "Ms. Lundquist—she doesn't like to be referred to as *Mrs.*—and her friend Ms. King, who was visiting her that day, came in just a few minutes after Mrs. Corwin left the table. And Todd came in only a couple of minutes after that."

"I don't suppose you were dusting a clock then, too."

The housekeeper smiled again. "I'm afraid not. But I'd guess it was just before nine o'clock when they sat down, if that's what you want to know."

"It is. And they finished—when?"

"Todd ate in ten minutes—he shovels his food down. But I'd say Ms. Lundquist and Ms. King were at the table until close to nine-thirty."

"What did you do when they'd finished eating?"

"I spent a little while cleaning up the kitchen and the breakfast room, you know, doing the dishes and wiping the table and counters—the usual. And after that I just went about the rest of my chores." She hesitated, looking doubtful. "Do you want me to tell you just what it was that I *did*?"

"I'd appreciate it."

The shrug was almost imperceptible, but it was enough to notify me that the opinion here—although delivered very politely—was that I really didn't know what I was doing. And, to tell the truth, I didn't. Murder cases (even when they're not actually murder cases, as in this instance) aren't exactly my field of expertise. But there's one thing I do know. It's something I learned the hard way, and it applies to every kind of investigation there is: The most important questions always turn out to be the ones you didn't ask.

"Well, all right," Luisa was saying—and without even making it sound too grudging. "The first thing I did when I was finished in the kitchen was throw a load of towels in the machine. The woman who comes in four days a week to do the wash and all of the heavy work was home sick most of that week, you see. Then as soon as I was through in the laundry, I went upstairs and straightened up a bit on the second floor."

"You were in Catherine's room?"

"Yes, of course."

"And she seemed all right then?"

"She was *perfectly* all right," the housekeeper replied tersely, not quite able to conceal her irritation at what she thought the question was implying.

"The upset stomach was gone?" I persisted.

"It was. She wasn't even feeling that bad the night before. Just a little queasy, that's all. Believe me, if there had been anything wrong, I would have telephoned the doctor immediately." Her mouth was set in a straight, hard line.

"I'm sure you would have," I said in the most placating voice I could dredge up. "I'm just trying to get everything clear in my mind, that's all." This seemed to mollify her somewhat. I forged ahead. "What was Catherine doing when you went in there?"

"She was lying across the bed, reading."

"Did you talk to her?"

"I just asked how she was, and she told me, 'Fine.' That was the extent of it."

"What did you do next?"

"When the upstairs was at least presentable, I went into the laundry room again to throw the things into the dryer. And after that I dusted and vacuumed the sitting room—this room." She gestured with a quick semicircular motion. "And then I cleaned the small powder room, and when I was finished in there, I went and got the towels out of the dryer and folded them."

At this point Luisa lowered her eyes and began nervously plucking at her skirt, so I knew that her recollections were becoming increasingly upsetting to her. Then, looking up and swallowing hard, she said, "Catherine came back downstairs just as I was carrying my cleaning supplies into the library; she met me at the library door, in fact. She usually has her lunch at one, but she told me she was hungry, and, well, I was so glad to hear it, I dropped everything and ran into the kitchen to fix something for her." The woman paused now in an apparent effort to collect herself, and I saw that her eyes had misted over. "The poor thing didn't do much more than pick at her breakfast that morning, you see. The truth is, her appetite was just terrible since the day she was almost hit by that car. You know about that, I suppose?" And when I nodded, she added softly, "Not that Catherine was ever much of an eater, God rest her soul."

"What time would you say it was when she came down for lunch?"

"I'm afraid I can't tell you exactly, but I think it must have been about twelve-fifteen, because I'd checked the clock only a short while earlier—right before I took the things out of the dryer—and it was just past twelve then."

"When you went to the kitchen, Catherine went into the library?"

"Yes, that's right. She said she thought maybe she'd read for a while, and I told her I'd let her know as soon as lunch was ready."

"And then ... ?"

"I was really hoping she'd be able to eat a decent meal that day. So I started heating up some soup, and I made her a good-sized ham sandwich with lettuce and tomatoes and that Miracle Whip dressing she used to want on everything. Then I put the potato salad out on the table and went to pour her a glass of milk. But there was nothing in the carton. Well, it had been at least half full when I finished serving breakfast, so I knew Todd must have gotten thirsty again before he went upstairs and polished it off." I noted that the housekeeper's voice had hardened almost imperceptibly with her mention of the boy's name.

"What makes you think it was Todd who finished the milk?"

"Every once in a while he goes in and helps himself to two or three glasses of milk like that—I think he spills more than he drinks, actually; Todd isn't the most careful boy you've ever seen." She scowled for the merest fraction of a second. "He used to drink right out of the carton, too, until his grandfather—Catherine's father—caught him at it and put a stop to it. I suspect he still does it, though, when nobody's around. But, anyway, he has this habit of putting empty containers and bottles and things back in the refrigerator."

"You don't care much for Todd, do you?"

"That's not true," Luisa denied, flushing. "He's a nice boy, really. All boys that age are a bit of a handful, you know; you can't really expect anything else." A pause. "Actually, I'm quite fond of Todd."

Sure you are, I stopped myself from responding. "So you had to go out then and get some milk," I said instead.

"That's right."

"How far away is the store?"

"There's a place about two blocks from here."

"Did you see Catherine again before you went out?"

"No, but I know she was still alive when I left."

"How can you be so positive?"

"I left by the front door so I could tell her I was going to the store and that I'd be back in a little while. I hollered out to her, but I was in such a hurry that I can't be sure whether she answered me or not; I didn't want to find out. But, the thing is, a few seconds earlier when I was coming down the hall—before I even *got* to the library—I heard her laughing. Must have been something funny in that book she was reading." After a moment, the housekeeper added sadly, "That little girl had the most delicious sense of humor, and, believe me, she didn't have that much to laugh about."

"What do you mean?" I pounced. For some reason I was suddenly expecting a revelation of some kind—and don't ask me *what* kind. But, anyhow, I didn't get one.

"Well, you probably already know that she lost her father recently—they were very close. And I imagine Mrs. Corwin told you how frail Catherine was physically. That can be pretty difficult for a child to handle."

I mumbled something to the effect that I had heard about those things, and then, disappointed, I got back on track. "You're sure it was Catherine who was laughing?"

"Believe me, it was Catherine. She had this high-pitched little voice; it sounded almost like a bell when she laughed," Luisa recalled, her tone close to reverent.

"It couldn't have been the television?" I nagged. (Well, this was *important*.)

"No. It was Catherine, all right," she insisted.

"Could anyone have been in the room with her at the time?"

"Well, it's possible, I suppose," she conceded reluctantly. "But I didn't hear anyone else."

"Any idea what time it was when you went out?"

"I suppose it must have been about twelve-thirty. Certainly not much later than that."

"One more question. When you left, was the library door open or closed?"

"It was open; I just didn't look inside. But Catherine *was* alive when I went out to the store," the woman maintained almost tearfully. With that, apparently taking me at my word, she started to rise.

She found out soon enough that, for me, "one more question" is only a figure of speech. "About how long before you got home from the market?" I asked then.

"Maybe fifteen minutes or so," she said, settling back—not too happily, I suspect—in her chair again.

"Did you see Catherine when you came in?"

"No, I used the side entrance then; it's right off the kitchen."

"And you called Catherine in to lunch as soon as you returned?"

"Well, not right away. Maybe about five minutes later. Ten, at most. I had to get out of my coat first and then reheat the soup and take the things out of the refrigerator again. Oh, and there was this phone call from the plumber saying he'd stop by the next day to fix this leak we had in one of the bathroom sinks. But that only took a minute or two." Then she added somberly, "I know, though, that it was only a little after one when I telephoned emergency."

"What did you do when lunch was ready?" I asked gently.

"I walked partway down the hall and called out to Catherine. But she didn't come and she didn't answer, so I tried again. And then when there was no answer *that* time, I went to the library to get her. I was *annoyed* with that dear, sweet little girl. Can you imagine that?" The woman's voice was close to breaking, but I was spared the need to search my brain for some reassuring platitude, because she added hurriedly, "At any rate, when I opened the door, I—"

"Wait," I interrupted. "The library door was open when you left the house, wasn't it?"

She took a moment to respond. "That's right, it was," she mused. "I hadn't thought about that." And a second or two later: "I guess Catherine must have gotten up and closed it. Sometimes it gets chilly in there with the door open, because the hallway's usually pretty cold."

"That was probably it. Go on."

"Well, when I saw little Catherine facedown on the floor like that, my heart stopped. I ran over to her, and I think I said her name; I'm not really sure. But she just lay there, so still. . . . Well, then I screamed. I must have screamed my head off, too, because Todd and Ms. King—they were both upstairs in Todd's room at the time—they came racing down the stairs as if someone was chasing them with an ax. Ms. King's face was white as chalk, and even Todd looked frightened. And it takes a lot to frighten *him.*" Aware that she'd allowed her dislike of the boy to creep into her voice, the housekeeper turned a very becoming shade of pink before quickly taking up her story again. "Anyway, Ms. King rushed in and felt for a pulse. And after that she started to roll Catherine over—to check for a heartbeat, she said—and I shouted not to touch her, that I was going to call for an ambulance. And, of course, I did. They were here not much more than five minutes later." The woman closed her eyes then and sighed deeply. There was a brief, silent interval before she finished with a whispered, "But it was too late."

Now, somehow I'd gotten it into my head that only Luisa and the victim had been in the house at the time of the tragedy. Well, it looked like I'd engaged in some more conclusion-jumping. Cursing myself silently, I vowed—as I had so often vowed before—that this was positively the last time I would ever assume anything. But just as I was about to ask to see the library, I realized it had almost happened again. "Uh, was there anyone besides Ms. King and the boy in the house then?" I finally thought to ask.

"No. that's all."

"What about Ms. Lundquist? Where was she?"

"At work. She works for an advertising agency, and there are many times she has to go in for a while on Saturdays."

"And her friend remained here? With Todd?" It sounded a little strange to me, and I just wanted to make sure I'd gotten it straight.

"She was tutoring him. Ms. King used to be a teacher, and Todd is . . . well, he's bright enough, I guess, but he doesn't always apply himself. And it's beginning to show in his grades. Actually, I think she was here partially to tutor him but mainly to keep an eye on him and make sure he kept his word to his mother and really studied."

"And the other members of the household—where were they?"

"Mrs. Corwin was shopping. And Terry—she was Catherine's nanny—it was her weekend off. And, oh yes, Nicholas was chauffeuring Mrs. Corwin."

"And Nicholas is . . . ?"

"The chauffeur."

Naturally. Who else would be doing the chauffeuring?

"Also, he's my husband." It sounded almost like an afterthought.

"Just one last question. If someone had rung the doorbell that day when you were out, how likely is it that Catherine would have let him—or her—in?"

"Do you mean someone she knew?"

"I'm not sure what I mean. Let's say it was someone she didn't know."

Luisa gave it a few seconds' thought. "I can't really see her doing something like that. She was always told not to let a stranger into the house. No, I'm certain she wouldn't have opened the door to any stranger."

Not quite trusting that my "last question" *was* my last question, the housekeeper wisely did not attempt to get up this time. She was, however, still optimistic enough to edge forward in her chair a couple of inches.

"Luisa, can you think of any reason at all why someone would want to murder that little girl?" I proceeded to ask.

"Of course not!" Her eyes opened wide, and she seemed to physically recoil from the very thought. "I know that's what Mrs. Corwin—the older Mrs. Corwin—suspects, but Catherine was the sweetest, the *dearest* . . . Only a monster—a *maniac*—would have wanted to harm that child!"

Only a maniac . . . Could that be what we were dealing with here?

No, forget it, I immediately told myself. What we were dealing with in this case was an old woman's mistaken conviction that had grown out of a coincidence and been nourished by her feelings of grief and guilt. And right now Luisa was going to help me further that conclusion. "I understand Catherine used to watch a lot of television," I said.

"That's right."

"And you mentioned earlier that she was an avid reader."

"That's true enough. With her health the way it was, Catherine spent a lot of her time indoors, reading and watching TV." There was a perplexed expression on the housekeeper's face.

"Just one more question. Would you say Catherine had an active imagination?"

The perplexed expression vanished. We were on the same wavelength now. "Oh, yes, very," she responded, eager to embrace what I was suggesting. (Evidently, the little girl's death had given Luisa second thoughts—at least on some level—about that almost car accident.) "She was always making up little stories—from the time she was just the tiniest thing, in fact. She'd say that someone was after her to sign a movie contract or that that teenage boy on the TV show *Blossom*—you know, his name is Joey Somebody-or-other—had just called to ask her out. Once, a day or two after her grandmother took her to the Museum of Natural History, she claimed that a dinosaur had come into her room in the middle of the night and swallowed her whole. But she made such a fuss in his stomach, she said, that he spat her right out again. It was all playacting, of course. I suppose it came from not being able to do a lot of the things other little girls her age could do. But she really did have quite an imagination. That thing about the car *aiming* at her ... well, it must be that she just got carried away, and believed one of her own stories. That's what her mother thinks. And I'm sure she's right." The housekeeper looked at me in anticipation, waiting for my next question.

This time I fooled her. "I'd appreciate it if you could take me into the library now," I said.

Evidently, the woman couldn't quite accept that we were finished in here. She waited for me to stand before making even the slightest move to get out of her chair.

Chapter 4

I stood just inside the entrance to the handsome wood-paneled room, looking around me as the agitated house-keeper related again how she'd marched impatiently to the library that day, only to discover the object of her annoyance lying motionless on the floor.

"Did you happen to see where Catherine was sitting before you went into the kitchen?" I asked.

"No, I went straight in to fix her lunch. But she always curled up on that sofa over there." She tossed her head to indicate the brown leather Chesterfield sofa that was part of a furniture grouping at the far end of the room. "And that's where they found her book, too—on the seat cushion."

"She was lying where?"

"I'll show you."

I followed as Luisa walked about thirteen feet into the room, stopping alongside the round cherry table at its center. "Right over here." The table was maybe forty inches in diameter. And on it was a modern telephone/answering machine setup. "I think that when she became ill, she tried to get to the telephone to buzz me," the housekeeper said. "I understand that's what the police think, too." Then, in a strained voice, "But she couldn't make it, poor little thing."

I bent down and examined the carpet. Nothing at all. "Would you know if Catherine bled when she fell?"

"No. I don't think so. Although she banged her head a bit, from what the family was told."

"What was the name of the book Catherine was reading? Do you remember?"

Luisa seemed surprised by the question, but she scrunched up her eyes for a moment, trying to recall the title. Then she shook her head. "I'm sorry. I can't think of it." A pause. "No, wait! It was *The Boy from Planet Pluto*. That was it. I'm sure it was."

"And she had it with her when she came into the room?"

"I'm afraid I didn't notice. She might have taken it out of the bookcase; there's plenty to choose from in here." She gestured toward the area behind me, where floor-to-ceiling bookcases covered an entire long wall. "About six shelves of children's books are in that section at the end," I was informed.

"Luisa, can you tell me if there was anything in this room that day that isn't here now?"

She glanced obediently around the room. "Well, there was a bronze lamp with a black lacquer base on this table here. It was probably knocked over when Catherine was reaching for the telephone. Anyway, it's out for repair now; they're taking forever to fix it. And there were my cleaning things, of course. But nothing else as far as I can tell."

"A chair was overturned, I understand."

"Yes, one of those by the card table."

I took note of the fact that in order to get from the sofa to the phone, it would have been necessary for Catherine to pass the card table. "Which chair was it?"

Luisa walked over to the leather-topped table and rested her arm on the back of one of the four Sheraton chairs surrounding it. "This one." The chair she indicated was parallel to the cherry table but three or four feet closer to the sofa. If Catherine had been trying desperately to reach the telephone, it's not unlikely she would have stumbled against this chair.

I couldn't think of anything more to ask, so I finally told the housekeeper what I knew she'd been longing to hear. "I guess that about does it," I said. Then I thanked her profusely and asked her to point the way to the living room.

Evelyn Corwin put down her book as soon as I walked in. "Well?" she demanded.

"Well, as of now," I told her gently, "there's still nothing to suggest that we have a murder here." Mrs. Corwin's response to this was immediately telegraphed by her eyes; they were blazing with anger. It was becoming increasingly plain that this wisp of a woman had a spine of steel. But, anyway, I really hadn't said all I'd intended saying, so I hurriedly added, "I've just begun to look into things, though. There's a lot more I want to check out."

The blaze extinguished itself, and she nodded, apparently somewhat satisfied.

"I wonder if I could see your daughter-in-law now?" I asked then, anxious to move things along.

"She isn't in. None of the family is here tonight. Donna's at a friend's house for dinner—the first time we could get her to spend an evening out since Catherine was murdered. And Barrie—my granddaughter, Barrie Lundquist—and her son, Todd, left for Vermont this afternoon. This friend of hers has a cabin there, and she invited them for the weekend."

"Would that be the same friend who was here the day your granddaughter died?"

"That's right. Saundra King, her name is."

"I'll want to talk to her, too."

"That won't be a problem. I'll get her phone number from Barrie and give you a call Monday morning."

Well, it seemed there was nothing more I could do at the house that night, so I left just minutes later. Right after Mrs. Corwin's promise to have her daughter-in-law contact me the following day.

But I don't mind telling you that I was worried. I mean, even when all the results were in, *how in God's name would I ever be able to convince this implacable lady that her little granddaughter had not been a murder victim?*

Chapter 5

On Saturday I met my friend Pat Martucci for lunch at a little Italian restaurant in the east Fifties. Pat was not feeling too chipper. She was between husbands—having already worked her way through three—and at that precise moment in time there wasn't a potential "significant other" in her sights. I tried not to let the downbeat tone of the conversation affect my appetite, but when the food came, I realized it would probably have been better if it had. Adding to our dissatisfaction with the meal was the fact that the place itself practically demanded to be closed by the Board of Health. Still, the most unfortunate thing of all about the restaurant was its proximity to Bloomingdale's.

As soon as we finished eating, we made a beeline for Lexington and 59th. Pat didn't purchase anything at all in the almost two hours we spent at the store. Which I thought showed remarkable strength of character. (When I'm depressed, I itch to buy everything in sight.) I, however, managed to make up for my friend's restraint, celebrating the slight upsurge in my business by buying an expensive pair of gold and coral earrings that didn't go with a thing I owned and a pair of Italian shoes I didn't need, couldn't afford, and that pinched my toes, besides.

When I returned to the apartment at around five, there was a message on my machine from Donna Corwin, asking me to get back to her. I returned the call as soon as I was out of my coat, hoping to set up a meeting for some time that weekend. But when I suggested it, she put me off with a vague remark about having a lot to do. Monday night would be much better for her if it was okay with me, she said. I let it go at that. Anyway, what choice did I have?

In the evening I went to a movie with Barbara Gleason, who lives in the apartment next door.

Now, I like Barbara. I really do. But there are times that I have to remind myself of that. This was one of those times.

She rang my doorbell right on schedule at ten after eight, and I was already in my coat when I answered. As soon as we were going down in the elevator, she squinted her eyes and looked at me appraisingly—all she needed was one of those jeweler's loupes—and then with one thin finger on her sunken cheek, she made a pronouncement. "You know," she said, "a dark color would be much more flattering to your figure." Apparently, this was with reference to my two-year-old beige wool coat, which, it just so happens, I am passionately fond of. Besides, I couldn't swing another coat even if I wanted one (particularly after the earrings and the Italian shoes, neither of which unnecessary purchases I had any intention of returning). I started to tell Barbara what I thought of her gratuitous opinion, but she didn't give me a chance. Stepping back in the empty car for a better view and knitting her brows together in concentration, she shared another invaluable observation. "And, too, the cut's all wrong for you; it's much too full." *This from a living fashion statement, a woman dedicated to wearing knee-high stockings—which are always peeking out from under her skirts when she sits down!* Anyway, I was once again phrasing a response when, as we exited the elevator, she added this bighearted offer: "Maybe we could go shopping next week, if you like."

I restrained myself from saying something I might later regret. "I don't need a new coat, and I don't want a new coat," I finally got out, gnashing my teeth together.

"Well, of course," she responded in this extremely chilly voice, "that's entirely up to you." And an instant later: "But if you should change your mind, well, you know where I live."

At that moment there's nothing I would have enjoyed more than pushing Barbara to the floor and then plopping myself down on her skinny bones for maybe an hour or so right there in the lobby.

I wasn't any more favorably disposed toward her after the movie, either. It was a talky black-and-white Swedish production with subtitles that she pronounced "a classic" as soon as we left the theater and which I found a pretentious bore. To tell the truth, I didn't have even the slightest clue as to what the whole thing was supposed to be about. Later, over coffee, Barbara really took pains to explain it to me. But it wasn't long before I realized—with a kind of spiteful glee—that my friend, with all her intellectual pretensions (and I do like her, honestly), didn't understand the picture any better than I did.

I spent a little time on Sunday doing a cursory job—a very cursory job—of housecleaning, then devoted myself body and soul to doing pretty much nothing at all.

At eight o'clock I turned on the TV for *Murder She Wrote,* which, by the way, I wish real life would imitate. I mean, never once, as long as I've been watching that program, has Jessica Fletcher ever accused anyone of a crime without the perp spitting out a confession right then and there. But anyway, what I started to say was that I couldn't concentrate on the show because all I could think of was Catherine Corwin's death. It was that damn conscience of mine, which I can always depend on to dump on me without the slightest provocation.

Okay. It's true I'd accepted the case knowing that the police had already investigated and ruled out foul play. I also admit that I hadn't expected to learn anything to dispute that finding (and, so far, nothing had). But, as I told you, I'd taken it on with the very best of intentions.

Yet now, tonight, that irritating little voice inside me starts in, forcing me to do some soul-searching.

Had my attempt to dissuade Mrs. Corwin from hiring me been only halfhearted? it demands to know. Had I, in fact, actually been anxious to acquire her as a client so I could pay some bills—and then fooled myself into thinking I had a more altruistic purpose?

I hoped not. But the truth was, I couldn't be sure.

I went to bed that night extremely troubled.

Things looked a little brighter in the morning, mostly because between bouts with my pillow that lasted well into the early hours, I'd managed to convince myself—correctly, I like to think—that my motive had been, at least for the most part, a compassionate one. I had honestly hoped that the results of my investigation would make it easier for Mrs. Corwin to live with the death of her granddaughter.

I grabbed a quick shower before work, and when I got out of the bathroom, my answering machine was winking at me. Barrie was back from Vermont, Evelyn Corwin informed me, so she could give me Saundra King's phone number now. She proceeded to recite it. "Oh, and I told Barrie you'd want to talk to her, too, so be sure and give her a call this morning," she instructed—just a little imperiously, I thought.

Chapter 6

I didn't get in touch with Barrie Lundquist that day. Mostly because I had the idea that Mrs. Corwin was trying to tell me how to do my job, and I'm just immature enough to want to retaliate—even if no one knows I'm doing it. But there was a call I did make just as soon as I got to the office. . . .

Tim Fielding—Sergeant Tim Fielding, that is—works homicide out of the Twelfth Precinct here in Manhattan, and he's a good friend of mine, as well as having been a buddy of my husband Ed's. (I'm not sure I mentioned this, but Ed had been a P.I., too, and before that, a member of the force.) And since I needed a favor from the police, who else would I call?

The phone was answered on the first ring. "Fielding," growled my friend.

"Shapiro," I growled back.

"You mean that little red-haired, know-it-all witch *Desiree* Shapiro?" A typical kind of greeting from him.

"Ahh. I see you still resent me for being such a superior investigator. Reminds you of how inadequate you are, doesn't it?"

"Listen, the only thing talking to you reminds me of is that I'd better check my supply of Tylenols—*extra-strength* Tylenols."

We continued in that same vein for another round or two. It's practically a ritual with us by now, a way of covering up the genuine respect and affection we actually feel for one another. Finally, I got around to saying that I had this little problem I hoped he'd be able to help me with.

Fielding was instantly wary. "What kind of a little problem?"

"Well, I've just taken on a case that might turn out to be a homici—"

"Christ! Not again!" (I guess we *had* gotten on each other's nerves a few times when I was involved in those two other homicide investigations I mentioned before. Or maybe I should say that *I* had gotten on *Tim's* nerves.)

"You can relax," I told him. "It didn't happen in your precinct."

It wasn't until he let out this long wheezing sound that I realized he'd been holding his breath. "Well, thank the Lord for small favors," he muttered rather unkindly. "Whose hair will you be getting into this time?"

"It's Manhattan Central's case, if that's what you mean," I responded haughtily. Then I sweetened my tone a bit; after all, I was trying to get him to do me a favor. "Seems the M.E. determined that death was due to acute respiratory failure, but my client is certain it's murder—although, frankly, that doesn't appear very likely at this point. Anyway, I need some information from the police, and I don't really know anyone in the precinct. No one who'd be willing to help me out, I mean."

I could actually *hear* the grin. "So you've already had a run-in with some of those guys, huh? What kind of case were you working? An old geezer misplace his false teeth or something?"

"Very funny. For your information, I never had a run-in with anyone up at Man Central." *Just a little disagreement once or twice.* "Look, I really need someone to run interference for me—you know, put in a good word with the right person. I thought maybe you might know somebody there."

"As a matter of fact, I do know a couple of guys there, but I—"

"I'd appreciate it, Tim. I really have to find out what they've got."

"Geez, Desiree, you—"

"The victim's name was Corwin, by the way, Catherine Corwin." I played my trump card. "She was ten years old."

A sharp intake of breath. "Oh, Christ!" Then: "You at the office?"

"Yes."

"I'll make a phone call and get back to you as soon as I've got anything to tell you."

"Thanks, Tim. Thanks a lot."

"Yeah." It was a growl, of course.

I thought it might be a good idea if I talked to the police before I met with any of the other members of the Corwin household. So all morning—except for a very brief and necessary trip to the ladies' room at around eleven—I baby-sat my phone. By twelve-thirty I was trying to ignore the gripes of an increasingly vocal stomach. I was still hoping to get out to lunch—it was an absolutely gorgeous day—but I didn't want to miss Fielding's call. I finally threw in the towel at one-thirty and ordered from this new continental sandwich shop across the street. I'd eat out tomorrow, I promised myself. *When it would, no doubt, be pouring.*

After consuming the last bite of my skimpy, over-priced smoked turkey and brie, I got around to typing the notes I'd taken on my meeting with the Corwin housekeeper. It was just past two when I finished, and by then I absolutely *had* to leave my post. (My mother always used to warn me not to hold it in until the last minute.) I buzzed Jackie. "I'm going to the ladies' room now," I informed her hurriedly. "If Tim Fielding should call while I'm in there, tell him I'll get right back to him."

I passed Jackie's desk when I was returning to my office not more than five minutes later. "I have a message for you," she said, waving this pink slip of paper at me.

"Fielding?" I didn't really have to ask.

"You got it. He said to tell you he couldn't wait for your call, that he was on his way out."

"Damn!"

"Hold it; don't get crazy. He left word for you to get in touch with this detective at Manhattan Central, a Sergeant Jacobowitz. Fielding said Jacobowitz was the one who handled the investigation. I guess he's talking about this new case of yours, huh?" She didn't pause for my answer. "Here," she said, thrusting the paper into my hand. It had the sergeant's name and number on it.

Jacobowitz's line was busy the first time I tried him. Then when I tried again, I was told I'd just missed him but that he was expected back shortly. I left the message that Sergeant Fielding had said for me to contact him, and I asked that he return my call as soon as possible.

When I put down the receiver, I vowed that I would not make another trip to the ladies' room until I heard from him. Not even if I exploded.

The phone rang at 5:45, just as I was about to gather up my things and, very reluctantly, call it a day.

"Desiree? This is Frank Jacobowitz," I was informed by a voice so young it immediately conjured up peach fuzz and zits. "I understand you're looking into the Corwin case."

"Yes, that's right. Thanks for getting back to me."

"That's okay. But there isn't very much I can tell you. There's absolutely nothing to indicate that anyone did that poor little Corwin kid. Nothing at all. She had this serious lung problem, and that's what killed her."

"So I understand, but—"

"Believe me, we conducted a thorough investigation."

"Oh, I believe you. It's just that Mrs. Corwin—"

"She the one who hired you?"

"That's right. Mrs. *Evelyn* Corwin. The grandmother."

"It figures. Right from the beginning she was convinced it was murder—even with no evidence at all to support that and with the little girl being so sick and everything. The captain himself went over to see that lady, you know—he's a friend of a friend or something—and it still didn't do any good."

"I'm not surprised. Listen, I don't know if it's even possible to *un*-convince her, but I'm pretty positive the end result will be that I'll have to try. In fact, I told Mrs. Corwin when I took the case that I'd most likely come to the same conclusion the police had. But I did promise to check into things for her, so I'd appreciate it if I could come by and talk to you for a little while. It won't take long, honestly. Would it be okay if I dropped over now?

I could be there in about twenty minutes." The truth was that it would very likely be closer to forty minutes before I could make it uptown at that hour. But I figured I'd stand a better chance with twenty.

"I can't do it today anymore. It's my son's birthday, and I've gotta get home."

"How's tomorrow morning?"

"I'm off tomorrow and Wednesday," Jacobowitz said apologetically.

"We could—" I began, about to suggest we meet for coffee or something the next day, but he cut me off at the pass.

"Uh, I'm afraid I won't be available at all until Thursday. Why don't you call me in the morning just to make sure I'll be around?"

"Oh, I was hoping—" I stopped myself from testing the guy's tolerance level. "Okay, I'll give you a call then," I agreed. "And thanks. Thanks a lot."

In spite of how anxious I'd been to get the official version of things (and also in spite of being the most impatient person I know), when I hung up I realized I wasn't that upset about the delay.

What was another few days? And so what if I met with the family before talking to the police?

It wasn't as though I was dealing with a real murder here, was it?

Chapter 7

Evelyn Corwin wasn't at her daughter-in-law's when I arrived for my appointment that evening. Luisa showed me into the sitting room, where I found the younger Mrs. Corwin waiting for me. Then the housekeeper promptly withdrew, leaving us alone together.

Donna Corwin was seated in the same large black armchair her mother-in-law had occupied on my previous visit here. She stood up to greet me, extending her hand.

She was about thirty-five, a tall woman, five-nine or so, and very thin—far too thin to qualify for the euphemism *slim*. She had on a simple, V-necked white cotton blouse and baggy chinos that I suspected may have been fairly form-fitting not that long ago. She wore no makeup except for the palest of lipsticks. Her large brown eyes were bloodshot and underlined by deep blue circles. And her blond hair, which was a little shorter than shoulder length, was in desperate need of a touchup. Yet, for all that, you couldn't miss her basic good looks. In fact, with those high cheekbones, full lips and large, doe-like eyes, at other times and under other circumstances, Donna Corwin was probably regarded as a beauty.

"I'm so terribly sorry about your loss," I told her.

"Thank you," she responded evenly. "Please, make yourself comfortable. Can I get you anything?"

"No, nothing, thanks," I said, sinking once again into the now familiar cream-colored sofa. As soon as the insatiable down filling was finished swallowing up the greater part of me, I started to explain just why I'd taken the case. "Your mother-in-law—"

"Yes, I know," Donna interrupted, "My mother-in-law thinks my daughter was murdered."

"You don't agree with that conclusion, I gather."

She eyed me distrustfully. "No. Do you?"

"Frankly, it doesn't appear that there was anything suspicious about your daughter's death, at least not from what I've learned so far. Of course, I've just begun looking into things."

She seemed to relax a little. "Believe me, you won't find anything to suggest murder."

"There's a very good chance you're right. But maybe it would help if I confirmed that one homicide could definitely be ruled out—help your mother-in-law, I mean."

"I doubt that. While I'm very fond of her, my mother-in-law is an incredibly stubborn woman. And she's pretty much decided that Catherine was killed by some fiend. I don't think you'll be able to disabuse her of that no matter what." I was about to say that at least I could make the attempt when she added, "But look, I could be wrong. It's just possible you *can* get her to accept the truth. I'd like to see her let herself off the hook, that's all."

"I promise you I'll do my best."

"Fair enough. All right, how can I help you?"

"I'd like you to tell me about that Saturday—the day Catherine died."

Donna spoke quickly now, plainly anxious not to linger on the subject that was so painful to her. In a low, soft voice she repeated the basic facts I was already familiar with: how, in the nanny's absence, she'd intended to take Catherine to the park that morning and how nasty weather and the little girl's upset stomach of the night before had changed their plans.

"How often did the nanny have the weekend off?" I asked her.

"Every fourth week."

"And this was her usual weekend off?"

"That's right."

"You wound up spending the day shopping, I understand."

"Yes. Part of the day, at any rate. As long as Central

Park was out, I asked Catherine if she'd mind if I did a little shopping, and she said she wouldn't mind at all. She was such a good little girl, so ..." Donna bit her lip then in an obvious effort to compose herself. She was able to continue almost at once. "Anyway, since Catherine didn't object, instead of staying home and spending some extra time with her—which, God knows, she deserved—I went off on my merry way to Bergdorf's and Bendel's and Saks. By the time I came back, it was all over. And it was too late to spend any more time with her—ever." The sigh that followed this truth was accompanied by a tremor that ran through Donna Corwin's entire body.

"Look, how could—"

She cut off the attempt at consolation. "I'm sorry. I'll try to get hold of myself."

"Would you like to take a few minutes—maybe get something to drink?"

"No, I'm okay now." Then, with forced brightness: "So where were we?"

"When you came home ..." I prompted.

"Yes. By then these detectives were busy in the library, peering and poking and I guess checking for prints and doing whatever else it is they do. And Catherine was—" Donna broke off again, and her pale skin seemed to grow paler still, but she remained dry-eyed.

"The paramedics had determined that it was a matter for the police?"

"Oh, no. That was Evelyn. She walked in right after they pronounced Catherine dead. She's the one who insisted on homicide getting involved."

"And it was what time when you got back?"

"About two-thirty. Something like that."

"Your chauffeur had driven you around to the stores?"

"Well, he drove me to Bergdorf's, but I'm not so decrepit I couldn't make it from there to Bendel's and Saks under my own steam. When Nicholas—our chauffeur—dropped me off at Bergdorf's, I asked him to pick me up at Saks at one-thirty."

"But you didn't come home until two-thirty; isn't that what you said?"

"Yes, that's right. I *expected* to be ready to leave at one-thirty. But I should have known better. Once I'm in a store, I always wind up spending more time there than I planned to. I didn't get to the restaurant at Saks—that's where I had lunch—until close to one. And by the time I finished eating . . ." She spread her hands.

"Did you happen to charge your lunch?"

"No, I . . ." The doe eyes opened wide. She stared at me in disbelief. "You don't think . . . Do I need an *alibi*?"

"No, no, of course not. I told you; I doubt very much that this was even a homicide. But I'm committed to getting all the facts, regardless of what I think personally."

"Sorry. You're right."

"Look, I'm sure that in your shoes, I'd be just as resentful, but I—"

"It's okay, really. Go on."

I tried to make my voice a little softer as I continued the questioning. "Did you happen to run into anyone you knew at the stores?"

"Not a soul."

"Think any of the salespeople might remember you?"

"I doubt it. I looked around on my own. The only thing I bought was a blouse at Bendel's, and I'd be completely shocked if I made any impression at all on the woman who wrote up the sale. She seemed to be concentrating on staying awake."

"What time did you get to Bendel's?"

"Somewhere around noon, I'd say."

"And you left when?"

"Must have been about a quarter to one."

"And then you walked over to Saks?"

"That's right. And by that time I was very hungry—also pretty tired—so I decided to forgo any more shopping that day and just go straight upstairs to the restaurant."

"You say you paid for your lunch in cash. I assume you don't have a charge at Saks?"

"Oh, I have a charge, but I wanted to change this fifty-dollar bill I've been carrying around for two days."

"Do you think your waitress might recall your being there?"

"Waiter," she corrected automatically. "My server was a waiter. And I wouldn't think so, but, of course, he might. Let me ask you something, though. Assuming that, for some reason on God's green earth, I wanted to do away with my own precious child and assuming she died between twelve-thirty and one—which it certainly appears that she did—what would have prevented me from interrupting my shopping and taking a cab home and . . . and . . . doing it? And after that turning around and arriving at the restaurant in time for lunch?"

Nothing at all! And thanks for pointing it out to me. I mean, it's a real joy when you're conducting an investigation to have a suspect explain how it would have been possible for her to commit the crime (if anyone in this case could be termed a suspect, that is). After all, I was perfectly capable of reaching that conclusion myself, for God's sake, once I had the chance to even think about it.

"You're absolutely right," I finally conceded, trying not to sound as petulant as I felt.

"Listen," Donna said then, a sudden intensity in her voice. "I'm sure you've been told that Catherine was a sick little girl, but I wonder if you have any idea just how sick."

"Well, I'm—"

"Mrs. Shapiro, Catherine had this congenital lung condition. And as a result of that, she developed a severe case of asthma when she was only two years old. Her life expectancy—well, there was serious doubt she'd live to adulthood. Sometimes I'd hear my poor little girl gasping for breath during the night, and I'd run into her room absolutely terrified. It was so frightening that even after she used her inhalant and her breathing became easier, I'd spend the rest of the night in the chair next to her bed, afraid to leave her for a minute—even with her nanny.

"I'm distraught that I've lost my only child—devastated! But I have no right to be *surprised*. What I'm trying to impress on you is that Catherine's death was not unexpected; it's a sword that's been hanging over my head—over all our heads—for a very long time."

Now the tears began, cascading freely down the white cheeks and down her throat into the V of the blouse. She made a vague and unsuccessful attempt to brush them away with the back of her hand, then finally reached into her pants pocket and extracted a packet of tissues. A good two or three minutes—and a half dozen tissues—went by before she was able to stem the flow.

"I'm sorry," she murmured, mopping up the last vestige of her tears. "I seem to keep saying that, don't I?"

"Please, don't apologize," I told her, horrified to find that my voice was cracking. *God! What a wimp I am!* "Uh, Mrs. Corwin, I hope you won't resent this next question, but I do have to ask." Miraculously, I managed to get that out without embarrassing myself further.

She looked at me warily. "What is it?"

"Can you think of anyone who might have had a reason—no matter how far-fetched—to want your little girl dead?"

The answer was barely audible. "No one."

"I understand you lost your husband not long ago."

"Yes. He died of a heart attack. I promise you that's what it was—*a heart attack.*"

"I'm not questioning the cause of his death," I hastened to assure her, "I was wondering about his will."

"He left half of his estate—along with this house—to me. The other half was divided equally between Catherine, his daughter, Barrie, and his grandson, Todd, with the money to the children in the form of a trust fund." The next question was just beginning to form on my lips when Donna answered it. "I'll save you the trouble of asking. There was a little under two million dollars in the estate, not counting the house."

I nodded, a little taken aback. I mean, two million sounds just lovely to me; it could certainly buy a person a lot of Häagen-Dazs. Still, the Corwin lifestyle, from everything I'd seen, seemed to suggest a lot more than that.

"Not as much as you thought, is it?" Donna said shrewdly. She didn't really expect an answer. "Clark lost some money in the market over the last few years," she went on. "But actually, it's always been my mother-in-law who had the *real* money."

"What did your husband do for a living?"

"He was an architect."

It was at this point that I suddenly got myself an idea. Not a very good idea, you understand. But at least it was *something*. "I was told Catherine died just before her tenth birthday. Was there anything in your husband's will that made the birthday significant in any way? Some special provision maybe?"

"No, there was nothing like that," she replied, shooting down my only idea.

"Just one more question, Mrs. Corwin. Who inherits Catherine's portion of the estate now?"

"It goes to me," she responded flatly. Then, attempting to lighten the mood, she put in mischievously, "But call me Donna. It'll keep you from confusing me with my mother-in-law." I laughed, and a moment later she said, "Is it all right if I call you Desiree?"

"Oh, of course. Please do."

"Okay then, Desiree, are we through for now?"

For once, I'd been telling the truth. My last question *was* my last question. "We're through," I said.

As soon as I was back at my apartment, I settled in with the book I'd borrowed from Donna Corwin just before I left her. It was the story Catherine had been reading the day she died: *The Boy from Planet Pluto*. I didn't put it down until I'd finished it.

While the book had prompted only some tepid smiles from me, I could see where it might have caused Catherine Corwin to laugh out loud, just as Luisa had claimed. After all, it was late now, and I was tired. Also, I wasn't in the best humor imaginable. Plus—and I guess this is the important one—it had really been quite a while since I was ten years old.

Chapter 8

The following day I contacted Barrie Lundquist. She suggested I stop by the house at nine o'clock that evening, but when I arrived at the Park Avenue address, an apologetic Luisa had news for me. "Ms. Lundquist's been detained at the office," I was informed. "She just called five minutes ago. She said to tell you she's very sorry, but she was stuck in a meeting until now, and she couldn't get to a phone. She doesn't have any idea what time she'll be able to leave work, so she asked if you could please get in touch with her tomorrow."

"I'll do that, Luisa," I said, irritated in spite of myself. After all, it wasn't Lundquist's fault she got tied up. I was just starting to turn away when I heard this ridiculous voice coming from behind the half-open door. The range went from squeaky almost-soprano to scratchy close-to-basso. "Is that the fat lady P.I.?" it demanded. "*I'll* talk to her. I was there that day, too, Luisa—remember?"

"I'm not certain your mother would approve of that, Todd," the housekeeper cautioned, glancing in the direction of the offending sound.

"So?"

A split second later, the door was flung open and Luisa shoved not too gently aside.

The young male framed in the doorway was extremely skinny, with too small eyes and a long, thin nose. A deep scowl made his not very attractive face less attractive still. I can't tell you if he was tall or short for his age, because I have no idea how far up a twelve-year-old is expected to extend. But what I can tell you is this kid was some sight!

He had an absolutely outrageous hairdo (if the word

hairdo can be used for boys, that is), with his dark, greasy-looking locks frizzed out to *there* and a three- or four-inch strip of bright magenta down one side of his head. His feet were huge and encased in appropriately dirty designer sneakers. His hands, too, were extremely large, and the bony red knuckles covered with scabs and scars. He was wearing a pair of torn jeans and a T-shirt that said, DON'T SCREW WITH ME.

I had every confidence that the shirt was giving out some pretty sound advice. I mean, right from the start I knew Todd Lundquist was a weirdo. And it had nothing to do with his hair or his clothes. There was something in those little eyes of his, something in the way he stared at me that gave me the creeps.

"Well? You wanna talk to me or what?"

"Think his mother would mind?" I asked Luisa. Her response was a shrug and an uncertain smile. I made a quick executive-type decision. *Too bad if she did; I had a job to do, too.* "Sure, why not," I told him.

"Okay, shoot," the kid said. We were seated at the kitchen table, and Todd had just poured himself some milk, a good portion of which he'd shared with the table. Now, he opened up a package of Oreos, shoved at least three of them in his mouth, and took a healthy swig of the milk without bothering to swallow. His mouth, a bulging melting pot of Oreos and milk, was leaking out the overflow.

I began by asking, "What can you tell me about your cous—" I stopped short, suddenly realizing that Catherine was actually this kid's *aunt*! I felt idiotic referring to the little girl that way, so I settled for: "What can you tell me about Catherine?"—at the same time doing my best to avert my eyes from the disgusting mess dribbling down his chin.

"Little Miss Sickie?" he said after finally gulping the stuff down. (Since he hadn't offered me anything, I'd found myself wishing he would choke.) "The only reason everyone made such a fuss about her was because she didn't have long to live," he pronounced, while wiping the lower portion of his face with his forearm. "But she was pretty dopey, if you knew her. And she was always makin' up crap. I do it, and they say I'm lyin'. She did it, and they say, 'What a wonderful imagination our dear, sweet, darling Catherine has!" With this attempt at mimicry, the kid's voice rose so high it was practically out of human hearing range. A moment later, he tossed his frizzy curls to demonstrate how little he was bothered by this favoritism. "Anyways, I don't know why it's such a big deal, her dying," he went on. "She would of kicked off soon anyhow. We all expected it. My mother tole me a long time ago she wasn't long for this world."

The kid certainly had a nice, sensitive way about him, didn't he? "You think Catherine was a liar?"

"Bet your damn hooters, I do!"

Crude, too. "What about that incident with the car? Do you think she lied about someone deliberately trying to run her over?"

"Wanna hear somethin'? She might have been telling the truth that time, for once in her life." He laughed unpleasantly. "And wouldn't you know it? Nobody believed her."

"What makes you say that—about her telling the truth that time, I mean?"

"I got my reasons," he replied slyly.

"Well, what are they?"

"None of your business."

I couldn't decide whether the charming Todd was really privy to some pertinent information or just playing the big shot. From what I'd seen of him so far, I figured it was most likely the latter. Still, it was worth another try. "You know, Todd, I wouldn't want to tell the police you're withholding any facts," I threatened.

"Yeah? I'll deny I said nuthin'."

"Anyway, I think you're bluffing."

"You think so, huh? Well, maybe I am, but then maybe I ain't."

Throwing in the towel, I tried a different tack. "I get the feeling you weren't that fond of Catherine."

"Listen, all I ever heard since I come here was: 'Don't be so rough, or you'll hurt poor little Catherine.' And 'Don't play your stereo so loud, or you'll disturb the little darling.' And 'Don't be so fresh, or you'll make poor little Catherine cry.'" He sneered malevolently.

"Well, the hell with them! If she was so sick, they shoulda put her in one of them homes. That's the kinda place she belonged in, right?"

I clamped down on my tongue—hard. "You said something about since you got here. Just when was that?"

"Around two years ago. When my mother and father split."

"Your parents are divorced, then?"

"That's what I said, didn't I?"

"And you live here permanently now?"

"Not permanently. We moved in just till my mother could afford a place of our own. My grandfather—the old guy was alive then—said we could stay as long as we wanted. I don't think Grandma Donna's too thrilled with that idea, though." The *Grandma* was accompanied by a smirk.

"What makes you think that?"

"I got my reasons."

"Did she ever say anything to you?"

"She didn't have to. She knows that I know what's what around here, and she ain't any too happy about it."

"And what is it you know?"

"Never mind. That's *my* business," the brat told me obstinately—and infuriatingly.

"In view of the tragedy, Todd, I don't think it's a good idea to keep any secrets right now. It's possible that whatever information you've come across could have some bearing on Catherine's death."

"Yeah? Well, tough."

I have to tell you, my fingers were just itching to work their way around that little bastard's throat. I had to remind myself that it was not nice to kill a kid, even a kid like this. And it would probably get me a stiff penalty, besides. So I quickly moved on to another topic.

"You were up in your room with your mother's friend when Catherine's body was found?"

"Yeah, Saundra King. She was tutoring me in grammar, the ole busybody."

"I understand she was a teacher."

"Yeah. Useta be."

"What does she do now?" I asked for no reason I can think of.

"Got her own company. And save your breath; I don't know what kind."

"At what time did she start tutoring you?"

Todd hunched bony shoulders. "Who knows? Musta been about ten, maybe later."

"The two of you were together all morning? Right until you heard Luisa scream?"

"Yeah."

"You didn't take a break?"

"Just for a few minutes, that's all. I hardly even got a chance to listen to this new CD I got."

"Did either of you leave the room during that time?"

"She did." Then with a nasty little chuckle: "She couldn't exactly go to the bathroom in the middle of the bedroom floor, could she?"

It's not easy interrogating someone between clenched teeth, but I'm a trouper. "What time was that, do you know?" I pressed on.

"Look, I didn't check my watch. I wasn't expectin' the little princess to bite the dust that day, for chrissakes!"

I tried again. "All right. How long before Luisa screamed would you estimate it was that you took your break?"

The look Todd gave me held more than exasperation (which I'm used to); it bordered on menacing. And it sent shivers down my spine. "I told you, I don't know," he said, spitting the words out at me. "And if I was you, I'd stop raggin' me."

I could feel myself flushing. I was actually allowing myself to be intimidated by a twelve-year-old! In my own defense, however, I want to make it clear—if I haven't already—that this was no ordinary twelve-year-old.

At that moment the phone rang. It rang just twice— apparently having been picked up elsewhere in the house—but the interruption gave me the opportunity to regain some focus and remind myself that I was the adult here. "Miss—Ms.—King resumed your tutoring when she returned from the bathroom?" I asked Todd, speaking with a little more authority now.

"Yeah. For about a minute. But she was coming down with a cold, and she started sneezin' and coughin'. And who wanted her spreadin' her lousy germs? I don't need no diseases, you know."

"So Ms. King left the room again?"

"No such luck. The ole bitch said she promised my mother I'd get some work done that day, so she says she'll read while I study. All's she did was move her chair away, for chrissakes! I'm tellin' you, I felt like I was in jail. That woman's some pain in my ass! I couldn't get her to take a hike nohow!"

"It must be difficult being surrounded by all these women," I put in then, shifting gears. (Anything to get some insight into this rotten little person.)

"It ain't no picnic."

"You must miss your father a lot."

"You kiddin'? I see him every single week! And don't start askin' me what the divorce was about, either," he cautioned, his eyes narrowing.

That kind of threw me, since I had no intention of asking any such thing. But since he put it like that ... "I already know what it was about," I told him.

"Yeah?"

"Yeah."

"Well, what you think you know and what I really know is two different things."

"Is that so? It happens I heard from a very reliable source *just* what it was about."

It was a feeble ploy, and I wasn't exactly shocked that it didn't work. "Listen, lady, if you do know—which you don't because nobody does—I wouldn't advise you to say nuthin'. Or else," he warned, those tiny eyes of his mere slits now, "you'll have to answer to me."

Can you believe it? This young pipsqueak acting like the heavy in a forties gangster movie!

"Hey," he put in then, and a friendly smile suddenly dispelled the scowl that was in more or less permanent residence on his face. "You got a license or anything?"

The question took me by surprise, so unthinkingly I said, "Do you mean a driver's license?"

For a fleeting moment, a contemptuous expression crossed the kid's face. I'd have bet the generous retainer

his great-grandmother had given me that it took real
control for him to prevent his reply from beginning:
"No, dummy!" Instead, he clarified pleasantly, "Oh, no,
Ms. Shapiro. I meant a private investigator's license."

"Sure I've got one," I told him.

"Can I see it?" His tone was so ingratiating that I
know I should have been suspicious, and maybe I even
was—a little, anyway. But what harm could there be in
showing the boy my license?

It took a good few minutes for me to fish the thing
out of my suitcase-sized handbag, into which I always
cram about twice what it was designed to hold. But I
finally pulled the small leather case containing the license out of its hiding place—along with the scarf it had
somehow managed to wrap itself in.

"Here it is," I said, starting to open the case. But
before I could stop him, Todd snatched it from me and
in one swift movement bolted from his chair and jumped
up on the kitchen counter. Holding the case high above
his head, he taunted, "Want your license, fatso? Then
come up and get it!"

Well, of course, given the shape I'm in, that was out
of the question, so I tried grabbing his legs. But he was
much too quick for me, twirling and dancing his way out
of my reach whenever I came close.

At first I attempted to make light of this stupid caper
of his. "Come on, Todd," I coaxed. "What do you want
that for, anyway? You'd never pass for Desiree Shapiro." And then as I ran alongside the counter, huffing
and puffing while fruitlessly attempting to get a hold of
him, it was: "Let me have that, Todd, will you? I have
to leave now." Finally, barely able to catch my breath,
I wheezed: "Give that back to me, you little worm, or
I'll murder you!"

That's when this tall, fair-haired man in a chauffeur's
uniform made his entrance.

"Todd! What do you think you're doing?" the man
demanded. "Have you lost your mind? Get down from
there at once!"

"Who's gonna make me?" It was only necessary for
the chauffeur to take one step in the kid's direction to
get the answer. "All right, all right. Might of known no

one around here could take a joke," Todd grumbled, tossing the license in my general vicinity and then hopping down from the counter and racing from the room.

Luisa hurried into the kitchen moments after that ignominious retreat. "What were you shouting about, Nicholas?" she inquired of the back end of her husband, who was bending down to retrieve my license from under the kitchen table. "Is something wrong?" she asked him as he returned it to me. Then she took a look at my face. It must have been brick red; my cheeks felt as though they were on fire. "Oh, my! Are you all right, Mrs. Shapiro?" she asked, her own face mirroring her concern.

I nodded, since I wasn't quite up to getting any comprehensible sounds out just then.

"What happened here?" she demanded, addressing Nicholas. "Where's Todd?"

"You just missed him. He ran out of here a minute or two ago, probably to his room. He had something belonging to this lady, and he was fooling around, running back and forth up there on the counter trying to keep it away from her."

"My license," I said, scarcely managing to eke out the words.

"Are you *sure* you're all right?" the obviously distressed housekeeper asked again.

Another nod. "Just out of breath," I assured her, smiling wanly.

"It's my fault. I should have known not to leave you alone with Todd." I didn't have the chance to give her absolution. "I'll fix you some tea, huh?" she offered. "It'll make you feel better."

Now, I still have not discovered exactly what it is in tea that makes it a cure-all for everything from a cold to heartburn to hysteria. But ever since childhood, like millions of other people, I've been convinced of its amazing medicinal properties. "Thanks, sounds good," I murmured.

Nicholas left at this point—with my heartfelt gratitude—and Luisa put up the teakettle, then sat down at the table with me. "Nicholas is on his way to call for Ms.

Lundquist at her office now," she informed me. "But I'm sure she's exhausted; it's been a very long day for her, and she—"

"Don't worry. I'm not up to doing any more questioning tonight; I'm pretty tired myself," I said to the woman's obvious relief. "In fact, I hope you won't mind, but I think I'll skip the tea, too. I think I'd rather go right home."

I suddenly realized that at that moment, there was nothing in life I wanted more than to put as much space as possible between me and Kid Dillinger.

Chapter 9

Barrie Lundquist didn't wait for me to get in touch with her again. I got a call from her at my office just after nine o'clock on Wednesday morning.

"I understand my son gave you a pretty bad time last night," she began.

I let her off the hook. I could tell from her voice how embarrassed she was. Plus it really wasn't her fault she'd given birth to that awful little degenerate. And besides, it would have been nice if I'd gotten her permission before I talked to the kid in the first place (although I would have made it my business to question him, no matter what). "That's okay," I said magnanimously. "After all, he's practically a teenager, and at that age . . ." I let the statement dangle.

"Oh, I'm so glad you feel that way," she responded gratefully. "Todd's been kind of difficult lately, but he has a good heart. Honestly."

I had a feeling she was telling that to herself. "I'm sure of it," I said anyway.

"Listen, I know you're anxious to see me about the death of my sister, but I'm afraid I'll be tied up until all hours again tonight. The ad agency I'm with is making a new business presentation tomorrow morning," she confided, "and we've been working on the stuff almost nonstop for the past three weeks. We'll probably be making changes right up until the minute we walk into the client's office at ten o'clock."

"When do you think you will be available?"

"It should be all over by around noon tomorrow— one way or the other. We could get together tomorrow night if you're free."

I said tomorrow night was fine, and we rescheduled our appointment for then.

As soon as I hung up, I started thinking about Todd and his secret information. Did he really have any, I wondered, or was he just pulling my chain? The odds were about ten million to one that he actually knew something, I concluded. It was merely his way of making himself feel important and, at the same time, driving me up a tree. Then I realized that thanks to his war dance on the kitchen counter, there was one question I hadn't gotten around to asking him: Did he think that Catherine had been murdered?

Of course, I was prepared to get some smart-ass rejoinder. I mean, it didn't figure he'd tell me what he really thought—not that I could place much stock in his opinion, anyway. Still, for some dumb reason I felt remiss in not putting the question to him. Well, maybe I could take care of it tomorrow night.

A little later that morning, I called Saundra King at the number Evelyn Corwin had supplied. "Saundra King, Public Relations," announced the secretary or receptionist or whoever it was who answered. So now I knew what business the woman was in. I gave my name and the reason for my call, and I was put through almost at once.

"What can I do to help you, Ms. Shapiro?" King's voice was brusque and businesslike but not unfriendly.

I asked if it would be possible for me to come and talk to her that evening, and she responded that she was having a late dinner with an out-of-town client. "I could spare you about a half hour at lunchtime today, though, if that's okay with you."

Now, I really hate trying to get information from someone who's on a tight schedule. You always feel rushed, and my thought processes have, on occasion, been known to drag their feet. So I said I was tied up then and wanted to know if there was any chance she could see me Friday night. But it seemed she'd be away for the weekend, so we finally settled on the following Monday at 8:00 P.M.

* * *

Thursday began disappointingly. First thing in the morning, I called Sergeant Jacobowitz as he'd suggested (after spending a brief time convincing myself to resist the inclination to just pop right in on him). He sounded harried when he answered the phone. "I'm afraid we'll have to postpone things for a few days. There was a grisly double homicide not two blocks from here; in fact, I'm just on my way out now to visit the crime scene. Why don't I get in touch with you next week sometime? Hopefully, things won't be quite so frantic then."

Don't call me; I'll call you? No way I was going to leave things like that! "Oh, I don't want to put you to any trouble," I said without any truth at all. "How about if I phone *you* next week. Would that be okay?"

"Oh, sure. Absolutely. And I'm really sorry to do this to you."

"No prob—" But I was talking into a dead receiver by then.

Barrie Lundquist looked nothing like your ordinary businesswoman. Medium height and pencil-thin (which seemed to run in the family), her short, dark hair worn close to the head, she was, in her own way, as much of a spectacle as her progeny.

For starters, her makeup base had, no doubt, been put on with a trowel. And the green eye shadow and black mascara she was sporting had been so liberally applied that I figured she probably needed to replenish her supply almost weekly. What's more, her lipstick—a garish shade of fuschia—extended well past her natural lip line and was further accentuated with I don't know how many layers of gloss. And then there were the large red spots on her cheeks which were much too large and much too red. The total effect was that if you stared at her face for more than a second or two, you were in imminent danger of going blind.

As for the rest of her, the bottom half was squeezed into a pair of too tight jeans, while her top half was ensconced (some of it, anyway) in a too low-cut purple silk blouse. She wore very high beige platform sandals, poking out of which were fuchsia-painted toenails. Completing the picture were the eight assorted bracelets decorating her arms and the six rings—if I counted right—on her fingers. In spite of the outlandish getup, however, there was something quite attractive about Ms. Lundquist. Or maybe I was just feeling sympathetic toward her. Because of Todd, I mean.

We sat in the living room, where I opened by asking just what she did at the agency. (Ellen had mentioned going into advertising at one or two points in her sometimes precarious career, but I didn't really know that much about the business, and I was kind of curious.)

"I'm an art director," she told me.

"You paint?"

"No, not at all," she replied, smiling.

"Oh. Well, you must draw."

"Barely." The smile widened.

"Well, what *do* you do?"

"Art direct." She laughed, following which she allowed for a short pause before elaborating. "Everyone always has the wrong impression of an art director's job. Actually, we work with the writers on concepts—you know, ideas—for ads and commercials, and then we're responsible for the graphics involved."

"Oh, I see," I told her. (I didn't exactly see, but I didn't want her to think I was a dummy.)

We spoke about Catherine then. I offered my condolences, and Barrie Lundquist's eyes were moist when she thanked me. Unlike her son, she gave every appearance of having cared deeply for the little girl.

"Do you think Catherine died as the result of her condition?" I put to her.

"Of course. We all knew how sick she was. My grandmother—well, that business with the car, it just threw everything out of perspective for her. Grandmother's convinced that if she'd believed there *had* been an attempt on Catherine's life, she could have taken the necessary steps to protect her."

"Your son thinks Catherine might have been telling the truth about that car aiming at her."

"Todd?" Barrie scoffed. "Listen, he'll say or do anything for shock value. That's his schtick." She softened the remark with an indulgent smile.

"He hinted at a couple of other things, too. And I'd like to check them out with you—just in case."

"Sure." Then, with a dubious look on her face: "Just what did he tell you?"

"Well, for one thing—and I hope you won't think I'm stepping over the line on this—he mentioned that he knew the real cause of your divorce."

"My *divorce*? There's nothing to know about *that*. I was thirty-four years old when my husband left me two years ago; it was for a woman of twenty-five." She uttered a short, harsh laugh. "Not exactly a novel situation, right?"

"That's when you and Todd moved into this house—after the breakup?"

"Yes, but it's only temporary—although I'm beginning to feel like that guy Whiteside in *The Man Who Came to Dinner*. How long was it he stayed on at that place?" She didn't wait for me to supply the answer. (Which was just as well, since I didn't have it.) "But anyway," she continued, "my father's estate was settled recently, so I think I'll be able to swing a decent apartment of our own—assuming, that is, I ever find the time to look around. In the meantime, Donna's been great. She keeps saying it's a big house and that we can live here as long as we like and that that's what my father would have said, too. But I'm still hoping it won't be too long before we're able to make the move."

"Todd also insinuated he had some kind of secret information concerning Donna."

A long, exasperated sigh. "There's one word for my son, Ms. Shapiro: *incorrigible*."

"You have no idea what he's referring to, I take it."

"I haven't got a clue. It's just another example of how he keeps on stirring the pot."

"You get along fairly well with your father's second wife, it seems."

"Very well. Only Donna was Daddy's *third* wife. You're forgetting Catherine's mother—Felice—aren't you?"

I think I must have gasped out loud then. "You mean Donna isn't Catherine's mother?"

"Oh, shit!" Barrie's hand flew to her mouth, and she

shook her head, clearly upset at her apparent indiscretion. "Sometimes I think I ought to have a padlock put on my tongue," she muttered when she took her hand away. "But I really thought you knew; I thought everyone knew." Hurriedly, she attempted to exercise some damage control. "Donna was Catherine's mother for more than nine years, though. She was certainly more of a mother to her than Felice would have been—than Felice ever was. And Donna and Catherine adored each other."

"I'm certain it was just an oversight that I wasn't told," I said. "So why don't you fill me in on this Felice?"

"Might as well. As long as I've shot off my big mouth already." A grimace and then: "My father married that gem a few years after my mother died. She left him when Catherine was just three weeks old. She wanted to get back into show biz. *Get back!*" Barrie reiterated with a snort."

"She's an actress?"

"A singer. And that's *was;* Felice is dead now. But at any rate, it seems she'd done a little professional singing—a very little—before she married my father. And then all of a sudden when Catherine came along, she convinced herself she was passing up the chance to become the next Streisand. But if you ask me, Catherine's condition had a lot to do with her taking off like that; Felice had no interest in raising a sickly child. Anyhow, she went out to L.A. to pursue fame and fortune and wound up drinking herself to death at the advanced age of thirty-one."

"Your father married Donna less than a year after Felice walked out on him?"

"About six months later, I think it was. But he and Felice hadn't gotten along for quite a while, so it wasn't as though he was on the rebound or anything. He really cared for Donna."

"There must have been a big difference in their ages."

"My father was close to seventy when he died; Donna's thirty-three. But they had a wonderful relationship."

I don't *think* I looked skeptical. But for some reason Barrie found it necessary to add, "They really did."

I was just about to ask *the* question when she said, an urgent note in her voice, "Please don't mention that I told you. About Donna not being Catherine's birth mother, that is. Not that it's anything to hide," she was quick to point out, "it's just that Donna and I are good friends, and she's been very kind to me. I wouldn't want her to think I repaid her by gossiping about her. Especially at a time like this."

I assured Barrie that while it would almost certainly be necessary to mention the information she'd given me, I couldn't see any reason to identify the source. That said, I finally got around to the big question. "I understand you were at the office the day Catherine died," I began.

"Yes, I was. At the time she . . . at the time it happened, anyway."

"Was anyone with you?"

"The copywriter I work with was there until after eleven; then she went home. But I had to stay and do up the comps a little tighter."

"So from eleven on you were at the office alone?"

"That's right."

"Is there anyone who could verify your presence, by any chance? A cleaning woman, possibly? Or a security guard?"

"No, the office is in a brownstone. There *is* no security guard, and the cleaning woman wasn't around."

"Did you receive any phone calls while you were there?"

"As a matter of fact, Saundra—my friend Saundra King—called me at about twenty of two to break the news about Catherine. But I'd already left; I wrapped it up around one-thirty or maybe a few minutes before." She looked at me intently. "Look, I didn't kill Catherine. *Nobody* killed her. My grandmother is a very peculiar lady, as you will, I'm sure, learn if you haven't discovered it already. But this insistence of hers that Catherine was murdered—well, it's way out, even for her. I just wish she'd let my poor little sister rest in peace, that's all."

And, with that, Barrie Lundquist put her head in her arms and sobbed.

* * *

I'd received Barrie's permission to speak to Todd for a few minutes. "I really have no objection to your talking to him; just don't believe anything he tells you," she'd cautioned.

He sauntered into the living room a short time later, scowl firmly in place.

"Luisa said you want to ask me something," he said, glaring at me.

"That's right. It'll only take a minute."

"And don't give Ms. Shapiro any of your crap, Todd," Barrie warned. "Answer her honestly." Then, to me: "I'll leave you two alone."

And sooner than I had a chance to yell, "No! Please don't!" she was gone.

Todd's first words to me were: "You got me in a lot of trouble the other night, you know that?"

"*I* got you in a lot of trouble? Listen, buddy, you're old enough to face the consequences of your own actions. And you behaved like a spiteful little jackass."

"I was only foolin' around. Weren't you ever a kid, fat lady?"

Now, I'm very familiar with that old saying about sticks and stones; still, that got to me. "Oh, I was a kid, all right," I hissed. "And I was no goody two-shoes, either. But I'm happy to say I was never the kind of . . . of *thing* you are." Then, while he was spewing out his retort, I came to my senses. As had been necessary on our last encounter, I reminded myself of Todd's tender years. I mean, here I was, engaging in a verbal duel with someone so young he was still undergoing a voice change, for God's sake! And I suddenly felt really foolish about it. Besides, how could I hope to get anything out of the little creep if he considered me his mortal enemy? So I interrupted his vitriolic indictment of me to say I was sorry he'd gotten into trouble—although I didn't go so far as to assume responsibility for it.

He took his time before giving me a grudging "Okay, whaddayawant?"

"I just want to know if you think Catherine may have been murdered."

"Maybe," he answered smugly.

"What makes you consider it a possibility?"

"Hey, you're the P.I.—that's what that thing in the leather case says, anyway. So why don't you find out?"

"Look, your mother said for you to cooperate with me. I'll go right out there and tell her you—"

"Yeah? And I'll tell her that all's I meant was that *anything* is possible." Then, with the sweetest smile you can picture, he concluded with: "So screw you, lady, and your whole freakin' family, too!"

Chapter 10

The first thing I did when I got to the office Friday (the second, really, but I don't consider consuming coffee and a croissant to be much of an activity) was to bring my notes on the case up to date. After that I went over them carefully. When I was through, I examined in my mind everything I'd learned that could possibly, in any way, point to murder.

There was that door business—you know, Luisa's statement about the library door being open when she left for the store and closed when she went to fetch Catherine for lunch. But the housekeeper's explanation had been simple—and in all probability, correct: Catherine herself had closed the door because the hall was so drafty.

Now, what about that miserable Todd's little collection of insinuations? I wondered if his allusion to possessing some sort of secret information about Donna Corwin had to do with her not being Catherine's birth mother or if something else—real or concocted—was lurking in that twisted brain of his. And, of course, there was also his hinting around that Catherine might have been telling the truth about the car incident after all. Well, I'd try to find out more about those things if I could, although given the source, I very much doubted there was anything to find out. According to his own mother, the little bastard wasn't to be believed.

At the thought of Barrie Lundquist, I was reminded of that reference Todd had made to there being some hidden reason for his parents' divorce. But how that could be relevant to the little girl's death was beyond me.

I turned my attention to what I'd found out about

Donna's relationship to Catherine. Okay. I know that a stepmother can be just as loving as a natural one. But to be honest, every time I read in the papers about a heinous crime a parent has committed against his or her child, I always find it a little easier to accept when the perpetrator is a stepparent. And don't forget, Donna would be inheriting Catherine's share of the estate; which came to more than $300,000.

But still, I couldn't see the woman as a killer. Her grief over Catherine's death had seemed so profound, so genuine. No way, I decided, she could be that good an actress. And then this little voice in my head piped up. "You've been wrong before, you know," it was kind enough to remind me.

Hold on a sec. Didn't Todd have a motive, too? You didn't have to be a Mrs. Freud to appreciate how jealous he'd been of his little relative. So let's say that Saundra King had been leaving Todd's room at the same time the housekeeper called out to Catherine that she was going to the store. With the door open like that, the boy could have heard her. Well, what would have prevented him from sneaking downstairs and doing away with his young nemesis then?

But here again, I had trouble buying it. As much as I couldn't stand the kid, he *was* only twelve years old. And don't tell me about children even younger than that turning out to be cold-blooded murderers. While I was certainly aware that it did happen, it was, I have to admit, a really big reach for me.

Besides, no matter how hard I tried to ignore it, whenever I considered anything at all in this investigation, the bottom line kept coming up and hitting me in the face: The police had rejected the possibility of homicide.

Once again, I was very anxious for that talk with Sergeant Jacobowitz.

I had Friday night all planned out. I'd stop off and rent a movie on my way home from work. And not just any movie. One of those good, old-time tear-jerkers like *Imitation of Life* (which I hadn't seen more than three or four times at most), or *Back Street* (I'd try the Susan Hayward version this time), and, of course, there was always *An Affair to Remember* (either version would do me just fine). I was really in the mood for a good cry. Why, I don't know.

But anyhow, I never made it to the video store that evening—thanks to a four o'clock phone call from Harriet Gould, who lives across the hall from me.

"I was wondering," she ventured hesitantly, "if you're free tonight, and if you *are*, umm, if maybe you'd have dinner with Pop and me."

Something in my chest constricted just then. "Pop?"

"My father-in-law. You remember him, don't you?"

How could I forget? "Oh, he's up from Florida again?" I asked foolishly. And with a shudder.

The next couple of sentences came out in a rush. "Till tomorrow morning. And Steve has a Masons' meeting tonight, so I thought I'd take Pop out to a deli for supper, and I was hoping maybe you'd join us."

Now, everybody has to die some time, right? Well, if I had my druthers, I'd like the cause of my demise to be cholestrol-clogged arteries, said cholesterol resulting from the greedy consumption—at a first-rate deli—of a nice, thick hot pastrami sandwich. Or, if they were out of pastrami, I'd settle for a corned beef on rye. But as much as I was practically salivating at the mere thought of delicatessen food, I couldn't think of anything more likely to ruin my enjoyment of it than Harriet Gould's *Pop.*

I'd met Pop Gould (aka Gus, aka "the ball-buster" —particularly among his immediate family) when he visited his son and daughter-in-law this past April and Harriet convinced me to join them for lunch one afternoon. Believe me, I was not about to make the same mistake again.

I promptly declined the invitation. "No thanks," I said bluntly. An explanation, I knew, was hardly necessary.

"He really seems to have mellowed since he was here the last time," I was told sotto voce.

"I'm glad he's behaving. But I still pass."

"Please, Desiree. I could use some moral support," Harriet whispered. And then, in a tone that bordered on the desperate: *"Please."*

I'm not certain whether it was Harriet who moved me

or the vision I was having of this absolutely gorgeous pastrami sandwich with cole slaw, French fries and a sour tomato on the side, but before I could censor myself, I heard my voice saying, "Okay, okay." And then, ready to shoot myself for relenting, I added, "But you owe me. *Permanently.*"

Harriet and the infamous Pop were waiting outside my office building at six o'clock. The instant he spotted me, Pop's face broke into an ear-to-ear grin, his false teeth gleaming brightly against his golden Florida tan. A nattily dressed little man in his eighties, he was wearing a well-fitting brown tweed overcoat, oxblood shoes that had been buffed to a high sheen, and a good-looking brown hat. He promptly whisked the hat from his silver head and held it politely in his hand. Standing there like that, drawn up to his full five-foot three-inch height and weighing in at not much over a hundred and twenty-five pounds, he looked so benign that it was hard for a moment to recollect what a terror he was.

"Well, Mrs. Shapiro," he told me cheerfully, "it's nice to see you again. You're lookin' good, you know that? 'Specially for a girl your age." This was accompanied by a wink and followed by a jocular jab in the rib cage with a manicured finger.

Harriet appeared to shrink an inch or two.

We took a taxi to a large, crowded deli on the Lower East Side, where, it seems, Pop had broken bread on a few of his other visits to New York.

The trouble started with the soup and went straight through to dessert.

"I'll have the mushroom barley soup," he announced to the dour waiter, a tall, skinny man who didn't seem to be that many years his junior.

"We're out of the mushroom and barley. The clam chowder's good today," the waiter informed him perfunctorily.

"Did I *ask* you about the clam chowder? I don't *want* no clam chowder. I came here for the mushroom barley."

"Look, mister," the exasperated waiter retorted loudly, "if *I* had the mushroom barley, *you'd* have the mushroom and barley. But I can't give you what I ain't got, can I?"

"That's the exact same thing they said here last time," Pop groused.

"Whaddaya think? We're savin' it for our *good* customers?"

"How should I know? I wouldn't put it past you."

At this point the waiter was very close to apoplexy. "I . . . told . . . you," he said slowly, emphasizing every word, "we . . . ain't . . . got . . . no . . . more . . . mushroom . . . and . . . barley." Then came the ill-conceived offer. "You wanna come into the kitchen and see for yourself?"

Pop, apparently never having heard of a rhetorical question, promptly got to his feet. "Let's go," he told the startled waiter, who had just put himself in the ridiculous position of having to take the world's most irritating restaurant patron on a tour of the kitchen.

"I'm sorry, Dez," a mortified Harriet was quick to tell me when her father-in-law was out of earshot. "He really did seem a little more civilized this trip."

What could I say? "It's not your fault," I responded grudgingly, at the same time picking up the menu and hiding behind it like the coward I am.

Pop returned a few minutes later, a dejected look on his face, the seething waiter close on his heels.

"Well?" Harriet asked angrily as soon as her father-in-law was seated again.

"I didn't see any," he admitted. An instant later, in an almost pathetic attempt at face-saving, he added, "But it's not even legal putting something on the menu when you never got it."

"Okay, so what'll it be, Mr. Miami?" the waiter demanded. "You wanna try the clam chowder or not?" There were now beads of perspiration on his forehead, and his lips were pressed together so tightly that the words came out with difficulty.

"I told you I don't *want* no clam chowder, didn't I?" was the high-pitched reply. "Look, just bring me a pastrami sandwich on rye. It's gotta be lean, though. Too fatty, and it goes right back, you hear me? And the bread should be nice and fresh. If it's stale, I'm not payin'. And bring me some French fries with that. But make sure they're well done; they shouldn't taste greasy, either, you got me?"

The waiter muttered something appropriately unpleasant under his breath before taking Harriet's order and mine. And when he shuffled away, he was shaking his head. But I had to give him a great deal of credit for restraining from physical violence.

The food came a few minutes later, and everything was really tasty, with Pop's order to his exact specifications. He seemed to be relishing his meal, but when the waiter had the misfortune to pass our table, Pop grabbed his arm. "A less reasonable person," he told the poor guy, "would have sent back the pastrami. It tastes—I dunno—it tastes from perfume."

I won't even attempt to go into the hassle over the apple strudel. All I'll say is that we left the restaurant by popular request.

When Harriet and Pop deposited me at my door that night, her expression was so apologetic I was almost sorry for her. *Almost.* "Will you ever forgive me?" she murmured as the old man started to walk away.

Before I had the opportunity to frame an ungracious response, Pop turned around. "Next time I come to New York," he told me, "we'll make a whole evening out of it. Get some delicatessen and go to a movie after. How does that sound?" Then he cocked his head to one side for a second in contemplation. "You know," he informed me, "maybe I'll even try the clam chowder. How bad could it be?"

Chapter 11

The persistent ringing woke me at seven-thirty. A truly obscene time to be calling anyone on a Saturday morning, don't you think?

Reaching for the phone in my semiconscious state, I knocked it off the night table. It fell to the floor with a nerve-jangling clatter. *Good,* I thought uncharitably. *I hope it breaks his eardrum—whoever he is.*

"Desiree?" *Her. It was a her.*

"Yes?"

"It's Mrs. Corwin—your client, remember?"

Uh-oh. I sat up in bed, fully awake now. "Oh, how are you, Mrs. Corwin? I was going to call you right after breakfast." Which wasn't exactly what I'd consider a lie. I mean, even though I'd been putting it off, I realized I'd have to touch base with her *sometime.* Who knows? Maybe it would have been then.

"I hope I didn't wake you," she said, feigning concern.

I matched her lie for lie. "Oh, no, I've been up for a while now."

"I haven't heard from you all week," she stated flatly. But it was definitely an accusation.

"Yes, I know. And I'm sorry." That much, at least, was true. The problem was, though, I just hadn't known what to say to the woman. It really didn't make sense to talk to her about any of the factors I'd considered as lending some support to a homicide theory. Especially since, on reflection, I'd concluded that none of these things was of any real significance. The way I looked at it, how fair would it have been of me to pump up her expectations for nothing? "I didn't call you earlier because I was waiting until I had something tangible to tell you," I added then.

"I gather that means that now you do have something,"

"No, I'm afraid not. I—"

"But you did say you intended calling me today, didn't you?" she challenged.

"Well, yes. But only because I didn't want to let any more time go by before making contact."

"I understand you've seen all the members of my family. Weren't you able to find out *anything* that could be of help?"

I think I might have hesitated for maybe a split second before responding with "Not really." But then I realized I couldn't leave it at that. So to demonstrate that I wasn't just sloughing everything off, I thought I'd discuss what I'd learned about her daughter-in-law. "I doubt very much that it has any bearing on Catherine's death," I told her, "but I did hear that Donna wasn't her natural mother."

"So?"

"You didn't mention that, and I wondered why."

"Because it's completely irrelevant, that's why. It has nothing whatsoever to do with the murder. Donna was devoted to Catherine; she was a wonderful mother to her."

"Look, you're probably right. But the fact that she was her *stepmother* does change the situation slightly, particularly when you consider that she did have a motive."

"A motive? What kind of motive?"

"A three hundred thousand dollar motive, unless I've been misinformed. I'm talking about Catherine's share of your son's estate."

"That's funny; it really is," Evelyn Corwin retorted. But she wasn't laughing.

"What is?"

"Donna stands to inherit many times that when I die—just like every other member of the family. And she knows it."

"Well, let's hope that will be a long time in the future."

"It won't be. And Donna knows that, too." This ominous pronouncement didn't even have a chance to sink

in before the old woman—apparently to preclude any
further discussion on this point—hurried on. "Besides,
I'm fairly certain Donna wasn't even aware that Catherine's portion of the money would be going to her. As
far as I know, my son inserted some sort of provision in
his will to that effect without even telling her about it."

I couldn't, of course, just come out and ask Mrs. Cor-
win what she meant by the reference to her own death.
(Maybe some other investigator could; I couldn't.) So all
I said was: "You sound like you're very fond of Donna."

"I am. She was by far the best of my son's three wives.
Diane—Barrie's mother—was all right but not really in
Clark's class. I know that makes me sound like a terrible
snob, but she was—I have to say it—coarse. A decent
person, you understand, but coarse. And when it came
to Felice, well, she was like a bad joke. I warned Clark
if he married that floozy I'd write him out of my will.
And I did it, too." This was related with more than a
little satisfaction. There was a brief pause before she
added, "I'm an old-fashioned woman in many ways, Desiree. And when a thing's not right, I don't reward it.
And it wasn't right that Felice should be the mother of
my son's children—or *anyone's* children."

"You reinstated him later? I mean in the will."

"As soon as Felice was out of the picture."

"Under the terms of the will, what happens when a
beneficiary is disinherited—or dies?"

"Their portion of the estate is divided between the
remaining heirs."

"And those heirs are . . .?"

"Donna, my granddaughter, Barrie, and my great-
grandson, Todd, with Todd's share held in trust for him
until he turns twenty-one. Now that Catherine is gone,
they get it all, except, that is, for a few small bequests to
the people in my household—my housekeeper, Frances,
who's been with me for years; Stella, my cook; and my
chauffeur, Karl."

"I see. Let me ask you this, Mrs. Corwin. I get the
impression you're very certain Donna didn't kill Catherine; am I right?"

"You are."

"Well, who *do* you suspect?"

"Nobody. Nobody occurs to me, at any rate. But it definitely wasn't a member of my family. I was hoping, though, they might be able to put you on to something. I thought that one of them might know something they weren't aware they knew."

Well, how do you like that? She sounded just like me! I must have said that same kind of thing myself hundreds of times. But she'd given me an idea. "What if it *should* turn out that a family member killed Catherine?" I put to her, trying to make her aware of the potential repercussions of a murder determination.

"It wasn't a member of the family."

"But if it was? If I found out anything like that, I'd have to inform the police, you know."

There was silence. "Well, then at least we'd have our answer, wouldn't we?" she responded at last.

Before terminating the conversation, I felt compelled to make a final effort to get her to accept the idea, at least, that her granddaughter might not have been a homicide victim. "By the way, I spoke briefly on the phone this week to one of the detectives involved in the case—a Sergeant Jacobowitz. He hasn't been able to see me yet, but I'm hoping to meet with him next week." I took a deep breath. "Look, I'll certainly continue to explore every aspect of this thing, but from what the sergeant said, the police investigated thoroughly and—"

"That's *their* story. Listen to me, Desiree. I'm well aware that since Catherine's death, everyone has me pegged as a crazy old woman. And maybe I am—but not about this. As surely as I know that night follows day, I know that my Catherine was murdered. And I'm depending on you to prove it." Then, very plaintively she entreated, "Please. Don't let me down."

I didn't even try to get back to sleep. I was no longer in the mood, plus it was past eight, anyway. So I headed into the kitchen.

I fixed myself a nice, hot cup of coffee (and the fact it was hot was the only thing nice about it, too, since I make the most putrid stuff you can imagine). And then over the coffee, I thought about Mrs. Corwin—sadly, at first.

Her plea really bothered me. I mean, the facts being
what they were, how could I possibly come through for
her? Well, the investigation was still ongoing, I answered
myself, and I'd have to try to keep an open mind.

But what about her remark that she didn't have much
longer to live? Now, *that* really threw me! Of course, I
could have mistaken her meaning. She might just have
been referring to her age; after all, she wasn't exactly a
young woman. Sure, that must be it, I decided. I hoped
so, anyway.

The truth is, that while she was stubborn as hell and
often overbearing, I admired Evelyn Corwin a great
deal. She had spirit. And determination. *And* ingenuity.
Believe me, I was going to keep in much closer touch
from here on in. And not only because it was what I
should do, but because it was certainly preferable to one
of her early weekend wakeup calls. Which was, I knew—
and I grinned then—exactly the way the old lady had
it figured.

I started getting dressed at ten for my twelve o'clock
date that afternoon with Stuart Mason, my accountant,
buddy, and on again/off again lover. When on again, as it
presently was, this physical intimacy—which had evolved
during a time of mutual need and long after we'd become close friends—gave our relationship an added and
very pleasant dimension. However, as much as I might
have wished otherwise, it did not mean we were in love.
While there are few people I'm fonder of than Stuart,
the fact is, tall, blond, attractive men with good incomes
and warm, considerate natures aren't really my type. I
prefer the short, scrawny, *needy* ones. (I know, I know,
I'm not too sound between the ears. But then, when it
comes to love, how many people are?) Anyhow, it was
just as well, since Stuart wasn't interested in me, either.
Not in *that way,* I mean.

At any rate, I was affording myself all this leeway
time-wise, because in a phone conversation we'd had
earlier in the week, Stuart had made a big thing about
my not being late. "This is probably against your reli-
gion," he'd said only half jokingly, "but try to be downstairs at twelve, will you? It's tough finding a place to

park in your neighborhood, and with all the street construction that's going on now, it takes about fifteen minutes just to drive around the block."

Even though I was forced to acknowledge that I hadn't given Stuart any reason to admire my promptness the last two or three times we'd made plans together, I managed to resent this chiding. "Don't you worry your little head," I told him haughtily. "I will definitely be on time Saturday—and you can take *that* to the bank!"

So because I happen to be about the pokiest person on the planet and also because it's a rare day when I'm taking special pains to look good that I don't encounter some kind of disaster—often of epic proportions—I gave myself a full two hours to get myself together.

This, however, turned out to be one of those rare days. I kicked off my preparations with a lovely twenty-minute bubble bath, following which I succeeded in putting on my makeup without a mishap of any kind. Even my mascara went on smoothly, winding up on my lashes, for a change, instead of under my eyes. And when I stepped into my dress—a blue wool A-line (for which I'd just bought a gorgeous blue, yellow and pink silk scarf)—I didn't get my foot tangled up in the hem or bust a seam or catch the zipper. But the big thing was that, wonder of all wonders, my hair behaved, too! In less than ten minutes of painstaking ministrations, it was ready for the customary mega-dose of spray, which would assure that not a strand could possibly go astray—even in the unlikely event I should be inclined to stick my head in a Mix-master.

Now I was ready to check myself out in the full-length mirror for spots, rips, and wrinkles.

You see, I have what I guess you could call an obsession about neatness. It probably has something to do with my weight. I mean, I know I can't do a damn thing about it if somebody calls me fat (although I much prefer "full-figured"), but there's no way I'll give anyone an excuse for calling me fat and *sloppy*. Anyhow, when I was satisfied that everything was in order, I inched up on my reflection, trying to determine whether I'd turned myself into the understated but positively irresistible woman I'd been shooting for. And that's when the phone rang.

"Aunt Dez?"

"Hi, Ellen." I glanced at my watch. Only 11:35. I had more than enough time for a little chat. "How's everything?"

"I don't think I've ever been this happy in my life," Ellen murmured.

It warmed my heart to hear her say that. Until now she'd had the worst luck imaginable in the romance department. "Mike okay?" I inquired, referring to the source of all this happiness of hers.

"He's better than okay. He's sensational! And did I mention brilliant? How's that for an objective, man-in-the-street opinion?" We both laughed—or I should say, I laughed and Ellen giggled—and then she asked, "How's everything with you?"

"Not bad, really. Stuart and I are driving out to New Hope this afternoon. You know, that little town in Bucks County, Pennsylvania, where they have all those arts and crafts and things."

"I know all about New Hope," she told me. "Mom and Dad used to go there pretty often when I was young. It's a great place, and today's a beautiful day for a drive. But listen, Mike's working this weekend, and I was wondering if we could meet for brunch tomorrow."

Now, I'm really uncomfortable making any reference to my sex life, even an oblique one and even to Ellen (although she's perfectly aware of the relationship between Stuart and me), but I did have to give her an answer of some kind. "We're probably staying over," I mumbled.

"What was that? I couldn't hear you."

I forced myself to speak louder. "I sa-id, 'We'll probably be staying over.' " You won't believe this—I know I don't—but I could feel my face getting warm! I hope it was the temperature in the apartment.

"Well, I don't know what you're so embarrassed about, for heaven's sake," Ellen responded, giggling again.

"I'm not em—"

"Oh, yes, you are! And I think it's adorable!" *Why,*

that little twerp! When somebody asks her intimate ques-
tions, she turns practically maroon! "By the way, how's
the new case going?" she said a moment later.

"Oh, I don't know. I don't even want to *think* about
it today."

"Good for you. Look, have a terrific time, and I'll talk
to you during the week."

It didn't take five minutes before the doorbell rang. I
peered through the peephole to see Pop Gould standing there.

"I thought you'd gone back to Florida already," I told
him as soon as I'd steeled myself to open the door.

"I was supposed to, but the kids"—he was applying
this designation to forty-something Harriet and fiftyish
Steve—"they pleaded with me to stay a couple more
days." I could just imagine! "Listen, is it all right if I
come in for a minute?" I opened my mouth to explain
that I was just getting ready to leave when he put in,
"A minute—at the most. Trust me."

What could I say?

Once inside, he took so long seating himself comfortably on the sofa that it looked like he was settling in for
the season. And I was really getting antsy. Finally, he
glanced around the room. "Nice place," he remarked
appreciatively, but I suspect it was mostly to provide a
decent segue into the reminiscence that was to follow.
"Edith and me, we had a chair that exact same color
when we first got married," he informed me. "You
shoulda seen the living room set we had! You wouldn't
believe . . ." He went on to describe just about every
stick of furniture in that apartment of theirs before I
could find the space to interrupt.

"I hate to cut you short," I got in at last, moving to
the edge of my seat, "but I have an appointment, and
I'm already late." I said it as gently as possible, at the
same time making a show of checking my watch—and
discovering to my mortification that it was now close to
twelve-fifteen!

"Oh. Well, no problem," he responded as I jumped
to my feet. "I only wanted to ask if maybe you'd wanna
go have a bite later. Just the two of us. Nothing fancy,

you understand. We could even do it Dutch treat if you want, so you wouldn't feel obligated or nuthin'—if you take my meaning."

My God! I think I'm being courted by an eighty-year-old! "Gee, Pop, I'm going away for the weekend, but I would have liked that; I really would," I assured him. After all, I didn't want to hurt the old man's feelings. Besides, in his own way, he was kind of cute. Well, maybe *cute* wasn't exactly the word; *impossible* would probably be closer.

"I shoulda realized," he said dejectedly, "seein's how you're all dressed up."

He looked so forlorn that to cheer him up, I added without thinking, "Maybe we can do it the next time you're in town."

He broke into a big smile. "You promise?" he demanded. I guess I'll just never learn.

"I promise," I replied.

I didn't make it downstairs until twelve-thirty. But you can see where it wasn't my fault, can't you? Anyway, Stuart was driving slowly past the apartment when he spotted me. He frowned when I got into the car, which even under those circumstances was very uncharacteristic, since he's normally a remarkably placid person.

"Do you have any idea how many times I've circled the block?" He barely glanced at me, and I could tell it was an effort for him to keep his voice even. "So much for your word that you'd be on time," he groused, driving away before I even had a chance to fasten my seat belt.

"I'm really sorry, Stuart," I said sincerely, "but this old man who's visiting my neighbors across the hall came in, and I just didn't know how to get rid of him."

"You might have tried telling him you had to meet someone at twelve and asked him to excuse you."

He was right, of course. Nevertheless, my back went up, and I was busy fishing around in my head for some kind of comeback when he reached over and took my hand. "I'm sorry, Dez; don't pay any attention to me. I didn't get too much sleep last night, and it's turned me into a real jackass."

Well, that explained it. Still, Stuart's reaction had been so unlike him that I wasn't completely satisfied. "There's nothing bothering you, then? Apart from my keeping you waiting for so long, that is?"

"Of course not," he said, turning toward me and smiling warmly.

Had he really hesitated before answering, or was I just looking for trouble? "You're sure?" I wanted to know.

"Yes, believe me, I'm sure."

We had a perfectly lovely time browsing along the cobblestone streets of New Hope. Within the first ten minutes or so, Stuart bought a watercolor. It was of an old woman seated in a garden, her ancient, gnarled hand resting on the large orange cat in her lap. It was a wonderful study, and for the remainder of the afternoon I was practically frantic looking for a little treasure of my own. Right before we were ready to call it a day, just so as not to go home empty-handed, I settled on a necklace I wasn't that crazy for and two pairs of earrings I could easily have lived without.

That evening we had dinner in a quaint old inn dating back to the Revolutionary War. And while conversation was for the most part relaxed and pleasant, a couple of times I sensed something a little different, a little strained, about Stuart's manner. But then a moment later, he'd be the same old Stuart again, and I'd tell myself I was nuts.

We spent the night at a bed and breakfast, and lying next to him, I was convinced I'd been imagining things. Or maybe, I reasoned, there was still a slight holdover of his earlier annoyance with me that he hadn't been quite able to shake.

The next morning, we had a leisurely breakfast before starting back for Manhattan. On the drive home, we chatted and joked around like the very good buddies we were. Nonetheless, there were a few fleeting instances when I again got the feeling that things weren't exactly right. I can't really explain it; it was as though Stuart wasn't altogether *at ease* with me.

* * *

He left me at my apartment at a little after three, having promised his nephew he'd take him to a Rangers game that night for his birthday. And for the rest of the day and all that evening, I barred from my mind any speculation about something being wrong between us.

But later, just before I fell asleep, the last thing I can remember thinking was that whatever was troubling my very dear friend—if there *was* anything troubling him, that is—it was bound to work itself out.

Chapter 12

Todd's "ole bitch" turned out to be a woman somewhere in her early forties. She was certainly not "ole"—at least, not be my standards. But, of course, the "bitch" part remained to be seen.

I was more or less comfortably settled on a worn leather sofa in the apartment that served as Saundra King's living room/p.r. office. The room I was in, which I took to be the largest room in the place (and it wasn't really all that large), was evidently where most of the actual business was conducted. Attesting to that, the walls were almost completely covered with simply framed publicity articles and photographs of minor celebrities—some of them so minor as to be unrecognizable to the average person, of whom I consider myself somewhat representative. Ms. King was seated in the matching leather chair at right angles to the sofa, having just set down on the rectangular wooden table in front of us a tray containing two cups of fragrant coffee and assorted miniature Danish.

I was really grateful for the coffee—I almost invariably have a cup with dinner, but I was running late that night. However, I declined politely when she handed me the plate of pastries. "They look wonderful, but I just had a big meal; I really couldn't manage another thing." About three seconds later, fighting off my embarrassment, I succumbed to an apricot Danish. (Well, it was *really* tiny, so how much space would it need?)

"Please ignore the mess," King apologized in this nononsense way she had of speaking. She was waving at the other side of the room, which consisted of two wooden desks, a complete wall of file cabinets, assorted office machines and equipment, and—strewn just about everywhere—manila folders on top of manila folders. "I keep meaning to straighten up, but I've been too busy lately, praise the Lord," she told me, smiling.

Saundra King was a large-boned woman, with short, curly auburn hair and wide-set blue eyes framed by long brown lashes. And while you wouldn't exactly call her pretty—her face was too broad, her nose was too wide and her complexion wasn't very good—there was something quite attractive about her. She carried her clothes well, too. Which that night consisted of beautifully cut navy pants and a pale blue wool turtleneck sweater that brought out the blue of her eyes.

She bent her head and took a sip of the coffee. While she was looking down like that, I surreptitiously helped myself to another Danish. Cheese, this time. "What is it you wanted to ask me?" she inquired, setting the cup back on the table.

I swallowed quickly. "I wanted to talk to you about the day Catherine died."

"Tragic, isn't it? She was a very sweet little girl. Barrie was all broken up over her death. She still is."

"They were close?"

"Oh, yes, and even more so after they began living in the same house. Barrie was like a second mother to her."

"I imagine you're aware that Donna wasn't Catherine's natural mother."

"Of course. I don't think anyone made a secret of it."

"Did you have much opportunity to observe the two of them together? Donna and Catherine, I'm talking about."

"Many times. I'm at the house quite frequently. They got along very well, as far as I could see. Donna seemed like an extremely caring parent. That *is* what you wanted to know, isn't it?"

"Yes, it is. I'm afraid I got sidetracked, though. I started to ask about the day Catherine died. I understand you and Mrs.—Ms.—Lundquist had breakfast together that morning."

"Yes. Barrie, Todd, and I—the three of us."

"And then Ms. Lundquist went to the office?"

"Uh-huh. And I went upstairs to tutor Todd. His

grades haven't been too good, and I was a teacher in a previous life, so Barrie pressed me into service."

"You and Todd were together all morning?"

"*All* morning. From about ten-thirty on. And believe me, it was no barrel of fun. That kid is something else." (I thought that was a very tactful way of putting it.)

"You didn't leave his bedroom at all until you heard Luisa screaming?"

"That's ri— No, it isn't. I did leave once to go to the bathroom."

"Can you give me an idea of what time that was?"

Saundra King shook her head regretfully. "I really can't."

"Soon after you and Todd went upstairs?"

"Fairly soon, I believe, but I can't tell you the exact time. Maybe Todd could tell you—if he's in the mood for truth, that is."

"I already spoke to him about it. He has no idea." Then taking her point, I put in, "Or at least, so he claims. How long do you think you were out of the room?"

"Not long. Not more than five minutes."

"Can you estimate how soon it was after you got back that you heard the housekeeper screaming?"

"Well over an hour, probably closer to two."

"What about Todd? Did he leave his room at any time?"

"Not unless it was when I was in the bathroom."

"Would you mind telling me exactly what happened when you heard the scream?"

"Well, Todd and I both fell all over ourselves getting downstairs—it was a bloodcurdling sound—and I rushed into the library. I saw Catherine lying there, and I ran over to her. She wasn't even moving a muscle, so I picked up her wrist and felt for a pulse. As you already know, I couldn't find one. And then Luisa called Emergency Services. I guess that's about it," the woman concluded, shaking her head. But two or three seconds later: "I forgot something. When I didn't get a pulse, I started to turn her over—she was lying on her stomach. I wanted to check for a heartbeat, but Luisa stopped me. She was probably right, too. After all, we had no idea what had happened to her. Suppose she'd had a fall and twisted something and had only passed out—why, I might have caused her permanent damage."

"Where was Todd all this time?"

"As I recall, he just stood in the doorway. Probably shaking in his shoes. It's only his mouth that's brave."

I grinned. "I get the idea you spend quite a bit of time with Todd. What do you think of him?"

She grinned, too. "I have—on many, many occasions—wanted to murder that little ferret face. Yet, in a funny way, I'm kind of fond of him. You probably find that hard to believe—and I can't blame you; Barrie told me what he pulled on you—but the kid is *so* bad, so determined to cause trouble, that there are times I find him really amusing. I don't know how he even conjures up some of those stories of his! Maybe I have a warped sense of humor or something, but I actually get a kick out of how hard that stinker works trying to drive everyone crazy."

Well, her sense of humor certainly *was* warped if she got a kick out of that little monster. "I don't even know how his own mother can stand him," I said, permitting a fair amount of acid to seep into my voice.

"It's not always easy for Barrie," Saundra admitted. "I can afford to be amused by him; I only have to take him in small doses." Then, noticing that I'd just set my empty cup back on the tray, she half rose. "How about some more coffee?"

"No thanks, I'm fine."

"You've got to help me out with these, though," she said, extending the plate with the pastries. "I got them for you. I never eat sweets myself." I thought I detected a smugness in the way she said that.

What do you want, a medal? I countered nastily—but only in my head. I refused, however, to be cowed by this holier-than-thou attitude of hers. Especially since I hadn't sampled the prune Danish yet. "Thank you," I murmured, promptly rectifying the omission, "but I'm only doing this to be obliging."

"And I appreciate it," King responded, laughing good-naturedly.

I took a dainty bite of the pastry. (Good. But not as

tasty as the cheese, I critiqued.) Another bite, and it was gone. Now I was ready to devote myself to business again. "Todd seemed to have been extremely jealous of Catherine," I commented.

"Don't doubt it for a minute. She was a lot more lovable—a lot more *likable*—than he is. And her being so frail only made her more precious to everybody. She was the hands-down favorite in the family."

"Do you think it's possible he might have wanted to harm her?"

"You bet. Only he didn't." Now came another rendition of the theme I'd heard from just about everyone else. "Look, Desiree—by the way, I hope it's okay to call you Desiree—nobody had any illusions about Catherine living to a ripe old age. She was sick right from birth; I'm talking *really* sick."

"You don't think there's even a possibility she was murdered?"

"*Nobody* thinks she was murdered. Not the police. Not her doctors. Not the family. Nobody! Only her grandmother. And, please don't quote me, but I think Catherine's death might have unhinged that poor woman a little. I don't mean that she's out of her mind or anything. It's just that it hasn't been that long since her son died. And now she's lost her granddaughter. That's very tough to take. And especially at her age. No wonder she's a little irrational on the subject."

"I guess her sickness hasn't helped, either," I said, putting out a feeler but hoping she wouldn't have any idea what I was talking about.

"Oh, you know about the cancer, then? I'm sure it contributes. It's bound to be preying on her mind."

I nodded, feeling lousy about the answer. "Just when did they discover it?"

"Only a month or two before Catherine died. You see what I mean? It's as though her whole world came crashing down at once."

"How much time does she have? Does anyone know?"

Saundra King hunched her shoulders. "Nobody can say for sure. Six months, maybe, a year at the outside."

"How long have you and Mrs. Lundquist been

friends?" I asked then, trying to shake off the sadness
that had come over me.

"About four years. We met when we were both working for the same ad agency."

"You were an art director, too?" Whatever that was.
(I think about the only thing I absorbed from Barrie
Lundquist's explanation was that art directors don't
paint pictures.)

"A copywriter. Barrie and I worked as a team."

"I hope you don't mind my saying this, but you two
seem totally unlike." Given Saundra's discreet use of
makeup and conservative clothes, it was a natural
observation.

"We're more alike than you think. I guess you've noticed that Barrie supports the cosmetic industry. But
don't let all that rouge and eye glop and those outlandish
getups of hers fool you. I'm no shrink or anything, but
Barrie didn't have the most attentive husband in the
world. I think it started as a way of saying, 'Look at me;
here I am.' "

I smiled. "Well, she'd certainly be hard to overlook
now; I'll say that." Then I decided to put out another
feeler. "I've been told there was more to her divorce
than her husband's taking up with another woman,
though."

Saundra seemed genuinely stunned. But after a moment, understanding looked out of her eyes. "Who told
you that—Todd?" she snorted. And when I didn't answer: "Who else would it be? He *loves* to get people
going. Look, Paul Lundquist had a roving eye; he treated
Barrie like a piece of furniture for most of the marriage.
Then when he found someone younger and sufficiently
better-looking, he picked himself up and walked out the
door. I give Barrie credit, though. She dusted herself off,
pulled herself together and moved on. The same thing
happened to me many years ago, and I still haven't gotten over it."

I guess I was wearing my sympathy on my face—I
usually do—because Saundra said quickly, "Oh, don't
get me wrong; I'm over *him,* that son of a bitch. It's
only the feeling of rejection that's lingered on. Not that
I dwell on it, but I just haven't been able to shake it

completely. It's probably why I haven't married again."
She laughed. "And for only a hundred dollars an hour,
I'll analyze you, too."

"I'll keep that in mind," I replied with mock solemnity. "But tell me, did Barrie's ex marry the other
woman?"

"No, they split up later. And I'm happy to say that
from what I understand, *she* left *him*."

"What goes around, comes around, they claim." (I
may not have the greatest command of the language,
but I'm terrific when it comes to clichés.) "Just one more
question. Is there anything that happened that Saturday
that was at all unusual? Anything at all?"

Saundra thought for a moment before answering.
"Nothing. It was more or less like any other day. Except,
of course, that poor little Catherine died."

Chapter 13

It was time, I decided that night, to tackle Sergeant Jacobowitz once again. I tried contacting him as soon as I got to work the next morning, and then I kept *on* trying, dialing him at frequent intervals right up until six at night.

"He hasn't come in yet," I was told on attempt number one. Then an hour later: "He's on another line." Ditto a half hour after that. (This time I tried holding but gave it up after ten minutes.) And after *that,* he stepped away from his desk—twice. At three o'clock he was out to lunch (lunch?—at *three o'clock?*), following which he was on another line (I held on again, only to get disconnected), following which he'd left for the day.

I was just about to do the same when Jackie poked her brownish-blond head into my office. "What are *you* still doing here?" I asked.

"Funny. That was supposed to be my line. Mr. Sullivan's due in court first thing in the morning, and he needed some last-minute changes on this brief he's been slaving over for the past couple of weeks. What's your story?"

I grumbled about my lack of success in reaching Sergeant Jacobowitz. "It's harder to get an audience with that guy than with the pope."

"You think he could be ducking your calls?"

"That would definitely be a possibility. Except I didn't give my name."

"I don't suppose you considered leaving a message."

"Of course I considered it," I retorted indignantly. "But if he didn't get back to me, I'd have to call him again. And I really hate having someone think I'm a pest."

"Right," Jackie said. And there was a really snide look on her face.

On Wednesday at exactly nine a.m., I was at it again. *I wonder where he'll be now—in the john?* I silently bitched while I was dialing. Then as soon as the phone rang at the other end, I entered my paranoid mode. *What difference does it make if I do reach him? He'll only come up with another excuse not to see me,* I informed myself with total conviction.

I was clenching my costly veneered teeth and manically drumming a pencil on the desk by the time Jacobowitz picked up on the fourth ring.

He sounded a lot less harried than during our last conversation, and when I asked when it would be possible to meet with him, he threw me completely by saying, "How about now?"

Sometimes it's a real problem for me to deal with anything positive. "You mean *right* now?" I responded stupidly. Luckily, I managed to recover before the guy could change his mind, quickly adding, "I'm on my way."

Frank Jacobowitz was thirty-something, short and round, with a prominent backside and an all but invisible waist. In fact, I'm not too happy to admit that the guy was shaped a lot like a male me (excluding the obvious places, naturally). The similarity, however, ended at the hairline. Except for the sparsest amount of something that looked like orange fuzz and which decorated the very top of his barren crown, Jacobowitz's forehead extended all the way to the back of his neck. Surprisingly, as far as I was concerned, the baldness only contributed to the sergeant's youthful appearance, reminding me of all the heads looking very much like his that were right now lying on their little lacy pillows in pastel-colored nurseries all over America.

"Take a seat, please," he was saying in his boyish voice, his pleasant face with its warm pink complexion now made warmer still by a bright, welcoming smile.

"What is it I can tell you?" he asked politely as soon

as I was seated—very uncomfortably—on the hard wooden chair next to his desk.

"Well, to start with, I know the autopsy report was 'acute respiratory failure,' " I began, "but what if Catherine Corwin was poisoned? I mean, aren't there some poisons that would produce the same diagnosis?"

"Look, I had a conversation with the M.E. about that. They did a very thorough toxicology screen. The blood was even sent to an out-of-state lab—in Philly, it was—for further analysis. There's no evidence at all that the little girl was poisoned."

"Well, what if it was an untraceable poison?" I speculated, more to myself than to Jacobowitz.

The sergeant answered me anyway. "Look, we talked to the woman—the housekeeper, I'm referring to—who prepared her breakfast that morning, and she swears no one could have put anything in the food."

"Well, suppose—"

"Naturally, the M.E. also considered the possibility she might have been injected with something," he broke in, anticipating me. "Says he went over that poor kid's body with a fine-tooth comb looking for puncture marks—even checked her scalp and under her fingernails." I shuddered then; I couldn't help it. I was just hoping Sergeant Jacobowitz hadn't noticed, but I got the feeling he had. (If so, though, he was polite enough not to make any cracks about women and squeamishness or anything of that stupid nature.) "And there were no suspicious marks of any other kind, either," he reported. "Nothing to indicate trauma." Then he reiterated somberly, "Nothing."

"I wonder if I could see the photographs of the crime—uh, the death—scene," I asked.

Jacobowitz hesitated. "I don't think ..." Then he broke off with a grin. "Okay. Why not?" he agreed. "I don't see how it can matter. Besides, I can always get a job in porno movies." I liked this guy's attitude!

He excused himself while I took the opportunity to squirm around in my chair in a vain attempt to relieve that wooden assassin's violation of my hindquarters. In a couple of minutes, he returned with a folder. Standing alongside me, he extracted a number of eight-by-tens,

which he unobtrusively slipped in front of me. "Here.
Take your time. Just try not to be too obvious about it,
huh?" Then, sitting down at his desk, he promptly
picked up the telephone.

While Jacobowitz was busy with his call, I bent over
the photographs, examining each of them in turn. Again
and again I had to steel myself to the sight of that tiny
form lying there so pathetically and irrevocably still.

The top photo was a medium close-up of the body. It
showed Catherine facedown on the carpet, the long
blond hair fanning out from her head. Her right arm
was extended in front of her as though reaching for
something, while her left arm was at her side, the small
fingers curled in a fist.

There were other shots of Catherine from different
angles, along with shots of the various sections of the
library and a long shot of the entire room. In one photo
I noted the overturned chair that was part of the card
table grouping. In another, I got a good look at the
bronze lamp Luisa had mentioned to me; it was lying on
the floor, right next to the round cherry table—on the
side opposite the body. And in a third, I saw the book
that lay in a corner of the brown Chesterfield sofa. I
could make out most of the title, too: *The Boy from
Planet* . . . I was able to supply myself with the one word
I couldn't see: *Pluto*.

I studied the pictures a second time, more carefully
now. And that's when you could have drawn a light bulb
over my head!

I was examining a close-up of the cherry table. On it,
of course, was the telephone system that just about everyone agreed the deceased had been trying to get to.
The phone was on that part of the tabletop farthest from
the Chesterfield sofa. On the side closest to the sofa—
and almost directly opposite the telephone—was a
feather duster. And to the right of the duster there was a
picture frame containing a collage of small photographs.

Now, when I was in the library with Luisa, asking
whether anything was missing from the room since Catherine's death, the housekeeper didn't tell me about any
picture frame. Yet the night I was there, it was nowhere
to be seen!

Oh, come on, will you? I chided myself. *What are we talking about here, anyway? It's a frame with some photos, for God's sake, not some valuable family treasure! Of what significance could a thing like that possibly be?*

Still, it was worth checking into. After all, what else did I have?

Sergeant Jacobowitz hung up the phone at this point. He turned and looked at me closely, as if trying to read my face. "I may be wrong," he said tentatively, "but, well, I get the impression you're not so convinced anymore that the kid died of her sickness."

"It's not that. I just want to make sure I cover everything, that's all. I told you that on the phone, remember?"

"I remember, but it seems—" He shrugged. "Never mind." A moment later, he leaned toward me. "Listen, I'm not saying that it's absolutely positive that kid wasn't whacked somehow—anything's possible, I guess. But what I am saying is that it's extremely doubtful. Like I told you before, that was a thorough autopsy they did, and there was nothing at all to indicate she died of anything but having the misfortune to be born a very sick little girl. And to be straight with you, I don't understand your client. She should be *thankful* of those findings, *thankful* her granddaughter wasn't murdered."

I opened my mouth to explain something of Mrs. Corwin's thought processes but promptly closed it when Jacobowitz began to tell me a lot of what I'd intended telling *him.* "Look," he said, his cheeks growing pinker and his voice becoming more impassioned as he warmed to his subject, "I can understand how she'd blame herself for not believing her granddaughter about that car business. Probably thinks if she *had* believed her, she could have prevented the thing from happening. And I guess if this was labeled a murder, it would give her an excuse for beating up on herself a little. But the fact is, if someone was out to get that kid—which I'd be willing to swear they weren't—they'd have found a way to do it, even if she went out and hired the kid a bodyguard."

I was certain he'd wound down then, so I was about to agree with him, gather up my belongings and thank him kindly for his time. But he picked up some more steam. "Let me tell you, if that old woman's in pain now, it's nothing compared to what she'd feel if she learned that someone really did go and whack that grandkid of hers. What I'm trying to say is that I've had my share of experiences with the parents and grandparents of murdered children. And take it from me, there's nothing worse you can go through than losing a child that way."

Jacobowitz leaned back, waiting for my reaction. "Normally, I'd agree with every word you said," I let him know. "And I do agree with most of it. But in this case I think there may be something else to consider. Mrs. Corwin is so certain Catherine was murdered and so distraught over not being able to convince anyone of it that to have the worst confirmed could actually help her—you know, give her some peace of mind." Jacobowitz eyed me skeptically, so I quickly put in, "Oh, not right away, of course; I'm talking eventually. It would bring a kind of closure to the thing."

"Assuming the perp is ever identified," he remarked dryly.

"Well, naturally. That goes without saying. But anyway, even if I'm wrong, I've made a commitment to the woman, and I have to see it through."

His response was a sigh, accompanied by a shake of the head.

"What?" I asked, already certain of the gist of what was to follow.

"You're looking for something that isn't there, Desiree," he told me kindly, maybe even a little pityingly. Then he glanced down at the pictures. "And I'm not just talking about these, either."

Preparing to leave, I picked up the attaché case at my feet. "Yes, uh, you're probably right," I conceded absentmindedly, my brain one step ahead of my mouth for a change, as I thought with a glimmer of hope about the picture frame that just shouldn't have been where it was. *But then again, it's equally possible that you're wrong,* I informed him silently, lifting my afflicted posterior from the chair.

And if that turns out to be the case, it's worth a sore rump any day.

Chapter 14

Now, don't misunderstand me.

It wasn't that I wanted it to turn out that little Catherine had been murdered—I agreed with Sergeant Jacobowitz; it would be hard to think of a more horrendous crime. But then again, given my client's mind-set, I didn't want to *not* find the evidence she was so desperate for. (And if that sounds like I was about as muddled as you can get, it's only because I was.) Anyway, what I'm trying to say is that the picture frame was the first concrete clue of any kind that I'd found, so I had no choice but to follow up on it. And even if it should wind up leading nowhere (I mean, as clues went, it had to be right up there with the flimsiest), at least it took matters out of my hands.

As soon as I left the precinct, I headed straight for a pay phone, finding one in actual working order on the third try. *Must be my lucky day.*

"Corwin residence," Luisa announced.

"This is Desiree Shapiro," I told her. "I called to check something with you."

Her voice was instantly wary. "Yes?"

"Do you remember when I asked if you noticed anything missing from the library since Catherine's death?"

Another wary "Yes."

"Well, I just went over some photographs taken by the police that afternoon, and there was a picture frame on that cherry table—you know, the one with the telephone."

"A picture frame?"

"That's right. A frame containing a collage of photographs."

"Ohh. My goodness! I never even noticed it in the

room that day. That frame is usually kept in the small downstairs study."

"Would you know if it's in the study now?"

"No. That is, I do know, and it's not there. I imagine Mrs. Corwin still has it in her room."

"You saw it in Mrs. Corwin's bedroom?"

"A couple of weeks ago."

"Is Mrs. Corwin home now, Luisa?"

"I believe she came in a short while ago. Did you want to talk to her?"

"Please."

Donna Corwin came to the phone just after I'd made New York Telephone—it wasn't called NYNEX yet—twenty-five cents richer. "I wonder if I could stop in to see you," I requested politely. "I won't take up much of your time."

"Of course. Did you want to come by tonight?"

"That would be fine."

"Around seven?"

"I'll be there."

"Oh, one minute," she said hurriedly as I was about to terminate the conversation. "Have you found out anything?" The thought had apparently just occurred to her, and now there was a trace of anxiety in her tone.

"Oh, no, I'd like to ask you about something, that's all."

"About what?"

"Some pictures." I didn't want to give her the chance to explain things away on the phone, so I quickly added, "I'll tell you all about it when I see you." And she let it go at that.

When I arrived at the town house that night, Luisa again brought me to the sitting room. I found Donna Corwin—dressed in baggy jeans and a blue-and-white-striped shirt—in the big black armchair her mother-in-law had occupied on my first visit here. She was knitting something using two balls of heavy yarn, a red and a cream, and frowning in concentration as she worked. The piece was a rectangle, measuring about eighteen by twenty-four inches, and she was so intent on her task—for which she was using the most outsize needles I'd

ever seen—that she was totally unaware anyone else was
in the room. Which was surprising, considering that
Luisa and I had been engaging in conversation—and we
weren't speaking in whispers, either—right up until we
came to the doorway. She finally looked up when the
housekeeper murmured a tentative, "Mrs. Corwin?"

"Oh, come in, Desiree! I didn't even know you'd arrived. Thanks, Luisa," she said practically in the same
breath. The housekeeper nodded, then turned and shut
the door soundlessly behind her. "Sit down. Please. I
just learned how to knit, and I've gotten totally caught
up in it," Donna informed me apologetically.

"A sweater?" I asked, settling into the sofa.

"God, no!" she protested, grinning. "I'm not ready for
anything like that. I'm just a beginner. It's an afghan."

"I like the colors."

"Thanks. It gives me something to do, anyway. A
friend of mine insisted on teaching me last week. Promised it would help take my mind off things. And you
know something? It has. I'm at it every minute I get a
chance." With that, she wrapped the two balls of wool
in her handiwork and gently tucked the project down at
her side, between the seat cushion and the chair. "Luisa
tells me you wanted to talk to me about the picture
frame—the one we used to keep in the study."

"Yes. But it was on a table in the library the day
Catherine died; I saw it in the police photos."

"There's no great mystery about that. The frame has
an assortment of photographs of Catherine—a collage—
and the night before she died, I took it off the bookshelf
in the study, intending to bring it upstairs with me. I
wanted to substitute a snapshot Barrie had taken of her
for another picture I never really cared for that much.
But then, on the way up to my room, I passed the library
and saw Barrie in there looking for a book. I stopped
in to chat, putting the frame on the table, and by the
time I was ready to go upstairs, I forgot about it." Then,
a sheepish expression on her face, Donna added, "And
I even stood it up on its easel so I'd be sure to notice
it on my way out."

"And you retrieved the picture frame after the police
were through in the library." It wasn't even a question.

"That's right. I like to keep it upstairs now so I can look at the pictures of Catherine whenever I have the urge. It's painful in a way, but in another way it makes me feel closer to her. I guess you'd call that kind of thing 'bittersweet.' "

I nodded. But the woman looked so stricken, I practically had to sit on my hands to keep from leaning over and patting her on the shoulder and clucking, "There, there," or something just as useless.

Well, anyway, that was that. The picture frame had led just where my more sensible voice had been trying to tell me it would lead: nowhere. And then I heard myself saying, "Do you mind if I take a look at those photographs?" I had absolutely no purpose in asking that. And to this day I can't imagine why I did.

Donna was obviously distressed by the request. "I'm sure there's nothing there that would help your investigation," she told me, her voice sharp, and two bright spots of color suddenly decorating the pale cheeks.

Now I was curious. "Is there some reason you'd rather not have me see them?"

"No, of course not. I'll bring the frame down in a minute." She got up and hurried from the room, her lips pressed tightly together.

When she returned, she was carrying a shopping bag and trying her best not to show that she was disturbed. She even favored me with a tense little smile. If the woman wasn't exactly thrilled to have me look at the photographs, she seemed, at least, resigned to it. She sat down, then removed the frame from the shopping bag, handing it to me facedown without comment.

The frame was larger than I'd expected from the police shots—about eleven by seventeen, I'd say—and bordered in a handsome inlaid wood that was probably an inch and a half wide. I was, of course, curious when I turned it over. I mean, from Donna Corwin's attitude, I knew I'd find *something* unexpected. Still, I was totally unprepared for what I saw.

There were cutouts of various shapes and sizes in the ivory matting,—eight in all—with little Catherine peering out of every opening. The pictures were a chronology of the child's brief life, dating from her infancy to close to the time of her death. Some of the photos were obviously the work of a professional, others candid snapshots. But they were all alike in one truly horrifying way:

In every photograph Catherine Corwin's small, delicate features were completely obliterated by an ugly red X across her face.

Chapter 15

"I felt sick the first time I saw it. Physically ill," Donna was saying in a trembling voice. "It was just so shocking. For a little while I thought that maybe Evelyn was right after all, that maybe someone did hate Catherine enough to want her dead."

"I gather you no longer feel that way."

"No, I don't. It was a nasty—no, more than nasty, a *hateful*—thing to do." Reaching into her jeans pocket for a tissue, she made a quick dab at her eyes. "But I don't think whoever did it murdered her," she went on. "And that's because I don't think she was murdered at all."

"Do you suspect someone in particular of defacing the photos?"

"It's hard to say. The frame was on my night table, right out in the open," she responded evasively.

"Yes, I know. But you must have some sort of suspicion," I prodded, trying to get her to say the name so I wouldn't have to.

"Well, I don't think it would be fair to speculate."

We could go on like this all night! "You think it was Todd, don't you?" I threw out.

The answer was so long in coming that I was beginning to think there wasn't going to *be* an answer. "Let's just call it a possibility," Donna finally replied.

"Have you asked him about it?"

"I can't do that," she said flatly.

"I don't understand."

"All right. Suppose I do ask Todd? He'll only deny it. And then I'll get even more upset. I'll say something, then he'll say something, then—" Making a face, she broke off. "The whole thing would only escalate," she continued a moment later. "Believe me, all I'd accomplish by confronting Todd would be to upset Barrie, and that would be cruel. She's worried enough about him as it is. And Catherine's death was her loss, too, remember?"

"I remember. And I also know you two are good friends, but I think it's important to get to the bottom of this." I waited for her to respond, and when she didn't, I plunged right in. "Would you mind if *I* had a talk with Todd?"

"Yes, I would. You have no idea what sort of family situation this could provoke. I've kept the thing hidden in a drawer since To—since someone did that to it." Then, reluctantly: "Look, Desiree, if my mother-in-law finds out about this, I don't know *what* she'll do. She might even disinherit Todd, for all I know. I just don't want to be responsible for anything like that."

"You won't be," I assured her. "I'd like to make a deal with you." Donna was shaking her head adamantly before I had a chance to say anything more. "Listen," I persisted, "you have to remember that I was hired to follow every lead. If you refuse to let me broach the subject with Todd, I'll have to report what he did to your mother-in-law." I knew that while this was true enough, it still sounded a lot like blackmail. And I don't deny that, in a way, that's just what it was. So I tried to lighten things up a little.

"I probably like this less than you do," I told her with what I hoped was an ingratiating smile. "I always hated the kids in school who ratted to the teacher—maybe because I was usually the one they ratted on." The silly little titter that followed was completely inadvertent. Nevertheless, when she didn't titter back, I leveled with her. "Seriously, like it or not, following through on everything is what an investigation is about. I have to see where this thing with Todd leads. But if it should turn out that—"

"I never would have let you set eyes on those pictures if I thought you'd go running to my mother-in-law with this," Donna broke in, bestowing on my person the sort of look one usually reserves for a cockroach. A *pregnant* cockroach. "Well, it shows you how smart *I* am. But then again, I didn't think there'd be any *reason* for you to do a thing like that."

"It's only that I—"

"I mean, why would you?" she demanded, stepping on my words again. "My daughter died of her sickness. I got the impression you agreed with that."

"I—"

"According to what you told me, you took this case mainly to convince my mother-in-law it *wasn't* murder. In fact, I can't see why you're still involved in this; it should have been all wrapped up by now."

I ventured a reply. "You're right," I said quickly. And when she didn't cut me off: "I did hope to persuade your mother-in-law that Catherine hadn't been murdered. But before I can persuade *her* of that, I have to be a hundred percent certain myself."

There was a long pause. I could almost read her mind (which was no great feat considering the expression with which she was regarding me). "Not only is this henna-headed bitch blackmailing me, but she's also milking this thing for all it's worth," is what she was thinking. But no matter what her feelings were toward me, she really didn't have much of an option, and I guess she realized it. So having had her say, Donna was finally ready to listen. "All right," she told me at last, "let's hear your deal."

"It's like this. I'll have a talk with Todd. But I won't mention the photos to anyone unless it should turn out Todd had something to do with Catherine's death."

"That's it?"

"That's it."

She thought it over for maybe a minute. "Okay, it's a deal," she grudgingly agreed.

"Good. Is Young Dillinger around now?"

"Last time I looked, he was in the kitchen. He usually is," she added tartly. "I'll see if I can get him to come in. You don't need me anymore, do you?" She was already fumbling around at her side for her knitting.

"No, but I do need this." I tapped my finger on the frame in my lap.

"Yes, well, just make sure you give it to Luisa when you leave. I wouldn't want anything *worse* to happen to it." Then, retrieving her handiwork, she started to get up.

"One more question."

Slowly, she sank back down in the chair again.

"Do you know when this happened?" I asked her.

"It was last week. Wednesday evening, to be precise." It was almost as though a cloud passed over Donna's face then. "Funny, isn't it," she murmured (and I know she was thinking aloud, since she wasn't exactly on speaking terms with me). "I had this snapshot Barrie took of Catherine for the longest time—it might have been close to a year. Yet I suddenly got the urge to substitute it in the collage on the very night before she died."

If anything, Todd looked even freakier than he had during our previous little chats. The greasy frizzed hair with the magenta streak was frizzier than ever—seeming to extend about a foot from his head on either side. He was wearing tattered jeans, ripped dangerously close to the crotch. These were topped with his classy DON'T SCREW WITH ME T-shirt, on which you could now make out the menu for his last half dozen meals. And to complete the disgusting picture, his huge feet were bare and none too clean.

Smiling nastily, he perched on the arm of the chair Donna had vacated, his arms crossed at the chest in a pose of self-importance. "What can I do for you, counselor?" he asked in his squeaky little voice. He was, apparently, trying to show off what must have been a new word for him—probably acquired while watching TV.

"I'm a private investigator, if you recall—not a counselor. A counselor's a lawyer." I provided this instruction with exaggerated patience, delighted with the opportunity to set him straight about something. (I know, I know; I'm a grown woman and here I was practicing one-upmanship on a boy. But I couldn't help it. This kid just seemed to bring out everything that's petty and mean and vile in my nature.)

Todd was unperturbed. "So?"

"So what do you know about this?" I challenged,

picking up the frame in my lap and practically shoving it in his face.

His answer rocked me. "You like my artwork?" he said, smirking.

"You admit you did it?" I gasped.

"Yeah, I did it. Me and my good ole magic marker." His changing voice picked then to change. "What of it?" he put to me insolently, his voice dropping for a second or two to a more masculine pitch.

"I know you hated Catherine, but *this*—this is sick."

"You think so? Sez who?"

"You need . . . it's obvious you need . . . you could use a *lot* of help," I sputtered.

"Yeah? Well, so could you if you got the idea this means I'm the one who croaked the little puke."

"But why would you want to do this to her pictures?"

"Because she useta piss me off all the time, that's why. Only I couldn't do nuthin' about it—see? She was everybody's little princess. Nobody knew what a pain in the ass she could be, a course. Anyways, now that somebody's croaked her—*if* somebody's croaked her . . ." He left the thought hanging in midair, but when I didn't fill up the void, he added, "Look, I didn't *hurt* her; she was already dead, f'r chrissakes! And this way I got all the hostility out of my system." He was looking very pleased with himself at springing this unexpected knowledge of psychology on me. But failing to get a reaction, he added almost petulantly, "Hey, that's supposed to be healthy, ain't it? Besides, she needed some color anyways; she useta walk around here lookin' like some pukin' ghost."

"You did your little dirty work last Wednesday, I understand."

"If that's what *she* says."

"What do *you* say?" I demanded.

"It was prob'ly Wednesday," Todd conceded nonchalantly.

"But Catherine's been dead quite awhile now. Why did you wait until then?"

"Because that's when I felt like it."

"You realize this is very serious, Todd, don't you?"

"Oh, come on," he scoffed. "It didn't have nuthin' to do with her dyin'."

"It shows a very deep hatred for her."

"Who cares?" Then, after a moment: "I'm surprised dear Donna took a whole week to squeal on me. She'd love to get me in trouble. She's worried, you see, on account of what I know about her, and she thinks—"

"Oh, come off it! Don't start *that* again. Donna didn't even want me to see those pictures. And she didn't accuse you of anything, either; I did. Donna—"

"All right, all right. But like I said, what I did got rid of my hostility and—"

"I'm not convinced."

"You got me all shook, you know that?" he shot back, glaring at me.

"And I wonder if your mother will be."

"Big deal."

"*Or* your grandmother. Your *great*-grandmother, that is—the one with the money."

At this, Todd lost some of his bravado. "Listen, lady," he put to me in a very reasonable tone, "if I'da killed Catherine, would I of made you suspect me by doin' that to the pitchers?"

"Maybe you didn't think about that at the time."

"And anyways, you think I'da *tole* you I was the one?" I was chewing that one over when he added, "Hey, that woulda been stupid. *Real* stupid."

He had a point there.

Chapter 16

I was having Ellen and Mike over to dinner the next night. I'd considered asking Stuart so we could make it a foursome, but—I don't know—it just didn't seem like too great an idea. Anyway, as soon as I got home from the Corwin place, I started preparing a few things. I figured that, for starters, I'd serve a salmon mousse, plus some tiny puffed pastry rectangles with a cheddar cheese filling. The main course would be roast loin of pork with sherry—a favorite of Ellen's—which we'd have with a sweet potato casserole. There'd be a nice big salad, of course, and then for dessert, my cold lemon soufflé—another Ellen favorite. (I really didn't know much about Mike's tastes in food yet, so I concentrated on pleasing Ellen and hoped Mike would like the menu, too.)

I was rolling out the pastry for the cheese appetizers and up to my elbows in dough—I'm not the neatest cook in the world—when the telephone rang. I quickly wiped a little of the sticky mess off my hands and picked up, getting a lot more of the gunk on the phone than I had on the paper towel.

"Desiree," my neighbor Barbara said without preamble, "I was wondering if you were busy tomorrow night."

"I'm—"

Listening is not Barbara's thing. "There's this wonderful foreign film at the Coronet," she went on, "and tomorrow's the last day."

"I'm sorry, Barbara, but my niece and her, uh, friend are coming over for dinner tomorrow night."

She didn't seem too perturbed. "That's okay. Guess I'll give one of my colleagues a ring," she replied, referring to her fellow teachers and sounding quite cheerful. Somehow, that made me feel very expendable.

I was just digging my fingers into the dough again when I got another call. I hurriedly wiped my hands as best I could—doing just as lousy a job of it as I had before—and said hello, checking my watch at the same time. It was twenty after ten.

"Hi, it's Pat," my friend Pat Martucci announced. "I hope I didn't wake you or anything." To her credit, she waited until I assured her she hadn't before continuing. "If you don't have any plans for tomorrow night, I thought you might like to go to the ballet with me. A ticket just this minute became available." With that, she began to cry.

"What's wrong, Pat?"

"It's this—this man I met," she blubbered.

That figured. "What man?" I asked. I mean, when we had lunch just a couple of weeks ago, she'd been bemoaning the fact there was no one in her life.

"His name's Duane. Duane Provost," she told me, loudly blowing her nose. "I met him at the supermarket last Monday. He asked me how you could tell if a pineapple was ripe—that's how it started."

"And?" I said a little impatiently, as I thought with something like despair of the hours of work still ahead of me. Which made me feel guilty as hell. I mean, my friend here was in emotional distress, for God's sake. (Never mind that with Pat this occurred almost as regularly as the sun's rising.)

"Naturally, I told him that the first thing you have to do is smell it, and then you check the leaves to—"

"You can skip that part," I put in hastily.

"I'm sorry. That was silly of me." A little laugh. "I guess it's because I'm upset. Well, at any rate, we hit it off right away. Right after my lesson in pineapple, that is." Another little laugh. "Honestly, Dez, I've never been that immediately attracted to *anyone*."

Now, I am not a mean enough person to have reminded her that this was an echo of what she said practically every time she took up with somebody new. So I just responded with "What happened?"

"Well, we saw each other every night since the A&P, and one night—Friday, I think it was—he mentioned how he loved the ballet, so I thought I'd get tickets and surprise him." She snuffled, and then there was a brief interval, during which all I heard were a couple of loud honks. "But," she resumed, her voice taking on a dramatic timbre, "it seems that when Duane went home last night—at five a.m., I might add—there was a message from his wife."

"His what?"

"I did tell you he was married, didn't I? But anyway, they were separated. They've been separated for *weeks* now."

It was all I could do to keep what I was thinking from leaping onto my tongue.

"And when he called her back this morning," Pat was informing me, "she said how much she missed him and begged him to give the marriage another chance." This was punctuated by a new round of snuffles. "And even though he swears he doesn't love her, he feels that for the sake of the children—they have five—he should give it another try. He called me just a few minutes ago to tell me all this—claims he just got up the courage and that it's been tearing him up to think that what we had is over."

Oh, Pat! I wondered if she could really believe that, then decided she probably did and that maybe it helped.

"Anyway," she concluded, "here I am with two third-row orchestra seats to *Coppelia*. So I wanted to know if you're free to be my date for the ballet tomorrow evening."

I'll say this for Pat, she's a damned practical woman. Crushed as she was over this latest romance gone awry, she was not about to let two perfectly good ballet tickets go to waste. And, it appeared, she had no intention of just giving them both away, either. "Gee, Pat," I told her regretfully, "I'm afraid I can't make it tomorrow night. Ellen's coming over for dinner." I purposely avoided mentioning Mike, thinking that if she found out Ellen had a significant other, it might rub salt into Pat's still raw wounds.

"Maybe you could switch Ellen to another night," she suggested hopefully. "They're sixty dollar tickets, Dez. Sixty dollars *apiece*."

Now, I ask you, what could I do? "It's not just Ellen," I admitted then. "This friend of hers is coming, too."

"What kind of a friend?" she demanded suspiciously. "A man?"

"Yes, a man."

"So how long has *this* been going on, anyway?"

"For quite a few months."

"Is it serious?"

"Well, I guess it *could* be."

"That's nice. I'm happy for Ellen. I really am. Not that I know her that well, but being she's *your* niece—" She broke off for a moment before adding with false perkiness, "I really *am* happy for her. In fact, it's actually giving me a lift."

"Good," I responded, hoping she'd manage to talk *herself* into this newfound state of bliss. "And I'm sorry I can't make it tomorrow night. Is there anyone else you think might be able to go?"

"I'll call Sylvia. She'll come with me; she never has anything to do."

Meow! "That's a good idea," I told her.

For some reason this produced a few more tears, accompanied by Pat's solemn vow that she was through forever and all time with individuals of the masculine persuasion. "You know," she pronounced then, "it serves me right. I should never have taken up with a Sagittarius."

I was up until close to three o'clock, finishing all of the parts of the Ellen and Mike dinner that I'd made up my mind to take care of in advance. I was practically mummified when I crawled into bed—and then I couldn't sleep. I guess I must have been overtired. Anyway, I tossed and turned for what seemed like a year. I'll bet it was after five when I finally dropped off. And when the alarm went off at seven-thirty, I reached out my arm, fumbled around my night table, found that damn, shrill little bastard, and pushed in the lever. All without actually waking up.

What finally did wake me, however, was the incessant ringing of the telephone.

"Hmmm?" I said. (It was supposed to come out "hello.")

"Desiree? It's Jackie. Is anything wrong?"

That woke me, all right! I sat up in bed and looked at the clock. It was after eleven—and I was about to be reprimanded as only Jackie *can* reprimand. "No, no, Jackie, I—"

"Don't tell me you're going to start pulling *that* stuff again," declared Ms. Master Intimidator. "I thought we agreed you'd call if you weren't coming to the office on time."

"We did, Jackie, and I—"

But she was only warming up. "Christ, Desiree, you know I worry about you. I can really live without a vision of you strangled in your bed by one of your murderers." (*I like that! One of "my" murderers!*) "It would just be plain, ordinary courtesy to let me in on your plans, you know."

"But—but I didn't *have* any plans," I stammered, surprised that she was actually letting me put a complete sentence together now. "Listen, Jackie, I fully expected I'd be at work on time, and then I overslept. I'm really sorry if I caused you any worry."

Jackie, however, was in no mood to forgive. (I swear, if she didn't possess such sterling qualities as both a secretary and a friend, I would have fired her from both positions a long time ago.) "Well, you might try going to bed at a decent hour," she sniffed. "What time should I expect you? I have to know what to say if anyone calls."

I'd intended leaving the office about an hour and a half early to get ready for my company. But in view of how late it would be before I even got there, it suddenly made sense to skip work altogether. Which is what I explained to Jackie.

"Whatever you say," she replied magnanimously. "After all, I'm not your boss."

But you know, don't you, that she didn't believe that for a minute.

By the time Ellen and Mike arrived at seven-thirty, everything was ready. But just barely.

I'd had my normal quota of disasters that day: When I opened the refrigerator door in the morning, the mayonnaise jar flew out, splintering all over my beautiful black and white ceramic tile floor and chipping one of the tiles in the process. For my next trick, I spilled an entire can of Comet on the bathroom floor, which—as everyone who's ever been sloppy enough to do a thing like that knows—is really a bitch to clean up. And then later I had this lengthy and violent confrontation with my hair. It ended with my going to the closet for my wig. Which I should have thought of a whole lot earlier, since the wig looks just like my own hair but is usually considerably less mulish. I managed to get myself together only minutes before my company arrived.

Ellen and Mike look just perfect together. She's five-six and boyishly slim, with dark eyes, silky brown hair and a terrific smile. I think she looks a lot like Audrey Hepburn. Well, maybe not a *lot,* but if you keep an open mind, there's a definite resemblance. Mike's well over six feet and he, too, is lean, with sandy-colored hair and blue eyes. I supposed their children would be brown-eyed like Ellen.

While we were sitting in the living room nibbling on our hors d'oeuvres and sipping wine—Ellen and Mike brought a delicious Chilean sauvignon blanc—I was surreptitiously taking stock of Ellen's intended. I'd seen him only a couple of times since our first meeting, and then just briefly. There was something truly gentle about his face, I decided. In fact, he was really nice-looking, not merely pleasant-looking as I'd thought initially. But no wonder I hadn't realized that before. I mean, with him being so tall, it was hard for me to get a very good look at his face. Unless, of course, he was sitting down, as he was now.

"Mike had to work last night," Ellen was saying. "This other resident broke his ankle, so he filled in for him. And then he put in a full day today."

"His wrist," Mike corrected good-naturedly, grinning indulgently at her.

"Anyway, he's kinda beat, and he's worried he'll fall asleep in his soup or something."

"Not quite," he told her. And to me: "But I am a

little tired, so I hope you'll excuse me if I'm not very good company."

"Don't worry about it. I'm not very good company even when I'm wide awake. Just ask Ellen."

Mike threw me a grateful smile, after which he turned to Ellen. "Oh, I almost forgot," he said. "Today was your day off, wasn't it? Any luck finding a dress?"

"Uh-uh, I didn't see a thing." Then coloring becomingly, she told me almost reluctantly, "Mike invited me to his cousin's wedding, and I want to get something new. It's almost two months off, but, I figured I'd better start looking."

He's taking her to meet the family! I thought, positively ecstatic.

Ellen had evidently developed a talent for mind-reading, because she gave me kind of a dark look and informed me pointedly, "Mike's parents will be in Europe then; his father has some kind of convention. They're really disappointed about missing their nephew's wedding."

I was not about to let her put a damper on things. After all, she'd be meeting the rest of the family—aunts and uncles and cousins—wouldn't she? *When you make a match, you really make a match!* I congratulated myself (ignoring, of course, the long string of disasters for which I also bore responsibility.)

Mike said something about how his father was one of the principal speakers at the convention, so there was no way his folks could get out of their trip, and then the timer rang to let me know the meat was ready. A few minutes later, we made the trek to the other side of the living room and sat down at the folding table I'd set up for dinner.

The meal was a complete success. Mike, it seemed, loved loin of pork, too (those two were *so* compatible); in fact, like Ellen, he was extremely complimentary about everything I served. And my kitchen prowess being one thing about which I'm totally immodest, I can say with absolutely no shame that I deserved every last syllable of praise.

After coffee and dessert (Mike, I noted with pleasure,

had three helpings of the soufflé), Ellen and I cleared away the dishes, insisting that Mike relax on the sofa; you could tell he was really exhausted. When something that was a cross between a whistle and a groan emanated from that area soon afterward, we glanced over at him. He was sound asleep, and making the strangest noises you've ever heard. Ear plugs would definitely be requisite to the survival of my niece's impending marriage.

"Doesn't he look adorable?" Ellen whispered.

Now, just then Mike's mouth was wide open, and at one corner there was a trickle of spittle that was poised to run down his chin.

Adorable was not the word I would have used. "Mmmm," I said.

"Let's go into the kitchen so we don't wake him," I suggested. We tiptoed out of the room, sat at the kitchen table and, over another cup of coffee, talked about Mike, with Ellen insisting the invitation to the wedding didn't mean a thing, but wasn't he just wonderful? and with me, in deference to her protests, trying to put a lid on my enthusiasm.

Sometime later, she suddenly popped up with: "I was thinking I might be seeing Stuart here tonight."

So I told her how I'd had the feeling off and on all that weekend we were away in New Hope together that something wasn't quite right between us.

"Maybe he was in a funny mood," she offered. "Or maybe you were just feeling a little sensitive. If there was anything bothering him—anything to do with you, I mean—why would he ask you to go away with him in the first place?"

"We made our plans weeks and weeks ago. Who knows what may have happened in the interim?"

"Like what?"

"Like maybe he met someone."

Ellen chewed that over for a while. "Oh, I don't think so ..." she finally responded uncertainly. "But listen, if you really feel there's something funny going on, why don't you just call him up and ask him what's what?"

I told her I'd probably end up doing just that.

"I want to hear about the investigation," Ellen said then. "How is it going?"

"It seems to be over."

"Really? Why? What happened?"

I brought her up to date. "I've gone as far as I can with this," I concluded. "I haven't been able to uncover any evidence at all to support my client's contention that it was murder. And now I'm going to have to work up the courage to tell her that. But I know she won't believe me no matter what I say."

"You don't think Todd could have done it?"

"Anyone could have done it; I just don't believe anyone did."

"But that horrible thing he did to those photographs—doesn't that mean anything?"

"Sure it does. It means he hated Catherine, which everyone already knows. And that he's a sick little bastard, which everyone also already knows. And that's all it means."

"Well, if that's how you feel . . ." She let it go at that.

"What's the matter?"

"I probably shouldn't say this; after all, I didn't want you to take the case in the first place and—"

"*What* shouldn't you say?" I demanded impatiently.

Ellen took a deep breath. "All right," she said. "It's just that you're a terrific investigator—the best one I know." (No doubt because I was the only investigator she knew.) "The way you solved some of your other cases—well, it was positively brilliant. But, umm, the thing of it is . . ."

Uh-oh, here it comes!

And then in a rush: "I don't really think you gave this your best shot. Do you?"

"What are you talking about? Of course I did!" I bristled. "Why in the world would you say something like that?"

"Look, Aunt Dez—and don't be angry—from what I could see, you went about this case entirely differently from anything else you've ever worked on."

"What's that supposed to mean?"

"It means that with only a couple of exceptions, everything you did was to prove to your client that there hadn't been a murder at all, instead of starting with the premise that there *had* been a murder and then trying to find out who committed it."

"That's ridiculous!" I fumed. "When I saw that picture frame in the police photos, I went right to—"

"I *said* there were a couple of exceptions. And that was the main one. But by and large, if you really want my opinion, you, well, you weren't nearly as thorough this time."

"That's not true at all. And I think I know more about my business than you do," I countered in this tone that was frigid enough to give my poor niece pneumonia.

"Okay, have it your way. But it's true." Ellen can be a very stubborn person. "Anyway, I don't suppose there's much chance of getting a CARE package now that I'm on your shit list," she ventured with a tentative smile.

I went along with this transparent attempt to change the subject, and we chatted amiably enough for a while after that. But underneath, I was still smarting from her assessment—all the more so because I was aware that she didn't know what she was talking about. I was greatly relieved when she woke Mike up at eleven-thirty and they headed for home. (And yes, she did get her CARE package—and with nothing lethal added, either.)

I was through straightening up and putting things away by a little before one and in bed twenty minutes later. But I couldn't sleep. I heard somewhere that the best remedy for that is to get up and maybe read or watch TV or have some hot cocoa or something. But what I know I should do and what I actually do are not often the same thing.

For the second night in a row I rolled around in bed, punching the hell out of my defenseless pillow. Finally, more than an hour later, I gave it up, exhausted. And since I had no patience at this particular time for reading or television, I dragged myself into the kitchen.

There was no cocoa in the apartment, so I did the next best thing: I put up the coffeepot. And then over a cup of my horrendous brew—which could keep a less hearty person on edge for days—I began thinking about

Ellen's vicious, unsolicited and totally unjustified attack on my handling of the case.

The longer I thought about it, the angrier I became. I'd done everything that *could* be done to learn the truth about that little girl's death. And what did she—Ellen—know about investigations, anyway, the little snot nose? What's more, whatever little she did know she'd learned from me, damn it, and now here *she* was telling *me* how to run things.

But if there was anything more bitter than the coffee I'd been drinking, it was the knowledge that finally hit me between the eyes when I was rinsing out the cup:

Ellen was right.

Chapter 17

Even before breakfast, I ate crow.

I called Ellen as soon as I got up to be sure of reaching her before she left the house. "I'm sorry," I said.

"About what?"

"About how pigheaded I acted last night. I thought it over, and you were right about the way I've been handling the case—completely right."

I could tell that Ellen was trying hard to keep the satisfaction from showing up in her voice. She almost made it, too. "Well, it's not too late to change things," she responded primly.

"I know, and I will. Friends?"

"Of course. And thanks for calling me. I'll talk to you in—"

"Hold it. Not so fast. I also have a bone to pick with you."

"What did I do?"

"It's what you didn't do. When did Mike invite you to that wedding?"

Ellen's voice dropped to a whisper. "Leek," she said. Or anyway, that's what it sounded like.

"What was that?"

Her voice gained a little strength. "Last week," she admitted sheepishly.

"Why didn't you tell me?"

"Can I be honest?"

"No, I brought it up so I'd be lied to," I answered sourly.

"Uh, well, I wanted to say something about it, but you *know* how you get—so enthusiastic and everything. I know you mean well," she was quick to assure me. "But I didn't want Mike to get spooked, that's all."

"I'd be the last person in the world to put a lot of stock in a thing like that," I responded huffily.

"I guess I *should* have said something. And I'm really sorry if I hurt your feelings, Aunt Dez. Believe me, I'd never do that intentionally. It's just that I was afraid you'd make a big deal of it."

Honestly. Sometimes I can't figure out where Ellen gets her ideas from.

A few minutes after arriving at the office that morning, I phoned Evelyn Corwin.

"I was wondering when I'd hear from you," she said, her tone just the slightest bit testy. "Anything new?"

"Nothing worth mentioning," I answered truthfully. "But there are still quite a few things I want to check out."

"Good."

"I'll need a couple of phone numbers from you: Barrie's husband and Catherine's nanny."

"I have Paul's number in my address book, but I'll have to ask Luisa for Terry's. I'll give her a call and get back to you in a few minutes."

She was as good as her word.

Terry Gilligan was now working for a family in Darien, Connecticut, and I contacted her there. As soon as I told her who I was and why I was calling, the cheerful note vanished from her voice. "Have you found out anything about what happened to Catherine?" she asked anxiously.

Now, what kind of a question was that from someone who, from what I knew, believed that Catherine had died of her lung condition? I made myself refrain from commenting. "Nothing definite yet," I answered. "Look, I wonder if I could drive out to see you for a little while. I'd like to talk to you about a few things."

"I really don't know anything that could help you. But I'd be glad to talk to you, if you think it would do any good."

"I'd appreciate it."

"Well, I'm going home to my mother's this weekend.

She lives in upstate New York—Monticello. Would you want to come up there tomorrow?"

I told her she could expect me sometime before noon.

I got up early on Saturday, but—and this never seems to surprise anyone but me—it took me longer to dress than I'd anticipated. Then besides getting off to a late start, it was raining fairly heavily that morning, and visibility on the Thruway was just awful. Which is probably why there was a three-car pile-up, resulting in bumper-to-bumper traffic and my not making it to the Gilligans until well after two.

"You must be Mrs. Shapiro," said the woman with the nice smile and the tightly permed yellow hair who opened the door.

"That's right. And I'm sorry I'm late, but—"

"Oh, don't be silly. We were worried about you; we heard there was an accident on the Thruway."

"Yes, but it happened earlier. At least six hours ago, according to the toll booth collector."

"I'm Viola Gilligan, Terry's mother," the woman informed me as she preceded me from the small foyer into the living room just steps beyond it.

"Sit anywhere," she directed after taking my coat. "Can I get you some coffee? Or tea?"

"Coffee would be wonderful, if you wouldn't mind," I responded gratefully.

"Of course not. In the meantime, I'll let Terry know you're here."

I sat down in a large armchair facing the sofa and took a look around me. The living room was a nice size, and while the furnishings were obviously far from new, it was a comfortable room, filled with faded chintzes and worn velvets and charming, if inexpensive, knickknacks. In a matter of seconds, a shaggy-haired dog of uncertain parentage ambled over. He just sort of materialized; I have no idea where he came from. I could have been looking right at him without noticing him, though, since his coloring was almost the identical shade of the threadbare rust carpet covering most of the floor.

Sniffing my hand, he (I didn't actually know whether it was a "he" or not since its hair was so long) apparently decided that I passed the litmus test—whatever the criterion for that might be. Because he put both paws on my lap and, with the largest tongue you have ever seen, proceeded to conscientiously wash my face.

"Muffy! Get down from there!" (*Muffy?* Oops! The "he," it seems, was a "she.") Just entering the room was a large, stocky girl somewhere in her twenties.

Muffy, ignoring the command, continued to see to my ablutions.

"I'm warning you!" the girl threatened. (I don't care; I refuse to use the term *woman* for anyone under thirty.)

Poor Muffy, it appeared, was totally deaf.

"Do you want me to sic Philomena on you?"

With that, the dog uttered one brief but hysterical yip, vacated my lap and scurried under the nearest end table.

"Desiree?" the girl said then.

I nodded.

"I'm Terry." She extended her hand. "I hope Muffy didn't frighten you."

"Oh, no, I love dogs," I told her. Which is true. I'm also very fond of cats. In fact, for years I've been considering getting myself a pet. But then I keep thinking that with the hours I sometimes have to put in, it might not be fair.

"I'm glad to hear it," the girl said, relieved. And her smile was almost an exact duplicate of the one that had welcomed me at the front door. She settled herself into the sofa, her hands resting in her lap, her legs properly crossed at the ankles. If I had to pick one word to describe Terry Gilligan, I'd say she was dependable-looking. (Or would you consider that two words?) Her curly brown hair, which was cut short, framed a plain square face with large, intelligent gray eyes. She wore very little makeup—pale coral lipstick and a touch of mascara; that was it—just enough not to frighten little kids. And her cream wool jumper and crisp white cotton blouse were not only positively spotless but wrinkle-free. Naturally, she was wearing the kind of sensible oxford shoes you'd expect to see on the prototypical nanny. Or my conception of one, at any rate.

"The only way we can ever get Muffy to listen is to threaten her with our cat," she was telling me.

"That would be the dreaded Philomena, I assume."

"Right."

"She must be quite a cat."

"She is," Terry agreed, grinning. "She can be very hostile. But I think that must be because she was abused when she was younger."

"That's awful," I responded, shaking my head.

"Isn't it? We found her shivering out by the back door one morning a few years ago. My mother brought her some milk, but she didn't even touch it. She just stretched herself out by that door and lay there. So my mother, who's a real softy, phoned my brother-in-law—who, it so happens, is a vet—and asked him to stop off on his way home from work. Anyway, he examined the cat and said she had the croup or something, and he gave my mother some medicine for her to take. But he told us there were burn marks on her body and everything."

"How can people do such things?" I murmured.

"Beats me. Anyway, Mother took her in, and she's been with us ever since, completely terrorizing everyone she comes in contact with." The girl turned in Muffy's direction and laughed affectionately. "Especially our fearless canine over there."

Well, it was pleasant chatting with Terry. But I'd just spent about five hours on the New York Thruway, and it wasn't to learn about Muffy and Philomena, fascinating though they might be. I was about to rectify things when, just then, something long and black sprang onto the magazine table right next to me and, from there, flew onto my shoulder. I think I shot at least a foot into the air. This, however, did not dislodge Philomena, who was now rubbing her face against my cheek and purring ecstatically. Animals do take to me, and I have to admit it's sort of flattering. I mean, they say our four-legged friends are fairly astute judges of character. On the other hand, though, when I consider some of the people whose pets are absolutely devoted to them, I'm not totally convinced of that. But at any rate, I would have been content to leave things status quo if it had not been for the excruciating pain in my right shoulder. You see, only a couple of seconds after Philomena started lavishing all this affection on me, she began digging her claws deep into my flesh.

"Theresa! Take that animal off that poor woman!" This from Viola, who was now gingerly approaching with a tray containing two cups of coffee that smelled like heaven, along with a sandwich and a plate of cookies.

Terry quickly stood up to address the problem on my shoulder. But her attempts to dislodge the cat were met with spitting, hissing and cries of outrage that I have no doubt featured a choice cat curse or two.

Setting the tray down on the magazine table, Viola took matters into her own hands. She picked up the small white pitcher on the tray, transferring some of the milk it held into one of the saucers. Then walking backward with the saucer extended in front of her, she headed for the door, making these little kissing sounds in Philomena's direction with every step.

She was almost at the threshold when the creature jumped down, missing the tray by *that much*. "I'll bring you some more milk in a second," Viola called as the fractious Philomena raced after her. Then as soon as the cat sped past her, she slammed the door shut with her foot.

In no time, she returned with a full pitcher. "Are you all right?" she asked, her forehead furrowed with concern.

"I'm fine, now that I've gotten rid of my epaulet."

Viola raised her eyebrows in puzzlement.

Her daughter chuckled politely before explaining: "You know, that's the ornament army and naval officers wear on their shoulders."

Apparently, Viola still didn't get my little joke. And what's more, she didn't care. Responding with a shrug, she turned her attention back to me. "I hope you like ham, Desiree."

"I do. But you really shouldn't have bothered."

"When was the last time you ate?" she demanded. I didn't get the chance to say. "That's what I thought."

The truth is, I was starved.

"Well, I'll leave the two of you alone to talk now," she told us, setting the pitcher on the tray. And to Terry: "Would you like me to take Muffy with me?"

Naturally, with my big mouth, I had to preempt the answer. "Oh, why don't you let her stay? She's not bothering us at all."

So, really, I was completely to blame for what happened next.

Terry waited patiently until I'd finished the sandwich. Then while we were sharing the delicious homemade oatmeal-raisin cookies her mother had provided, I figured I'd better start asking the questions I'd come here to ask.

"How long did you work for the Corwins?" I began.

"A little over two years."

"I understand you were with Catherine the morning she was almost run over."

"Yes, that's right. And it would have been my fault if she'd been killed!"

"Mrs. Corwin—Mrs. Evelyn Corwin—told me you felt that way, but she says you're the only one who does."

"I was so shocked when I saw that car bearing down on Catherine that I couldn't move. Instead of yanking her back, I just stood there—paralyzed."

I spent the next few minutes trying to convince Terry that her reaction, while not what she may have wished, had been a perfectly normal one. "And besides," I said, "Catherine wasn't injured. So why be so rough on yourself?"

"Because when parents entrust their children to your care, you have an obligation to protect them. I keep worrying there may be another crisis one day and that I'll freeze *again*."

I was about to try to allay her fears when suddenly this disgusting odor filled the room. I avoided looking at Terry. After all, she had to be terribly embarrassed.

"I'm sorry," she said, shamefaced.

I wasn't quite certain how to respond. Should I just tell her it was okay? Or would it be better to act as though I had no idea what she was talking about?

"Muffy," she informed me, "has a stomach condition."

By that time I'd forgotten Muffy was even in the room! My first reaction was relief at learning she was the culprit. But then I thought, *Swell. I'm cooped up in this room with a flatulent dog!* I glanced irritably at Muffy, who still lay under the table, her back end pointed in our direction. *Well, how do you like that! She makes the air in here completely intolerable, and all the while she has the gall to be sleeping peacefully!*

I tried not to breathe any more often than was absolutely necessary. "Where were we?" I asked. And then I recalled. "I think you were telling me that you were concerned you'd freeze again sometime."

"Yes, but that's *my* problem. You didn't drive all the way up here to act as my therapist."

"No, but I can appreciate how you feel, and maybe it would help you to talk about it. I'm a pretty good listener."

"That's very nice of you, but I'm okay. Most of the time, anyway. Occasionally, though, I have to remind myself that whatever did cause Catherine's death, at least it didn't happen when I was supposed to be looking after her. I'm grateful for that much."

"I understood you thought it was an accident—the car almost striking her, I mean."

"Well . . ."

When she didn't volunteer anything further, I prodded her a little. "You've had second thoughts, from what I gather."

"I guess I have. I didn't really see anything, you know; it was all over in seconds. But I figured it had to be a drunk driver. Or even just a careless one. The idea of someone actually trying to harm a little sweetheart like Catherine seemed preposterous to me at the time. But the more I look back on it now, the more I realize I may have made a mistake."

"Anything in particular cause you to change your mind?"

Catherine's former nanny fastened her eyes on me, and I could see the sorrow in them. "She's dead," she replied simply.

I moved on to other things then, first asking Terry if she could come up with any reason that someone might have wanted the child out of the way. "Any reason at all, no matter how far-fetched you think it might be."

"There's nothing. Catherine was a wonderful child!"

I asked about the kind of mother Donna was.

"She was a good, a very caring, mother."

"Tell me this," I said, because the new me felt that I couldn't afford to totally ignore Todd's allegations. "Did she seem at all secretive to you?"

"Secretive? She seemed like a pretty open person to me." A pause. "But I'm not exactly sure what you mean."

"Neither am I," I admitted.

I wanted to know about Barrie then.

"Ms. Lundquist's a very busy woman, so she didn't have much time to spend with Catherine. But from what I saw, she loved her very much."

Then we got to Todd. "I imagine everyone knows how Todd felt about Catherine," I said.

"He certainly didn't do anything to hide it."

"Do you think it's possible that *he* may have killed her?"

The idea was apparently not new to Terry, because she answered without hesitation. "To tell you the truth, sometimes Todd didn't seem quite, well, normal. But still, while he took real pleasure in making Catherine's life as miserable as he could, I can't actually picture him killing her. In fact, if you ask me, it would have spoiled his fun. Besides, what happened with the car—he couldn't have been responsible for *that*."

"No, but even if Catherine *was* murdered, that wouldn't necessarily mean the car business was deliberate. The two things may not even be connected."

"That's possible, I guess," Terry conceded. But it was obvious she didn't believe it. And for that matter, I didn't, either.

At any rate, by then I'd explored everything I'd intended covering with her. Besides, Muffy had been up to her favorite trick again, and I was desperate for fresh air. So I called it a day.

A few minutes later, Terry and Viola were walking me out to my car, and I was thanking them for their patience and hospitality.

And that's when Philomena scooted out of the bushes with her going-away present—a dead mouse—which she set down right in front of me before turning on her four heels and hot-footing it out of there.

And don't tell me that when that miserable, treacherous cat made this vile gesture there was no malice in her heart. Because I will never believe it.

You know, I'd still like to get myself a pet one day. But it was only after my afternoon upstate that I began giving serious thought to a guppy.

Chapter 18

Well, I'd finally come across someone—aside from my client, that is—who considered it a serious possibility, or maybe even a likelihood, that Catherine Corwin had been murdered. (I couldn't put any real stock in Todd's rantings.) The thing was, though, how much credence could I give to Terry's change of heart? By her own admission, it was only as a result of hindsight—"She's dead" was exactly what she'd told me—that the nanny was looking at Catherine's almost car "accident" in a different light now.

Okay. So I hadn't exactly discovered anything on my trip to Monticello—except that a fish might be a very desirable pet. But there was still Paul Lundquist, Barrie's former husband, to question. And there was no telling what I'd find out from him.

I'll say this. Ellen's talking-to had certainly given me a whole new outlook. *Who knows?* I said to myself. *Start looking for a murderer, and you just may find one.*

The next morning, I tried contacting Lundquist, waiting until a decent hour to make the call. (I consider ten forty-five very decent, even for a Sunday.) Unfortunately, it turned out to be *too* decent, since I'd apparently already missed him. I left a message on his machine to the effect that I was a private investigator working for Evelyn Corwin and that I'd appreciate his getting in touch with me as soon as possible. It was ten p.m. when I heard from him.

The voice was pleasant and sincere-sounding. Friendly, but not too friendly, if you follow me. You'd never be able to tell by listening to this guy that he'd dumped his wife for some chippie. "Sorry for not returning your call sooner," he said, "but I spent the day with my son. I just got back to the apartment five minutes ago. You're investigating little Catherine's death?"

"That's right. And I was wondering if you could give me a few minutes of your time. There are one or two things I'd like to check out with you."

"Sure, I'd be glad to. But I'm afraid there's nothing much I can tell you."

Someday someone's going to say to me, "Of course I'll meet with you; I have a lot of very important information to give you." Someday. Although probably not in this lifetime.

Anyway, Lundquist offered to stop by my office the next evening after he finished work. "It would be around six, six-fifteen," he told me, quickly adding, "if that's okay with you."

That was just fine with me.

Paul Lundquist was tall—not as tall as Ellen's Mike, but tall. He had a rather large nose, a slightly pockmarked complexion, and too small hazel eyes. What's more, he was walking testimony to some of the most unflattering physical characteristics middle age can inflict on people. His light brown hair was just beginning to recede, while his stomach was starting to protrude. And there was every indication he was on the verge of acquiring a full-blown second chin. Yet in spite of that—and of my predisposition to detest him—I decided that the man was not without appeal. His manner was good-natured and informal. And there was warmth looking out of those too small hazel eyes. All in all, Paul Lundquist gave me the impression that he was a very easy person to be with.

He was sitting next to my desk, excusing himself for arriving late for our appointment. (He'd walked in just after six-thirty.) "I was with a customer, and it took more time than I expected it to. I hope it hasn't affected your plans." (He was considerate, too—for someone who cheated on his wife.)

"Don't worry about that; I have plenty of time," I told him while I was busy checking out his nicely tailored gray suit with its coordinating gray and crimson paisley tie and wondering what he did for a living.

"I'm a salesman," he said in response to the question I hadn't asked. "Pharmaceuticals." And when I nodded: "But what is it you'd like to know?"

I wanted to discuss his miserable, lying son; also the breakup of his marriage. But of course you have to lead up to things like that, so I opened with: "How often do you see Todd?" Somehow, the tone of my voice was harsher than I'd intended, and it sounded almost as though I were accusing the man of being a delinquent father.

If Lundquist was offended it didn't show. "At least once a week. Sometimes more often," he answered, a quizzical look on his face as he tried to figure out, I'm sure, what the frequency of his visits with his son had to do with a young girl's death.

"Then you must be aware that Todd has a tendency to incite to riot." I wanted to be as uncritical as possible of the little bastard and still make my point. So I said it lightly, a smile of sorts plastered on my face.

"He's always pushing people's buttons, I know that," the father conceded. The uncomfortable chuckle that accompanied this seemed to be a cross between tolerant and exasperated.

"Well, do you think there's a grain of truth in any of the things he says?"

"You mean in those shocking little stories he's so fond of telling?"

"That's right."

"Look, every once in a while he comes up with something that has a basis in fact, which, of course, he usually embellishes on. But most often those tales of his are complete fabrications. He has quite an imagination, my son." *What a euphemistic way of putting it!* Lundquist was looking at me intently now. "I blame an awful lot of Todd's . . . his problems, I guess they are . . . on the divorce. He took it very hard." A thought seemed to occur to him at this point. "Is there anything specific you're referring to?"

"For one thing, he's been hinting that Donna Corwin is hiding some terrible secret."

Lundquist shook his head. "That gem he spared me. I really wouldn't pay any attention, though, if I were you."

"You say Todd's nast—Todd's attitude was the result of your breakup with his mother?"

"Not exactly. He was always a little difficult, almost from birth. But the breakup, well, it had its effect on him."

"That must make you feel pretty guilty." I flinched as soon as I said it.

Paul Lundquist frowned. "Sometimes those things can't be helped."

"I understand that the woman, uh, the woman you became involved with during your marriage is no longer in the picture."

He went completely white now. And for a moment I thought he might pick up and leave. Instead, he just sat there seething for a few seconds. Then he said, "I can't figure out how that's relevant to what happened to Catherine. But yes, you're right; we're not together anymore. I suppose Barrie supplied you with all the sordid details."

"She just told me you'd left her for a younger woman. And then her friend Saundra King said something about you and the woman having split up." I noticed that his jaw tightened when I mentioned King's name, so I remarked, "You don't seem to be too fond of Mrs. King."

"It wasn't supposed to show," Lundquist admitted, a smile turning up the corners of his mouth for an instant. "Actually, I don't really dislike her. I don't even know her that well; I only met the woman once. But she kind of got under my skin."

"I'm surprised. About your only meeting her once, I mean. She and your ex-wife have been good friends for quite a while, from what I've been told."

"Yes, but they became friends at work—that's where they saw each other mostly. Barrie did invite her to the house one weekend, though; we were living on Long Island at the time. And let me tell you, two full days of Saundra King were definitely enough."

"Why do you say that?"

"For one thing, she had to have all sorts of special foods—she's a health nut. Before she even came out to

the island, Barrie and I were shopping like crazy, going
from store to store to stock up on the kind of stuff she'd
eat. And for another thing, she carried on for the entire
weekend because she'd forgotten to pack this particular
blouse or something. And to top everything off, she's so
damned opinionated." I guess he figured he should explain that one, so he went on. "We invited a few people
over for dessert that Saturday night, and she started talking politics—she's smart enough to know better, too.
And nobody could get her off the subject, either; Lord
knows, I tried. At any rate, she wound up insulting two
of our closest friends because they didn't share her enthusiasm for some guy who was running for office."

I was a little taken aback. This hadn't been my impression of King at all. I mean, aside from the fact that she
didn't eat sweets—which even in my book didn't exactly
make her a health nut—it was as though he were telling
me about an entirely different woman from the one I'd
visited the week before. I said as much.

"I know exactly what you mean," Lundquist responded. "For the first hour or so after we met, I
thought she was great. Very forthright. Very down-to-
earth. But then—" Breaking off abruptly, he hunched
his shoulders. "Listen," he summed up a moment later,
"I'm not saying that she's not a nice person. I'm sure
she's a decent human being and all that. It's just that I
couldn't stand the woman." He quickly clarified that
with: "I didn't *dislike* her, you understand; I just couldn't
take her."

"So you didn't allow Barrie to have her to the
house again?"

"*Allow?* You have to be kidding!" he exclaimed with
a short, harsh laugh. "I never allowed or didn't allow
Barrie anything. No, the fact is, I lucked out. Seems that
Ms. Pain-in-the-you-know-what has all these allergies,
flowers among them. And fortunately, we had a beautiful garden at the time. So that first visit of hers was also
the last."

I had nothing left to ask except the question I'd been
leading up to all along. "I know it's none of my business,
but—"

He couldn't let that pass, I suppose. "That hasn't

seemed to be a problem for you so far," he interjected. But he was grinning.

"Yes, I know, but, uh, you see, this could really be important."

"Well, then, let's just get it over with."

I took a breath. "Was there another reason—apart from your being interested in someone else—that you and your wife divorced?"

"Where did you get an idea like that?" Lundquist asked mildly enough. But I found it difficult to reconcile that even tone of voice with the deep flush that was slowly working its way up from his neck. (Caused by guilt? Or embarrassment? Or just plain resentment at having his private life dissected like this?)

"Well, Todd sort of suggested something to that effect," I confessed, probably turning a little pink myself.

"*Todd?* And you believed him?"

The denial was already on my lips when he added, "Shame on you, Mrs. Shapiro." Then before I could put in even one word in my own defense, he repeated the admonition, but more softly this time. "Shame on you," he said again.

Chapter 19

It was the following morning that I realized I'd made a really unforgivable oversight. I couldn't even believe I'd been so slipshod! But the fact is, I'd never asked Nicholas, Donna Corwin's chauffeur, a single question about events on the day of Catherine's death. Or about anything else, for that matter.

Oh, had Ellen ever been on the money Thursday night! Mentally kicking myself, I dialed the Corwin town house.

I could almost hear Luisa stiffen at the sound of my voice. The housekeeper, I was sure, was not too pleased that I was still nosing around investigating Catherine's death. Especially since she was so certain it was a total waste of time. "Nicholas just left on an errand," she said when I told her I wanted to talk to her husband. And then: "Is there something wrong?"

"Oh, no. I wanted to ask him about a few things, that's all."

"He should be home shortly," she added a little reluctantly.

"Would you have him get back to me when he comes in?"

"Yes, of course."

The chauffeur returned my call about an hour later. "My wi—Luisa tells me you have some questions for me." I noticed now that he had a slight accent, one very reminiscent of his wife's.

"Yes. There are a couple of things I wanted to confirm with you," I answered.

"Certainly. What is it you want to know?"

"I'd rather not do it on the phone. Would it be convenient if I came over to see you sometime today? It won't take very long."

"I suppose that would be all right, although it might be easier if I stopped in at your office. I'll be driving Mrs. Corwin to East Forty-sixth Street this afternoon—Forty-sixth and Madison, that is. She has a three-thirty appointment."

"I'm not that far from there." I gave him the address.

"I'll be by as soon as I drop Mrs. Corwin off," he promised.

Nicholas arrived just before four. "I can't stay too long," he notified me. "I have to call for Mrs. Corwin at five."

"Oh, don't worry. I only have one or two questions."

"That should be fine, then." He had a soft, slightly stilted manner of speaking that was at once authoritative and polite.

I proceeded to ask him where and when he'd driven Donna Corwin on the day Catherine died. His account confirmed what Donna had told me weeks before.

After that, I sat there in silence for a brief time, with Nicholas looking on expectantly. I was trying to figure out the best way to phrase my next question. It wasn't an easy thing to do, because it wasn't an easy question to ask.

You see, something had occurred to me that morning concerning Todd's allusions to Donna. In fact, that's what had reminded me about the chauffeur in the first place.

Let me explain.

Now, I knew as well as anyone that the kid was a pathological liar. But according to his father, there *were* times when he told the truth. Or something close to the truth, at any rate. So it was just possible there was a grain of substance in those dark hints of his about his step-grandmother and that those hints didn't have anything to do with her not being Catherine's natural mother. After all, from what I'd learned since Barrie's revelation of that fact, it really didn't appear to be much of a secret. Anyway, if there *was* something Donna was concealing and if I had to guess at what that something could be, I'd say it involved a man.

Think about it. The woman was young and good-looking, and she'd been married to a guy thirty-five years older than she was.

Now follow me a little further with this.

Suppose Donna did have a lover before or even after her husband died. Wouldn't her chauffeur be in a position to know about it—or at least have his suspicions—either because he drove her to those rendezvous of hers or because he didn't? What I'm trying to say is that if she suddenly had him dropping her off at places she never used to frequent before (certain *kinds* of places, of course, like out-of-the-way restaurants or hotels), it might have made him wonder. Or if, on the other hand, she began taking taxis instead of having him drive her, it's likely he would have found that equally puzzling.

So you can see why I was half counting on Nicholas to help me uncover Donna Corwin's affair. If there'd ever been an affair to uncover, I mean.

Well, naturally, I was having all kinds of difficulty in finding a tactful way to bring up a sensitive matter like that. And while there was undoubtedly room for improvement, what I finally wound up saying wasn't nearly as bad as some of the gems I've been known to come out with.

"Listen, Nicholas," I began, "I realize that it would normally be considered bad form to discuss an employer's personal life. But in this instance it's vital that I know the truth if I'm ever going to determine how that little girl really died." The man's face was totally impassive. "You'll probably think the question I'm about to ask you is irrelevant," I continued, "and that could certainly turn out to be the case. But it's also possible it could help us learn what happened to Catherine."

I suppose I must have paused for longer than I thought, because Nicholas wound up prodding me in his quiet, gentlemanly way. "You were saying, Mrs. Shapiro?"

"Yes . . . well, it's been intimated to me that Mrs. Corwin had a lover. I really don't have any idea whether it's true or not, but if you know anything or suspect anything—anything at all—I can't impress on you enough how important it is that you tell me."

His answer came at once. "I don't believe a word of it," he stated evenly, a deep frown drawing his eyebrows so close together they almost touched.

I hastened to explain the rules we were playing by. "Please understand that unless it had a direct effect on Catherine's death, whatever you tell me will remain just between us."

Without changing his tone one bit, Nicholas managed to leave no doubt as to his opinion of my question—and for that matter, of me personally. "That's not necessary," he assured me. "Mrs. Corwin is a fine lady—a *really* fine lady—and she was devoted to her husband. They were devoted to each other. Just ask my wife." Then slowly shaking his head, he concluded, "If you ever saw the two of them together, you'd never say such a terrible thing."

"Well, maybe *after* Mr. Corwin's death. Maybe she was just awfully lonely after he was gone," I suggested weakly.

"She's been mourning him ever since he passed on," the chauffeur declared, his voice rising slightly. "You talk to Luisa about that." And an instant later: "You . . . that is, whoever told you such a malicious lie should be ashamed of themselves, considering all the tragedies that poor lady has had in her life. And anyone who repeats it—they should be doubly ashamed of themselves."

I'd certainly managed to loosen up that well-mannered restraint of Nicholas's, hadn't I? He was actually glowering at me when he said good-bye. First Donna and now him, I thought.

If I didn't wrap up this case soon, I wouldn't be able to question a soul. There'd be nobody still on speaking terms with me.

Chapter 20

I toyed with the idea of having another talk with Luisa to see whether I could learn anything from her about Donna's maybe lover. But I abandoned the notion almost as soon as it occurred to me. Nicholas had already made it clear where his wife came out on the subject, so really, what was the point?

Well, I'd hold the Donna thing in abeyance for a while until I figured out how I should proceed. Or even *if* I should proceed. In the meantime, there was an entirely different area of the case that I hadn't even touched on—which I set about rectifying on Wednesday morning.

Mrs. Corwin—it's the older Mrs. Corwin I'm referring to—had gone out for a walk, her housekeeper said when I called. She'd tell her I was anxious to speak with her.

I heard from Evelyn Corwin about an hour later. "Have you found out anything?" she asked eagerly.

"No, I'm afraid not. Not yet, anyway. But there are a couple of phone numbers I forgot to get from you on Friday."

"Ohh." For an instant it was as if all the air had suddenly left her body. Then she said briskly, "Just tell me whose numbers you need."

"Catherine's pediatrician and the pulmonary specialist she was seeing."

Evelyn gave me the doctors' names and phone numbers without comment, and I assured her I'd talk to her soon.

Dr. Mazelli, who had been Catherine's pediatrician, said that he'd be able to see me for a few minutes if I could make it to his office by eleven forty-five. I checked my watch: eleven-twenty. I assured him I'd be there on time. But I wasn't nearly as confident as I sounded. I knew it was going to be close.

I made an immediate four-minute trip to the ladies' room, following which I struggled into my coat while rushing toward the door—a three-minute sprint at most. After that I paced the hall for five minutes waiting for an elevator. When I finally got to ground level, I spent another five minutes doing battle for a cab, then wound up with the only one in Manhattan that didn't take the corners on two wheels. Needless to say, I arrived at the doctor's office just in time to make excuses to his receptionist.

"Doctor expected you at eleven forty-five, Miz Shapiro," the skinny blond receptionist with the enormous bust scolded. I started to explain about the elevator and the taxi (I thought it kind of crass to include the ladies' room), but Big Bust interrupted before I'd had a chance to utter more than three words. "Doctor is with a patient now. He'll *try* to see you before his next one. But of course, there's no guarantee he'll be able to. He's a very busy man, you know."

"Mrs. Corwin—little Catherine Corwin's grandmother—thought it important I speak to Doctor today," I told her. A lie, of course. "And I have back-to-back appointments almost all afternoon." A lie to keep the first one company.

She didn't seem impressed. "I'm certain Doctor will do his best. In the meantime, why don't you make yourself comfortable in there?" Indicating the adjacent waiting room with a toss of her bleached blond head, she dismissed me with a forced smile.

I'd never been in a pediatrician's waiting room before. At least, not in *this* century, and I couldn't believe the lengths this guy went to in order to keep his little patients entertained. Stenciled on the room's pale yellow walls were colorful representations of animals with human characteristics, some of them larger than life. There was a perky lady duck in a garish orange dress wearing spike heels and an outrageous red, green, orange, blue and gold hat. She was carrying an enormous

Bloomingdale's shopping bag that was overflowing with packages. There was also a dashing gray wolf in white top hat and tails, a bright purple cummerbund encircling his midsection. He was in the process of handing a bouquet of violets to the little red fox standing next to him. This foxy lady was decked out in a sequined ball gown in an almost blinding shade of red. And for a crowning touch there was a diamond tiara on top of her auburn upswept do. Similarly eye-catchingly attired were a giraffe, a kangaroo, a crocodile and some animal I swear the artist must have dreamed up. But anyway, you get the picture.

And the fun didn't end with the four walls. There were Lilliputian armchairs, a very small hobby horse and, in a corner of the room, a playpen filled with books and toys. All in all, the room did its best to make the kids forget they were here to get poked and pricked and to gag their little throats out on those abominable tongue depressors. And in some cases—mostly with the younger ones and those with the really pathetic I.Q.s— I'll bet the strategy even succeeded.

I settled myself into a tan Naugahyde sofa, alone in the waiting area except for a rather mousy-looking young woman seated on the far side of the room, near the playpen. She was so engrossed in the paperback she was reading that she hadn't so much as glanced in my direction when I walked in. I picked up one of the grown-up-type magazines on the end table next to me. Then I put it down and picked up another. And after that another. Eventually it became clear to me that the selection here was limited to publications with titles like *Today's Mother, Today's Children,* and *Today's Babies.* Which forced me into doing something productive with my time. Taking the manila folder from my attaché case, I began to study my notes. I'd only made it to the second paragraph when I heard the most godawful yowl.

My nerves not being as good as they used to be— and they were never anything to brag about—I almost suffered a coronary. I glanced over at the room's other occupant. The paperback was at her feet now, and one of the woman's hands was on her heart, the other over her mouth. Her eyes were wide with anguish. A moment later the yowling stopped, and she smiled faintly at me, embarrassed. "Adam's only four," she said before stooping to retrieve the paperback.

I returned to the notes. I even got to the second page, paragraph two, before the next commotion. This time the source was a tearful little towheaded boy who was being pulled into the room by a tall, very pregnant lady and who was struggling vainly to pull her back toward wherever it was they'd come from. I have absolutely no idea how old the kid was. Never having been a parent myself, I'm no judge of children's ages. He could have been anywhere from two to six, for all I know.

"Please stop carrying on like this, Brian," the woman urged softly. "The doctor isn't going to hurt you."

"I hate him! I hate him! I wish he died!" Brian screeched, giving me an immediate headache.

"Brian! Don't ever say a thing like that again!" his mother chastised, resolutely yanking him along.

"I don't care!" the kid yelled, still trying his damnedest to make a break for it.

"Behave yourself! And stop being such a baby."

"*Daddy* wouldn't bring me here," the kid whined, snuffling now. "My *daddy* loves me."

"Just calm down," his mother ordered. Dragging him almost off the floor, she marched resolutely past my Naugahyde sofa (thank God) toward a group of armchairs at the opposite side of the room while Brian kicked his legs and sobbed at top volume in protest. When she reached the seats, she bent down almost to her son's level and stroked his hair. "Tell you what," she said, "when we're through here, we'll go have ourselves a real treat at lunchtime."

"Ice cream?" the boy asked, turning off the waterworks and wiping his nose with the back of his sleeve as his mother lifted him onto a chair.

"For dessert." She began unbuttoning his little navy pea jacket.

"Choco-lit?"

"Could be." She was removing the jacket.

"And candy?"

"Don't push it," she told him, laughing.

Well, now, that the waiting room was comparatively

quiet again, I could concentrate on my notes. But in a matter of seconds I had a sofa mate.

"Hi," said Brian, hoisting himself with some difficulty onto the seat cushions. He got no help from me.

"Bri-an!" his agitated mother called to him. "Come sit down!"

"I *am* sitting," the kid pointed out.

"Well, don't bother the lady." She looked at me anxiously. "Do you mind if he sits there?"

"No, of course not." My third lie of this still young day.

"You'll let me know if he starts to annoy you, won't you?"

"Oh, no problem," I said graciously. Which, of course, bore no resemblance to what I was actually thinking. You have to keep in mind that it had been less than a week since Muffy and Philomena. And having to deal with a noxious-smelling dog and a guerrilla cat was bad enough, thank you. But then, practically before I had time to catch my breath, here was this pesky little kid in my life. I mean, I think that given the circumstances, Brian's presence would have tried anyone's patience.

At any rate, acting as though he weren't there, I made another attempt to read. It was not to be.

"What's your name?" he demanded.

"Desiree."

"That's a funny name."

"Yeah? Well, so's Brian."

"Is not," was the kid's rejoinder.

"Is too."

His lower lip started to quiver, and for a minute I thought he was going to take off. But I guess it was wishful thinking. "My mommy's getting me ice cream for lunch. Choco-lit," he apprised me.

Smiling sweetly (mommy was looking over at us), I told him it would give him a bellyache.

"Will not," he countered obstinately.

"Will too." Listen, under the proper conditions I can be as childish as the next three-year-old.

"Will not. And you're ugly."

Okay, that did it. "Listen, you wanna bet?" I said nastily, but still wearing this saccharine smile on my face for mommy's benefit. "You're gonna get these terrible, awful cramps and you'll double over and—"

"Maaa!" And scrambling off the sofa and almost tripping over his little feet, Brian rushed into his mother's arms.

Now, I know that was a terrible thing to do—and I should probably be ashamed to admit this—but I didn't regret it for a second.

I was able to read in peace until Big Bust ushered me into the doctor's office about a half hour later.

Dr. Mazelli was a man in his forties, with a kind face, thick glasses and very little hair. He was seated behind a large wooden desk, while I was occupying the comfortable leather armchair facing him.

"You said on the phone you were hired by little Catherine Corwin's grandmother."

"That's right," I confirmed.

"I was terribly sorry to learn of Catherine's death. It's sad when anyone that age is taken from us, but I was particularly affected by Catherine's passing. She was such a special little girl."

"Special in what way?"

"I just mean that she was very lovable."

"Were you surprised to hear that she'd died?"

"Well, yes and no. I didn't expect that she'd reach adulthood. She was suffering from a congenital lung disease, a very serious one."

"Something called alpha-1—um, something, wasn't it?"

The doctor smiled indulgently. "Alpha-1-antitrypsin deficiency."

"I understand she also had asthma."

He nodded. "That's right. Brought on by the other condition when she wasn't much past two. Her prognosis was not a favorable one, Mrs. Shapiro. However, I was hoping she'd have a few more years, but, well, you never know, do you?" He swallowed hard, and I thought I saw a tear in the corner of his eye, shimmering behind his glasses.

"No. You never do," I hurriedly concurred. "How long was Catherine a patient of yours, Dr. Mazelli?"

"Nine, ten years—ever since she was in diapers." Putting both palms flat on his desk then, he leaned toward me. "Now, do you mind if I ask *you* something?"

"No, of course not."

"Why would Mrs. Corwin have you investigating something like this? She was aware of the fragile nature of her granddaughter's health right from the beginning."

"It appears that Catherine was almost run over just a couple of weeks before her death. And there's some question about whether it was intentional. Mrs. Corwin believes the two incidents may have been related and that someone wanted Catherine out of the way."

Dr. Mazelli appeared stunned. "Does she have somebody in particular in mind?"

"No. That's why she hired me."

"I hope she's wrong. For anyone to deprive Catherine of as much as a single day . . . well, I hate to even think about it, that's all." He paused. "But what about you? Do you share Mrs. Corwin's opinion?"

I gave him the only answer possible. "I just don't know."

When I got back to the office, I called the pulmonary specialist who had attended to Catherine. Through his receptionist—or nurse or whatever she was—I was informed that Doctor was too busy to see me. "Doctor says to try in two or three weeks; maybe he can set up an appointment then."

"It's *the* doctor—*the!*" I wanted to shout in frustration. *What was with these people anyway?* Fortunately, however, I was able to contain myself. I even thanked the woman—although, I admit, not very warmly. And then immediately afterward, I got in touch with Evelyn Corwin. "I'm having a little difficulty persuading Dr. Pascal to see me," I let her know. "He had his receptionist tell me it could take two or three weeks before he could *maybe* find the time."

"*Did* he?" Evelyn scoffed. "Well, perhaps I can persuade him to do a little better than that. When would you like to go up there?"

"As soon as I can."

"Let me call you back."

We hung up, and I had just begun to pay attention to some of the bills I'd been trying to forget were in my desk drawer when she was on the line again. "How would five o'clock be?"

"Today?"

"Of course today," she responded, laughing, obviously taking pride in her success.

I spent no more than ten minutes and probably less in Dr. Pascal's office, during which time he must have glanced at his watch at least a dozen times. A slender, patrician-looking man of about sixty with wavy silver hair, perfect teeth and a deep, beautifully modulated voice, the good doctor had himself an attitude. No doubt this was compounded by Mrs. Corwin's having shoved me down his elegant throat. At any rate, he merely confirmed—brusquely and with one eyebrow raised—what I'd learned from Catherine's pediatrician.

And the fact of the matter was that neither of them was able to provide me with any more information than I'd received from Evelyn Corwin on the day I first agreed to take the case.

I left the doctor's office feeling terribly depressed. Unless I was missing something—which given my track record on previous investigations was not entirely far-fetched—my new, enlightened approach to the job had so far yielded nothing.

I was aware that, in a way, I should be happy *not* to have made any big discoveries. But I told you, when it came to this case, I didn't know *what* I wanted. I walked into the apartment feeling so down that I fleetingly considered skipping dinner that night. That's when the phone rang.

"Hi."

I recognized the voice immediately. "Stuart! How are you?"

"Uh, busy. That's why you haven't heard from me. And I really have to apologize. I've been meaning to call you since New Hope, but ... I don't know ... I got myself a couple of new clients, and everything has been so hectic and—"

I interrupted to put him out of his misery. "I know what you mean. I've been intending to call you, too."

"Anyway, how is everything?" he asked after what sounded like a sigh of relief.

"Not terrible, I guess. Working hard on my new case and getting nowhere. In other words, everything's as usual."

"You'll have to tell me all about it when we see each other. Uh, you wouldn't by any chance be free for dinner tonight?" Then quickly: "I know it's not much notice, but I wasn't sure if I'd be able to make it myself until now."

"It's your lucky day; I *am* free. And since when do you worry about notice?"

He chuckled—sort of—and we made plans to meet at this little French restaurant that had recently opened up in my neighborhood. "I'm looking forward to seeing you," I put in just before we hung up.

"Uh, yeah, me too, Dez."

If I'd had any doubts before about things not being right with Stuart, this call put an end to them. Now I knew for certain.

Well, anyway, in only a few hours I'd find out just what was going on.

And suddenly my mouth went dry.

Chapter 21

In light of Stuart's reaction to my delayed appearance the day we were driving to New Hope, I made sure I was on time when we met for dinner that evening. But when I arrived at Le Bon Mot not even a second after the agreed-upon nine o'clock, he was already seated at the table sipping a drink.

He stood up and planted a kiss on my cheek (awkwardly, it seemed to me), then pulled out my chair.

"You look very nice," he said. "New dress?"

"New*ish*." I had on a pale lavender A-line that I'd bought the week after New Hope. It was one of those cheer-yourself-up purchases that worked in reverse after weeks went by without my having anyone to wear it for.

"It's very becoming," he said, smiling warmly. *Could I have been wrong? Had my imagination been doing me dirt?* "What would you like to drink? I'm having a gin and tonic," he told me. Which gave me my answer.

Stuart, you see, rarely drinks. It has to be a special occasion: a birthday, an anniversary, a bar mitzvah, a christening ... I hurriedly scanned my brain. No birthday. No anniversary. No bar mitvah. No christening. Well, if it wasn't *that* sort of special occasion, maybe it was another kind—the kind that requires some quick artificial courage. Like, for example, a kiss-off?

I decided I'd precipitate a discussion and just get the whole thing over with. I'd ask him what had been troubling him lately, that's what I'd do. But no sooner had the thought entered my head when my throat closed up on me. "I assumed that was a Perrier you were drinking," I mumbled instead.

"From my past performances, I can see why you would. Well?"

"Well, what?"

"Tell the man what you're drinking," Stuart instructed, grinning.

I turned around to see a rotund little waiter lurking in the neighborhood of my right shoulder. "I'll have a glass of your house red wine, please," I said obediently.

As soon as the man walked away, Stuart asked about my case. Now anxious to postpone the inevitable, I replied in great detail, undoubtedly a lot greater detail than he'd bargained for. My dear, good friend listened attentively and responded to my concerns by saying all the right things. As usual. After which I asked about his new clients. His reply lasted less than three minutes, but I, too, listened attentively—and responded to a problem he expressed by making a couple of inane observations.

And then we ordered our dinners.

It took almost a full glass of wine to get the food past the lump in my throat, but pretty soon I was eating fine. Surprisingly fine, in fact. Abetted somewhere along the line by another glass of wine and then still another (which at least I had the good sense not to finish), I more than did justice to a bunch of my all-time favorite things: escargot for starters, then Caesar salad, roast duck à l'orange, wild rice with mushrooms, broccoli with hollandaise, and for dessert, chocolate mousse with some much needed coffee—black.

Now, since I'm not exactly one of your world-class drinkers, I don't often have even two glasses of whatever it is I'm drinking, much less three. So all the while I was sitting there, I had my fingers mentally crossed that I wouldn't start slurring my words or saying silly things or, worst of all, fall right off my chair. But the only one of the aforementioned catastrophes I can tell you for sure that I managed to avoid that night was the fall from the chair.

At any rate, over dinner Stuart and I seemed to talk about everything—and nothing. I remember babbling on about Ellen and Mike, gushing (undoubtedly) about how good things looked between them. And I remember, too, that later on Stuart said something in passing about how he hoped I was being more diligent this year when it came to saving my receipts for tax time (which I had not been, but probably didn't admit). I also recall his mentioning some movie or other and our having this discussion about who was a better actor: Robert De Niro or Al Pacino. But I can't figure out how I could have even ventured an opinion on a thing like that, since I've always had a problem telling the two of them apart. Anyhow, I don't have a clue what conclusion we reached or what other earth-shaking matters we covered. What does stick in my mind is that every time we exhausted another subject, I held my breath—and waited. But I guess Stuart was as eager as I was to put off the principal topic on the agenda. We were at the very end of the meal when he finally brought it up.

I'd just put down my spoon after having polished off the chocolate mousse when I noticed he'd begun chewing on his lower lip. *Uh-oh, here it comes,* I thought. And then, with wine-induced drama: *Well, at least the condemned woman ate a hearty meal.*

"There's something I want to talk to you about, Dez," he said.

I nodded. It seemed to be the best I could do at the moment.

"We've been friends—good friends—for a long time, and I hope that nothing will ever affect that. I don't see why anything should. But, well, it's just that I feel that certain *aspects* of our friendship will have to change now in view of something that happened recently. Do you follow me so far?" he asked, taking out his handkerchief and dabbing at the tiny beads of perspiration that were starting to form on his forehead.

"Not exactly; not just yet, anyway." But I was more than halfway there.

"Probably because I haven't really said anything yet," he admitted, grinning sheepishly.

It was almost painful seeing him struggle like that. So I helped him out. Reaching across the table, I laid my hand over his. "Are you trying to tell me that you've met someone, Stuart?"

"I suppose I am," he said, his voice close to a whisper. "And doing a lousy job of it, too."

"Are you also trying to tell me that because of that, you don't feel we should be spending the night together anymore?"

"No wonder I'm so fond of you." And then: "You are *something,* you know that?"

"Of course I know it."

"Look, Dez, you're very special to me. I love being with you, and I couldn't want a better friend. But I just don't feel it would be right if we continued to, uh . . . I think it would be fairer to Gretchen if we didn't continue to—"

I pressed my lips together to abort a smile. I mean, he was not doing at all well with this. "That was the problem when we were in New Hope, wasn't it?" I asked. I didn't have to wait for the answer. "Why didn't you just say something?"

"I thought I'd get around to it, but somehow I couldn't. You must have noticed that yellow streak down my back at some time or other."

"Look, Stuart, I'm happy for you," I told him then. And it was true. It was also true that at the same time I was sorry for myself. But I didn't mention that, of course. "I hope she's as good a person as you deserve. And who is this bimbo, anyway?" I joked, trying to make us both feel a little more comfortable.

"Her name's Gretchen."

"You already said *that.*"

"Yes, well, she's the sister of this new man—Conrad Nicholson—who came into the firm about six months back. He'd been after me to call her right from the beginning, but I'm not big on blind dates, so I never did. And then one day a couple of months ago, he invited me to his place for dinner. And guess who showed up?"

"You'll have to give me a little time with that one."

"Seriously, Dez, I don't know just where this thing with Gretchen is going yet, but I like her a lot—she's a wonderful woman—and I want to give it a chance. I hope you understand."

"Of course I do," I assured him, my mind going back a couple of years to an evening when the two of us were sitting in another restaurant having a conversation very much like this one. Only that time I was doing the talking, and Stuart was the one doing the understanding.

"Yes, of course you do," he said. And from the tone of his voice I knew that at that moment we were both thinking the same thoughts.

Chapter 22

I didn't get much accomplished at the office the next day. Mostly I just sat around alternating between depression and anger.

I went over the way Stuart and I had left things. We'd always remain friends, he had assured me at my door. After which he inserted my key in the lock, squeezed my shoulder and mumbled something about calling me soon before hesitantly walking away. A couple of seconds later, just as I was about to close the door, he was back. Without a word he bent down and kissed the top of my head. And then very quickly he was gone.

Well, in view of the amount of hair spray I'd spritzed on before our date—which was actually no more than the lethal dose I normally apply, so he should have known better—chances are he woke up with a cut lip this morning. But so what? Serves the louse right for dumping me!

Now, don't ask why, if I wasn't in love with him, I was carrying on like that. I hate change, that's why. I liked things the way they were. (Also, maybe—just maybe—there was a little wounded pride mixed up in there somewhere.)

And don't tell me I was being childish; I knew that myself. I even knew that he wasn't actually dumping me. I mean, I had no doubt we'd still be getting together—at least, for a while. But, of course, if things worked out between Stuart and this Gretchen person—and what kind of a name was Gretchen, anyway?—she might have a couple of words to say about his friendship with me. And eventually it could go by the boards.

Of course, it wouldn't be any big loss. Not if he was going to throw me over the minute a coworker waved some sister of his under his nose.

But even while I was so outrageously indulging my bruised psyche, I had my moments of generosity. I hoped Stuart's new relationship would fare better than my own romance of a couple of years earlier—the one that had sprung into both our minds last night. And believe it or not, that's the truth. Besides, if Stuart thought so much of this Gretchen person, she was probably, as my late husband, Ed, used to say, a mensch. And if that was the case, who knows? Maybe she and I would even wind up being friends.

Yeah? Don't hold your breath, I countered. *She's probably one of those cloying, possessive types that makes a complete cipher out of an otherwise intelligent man.* Sure, she'd have no objection to Stuart's seeing me for lunch occasionally. She might even feign some kind of friendship for me herself. Right until she walked him down the aisle, that is. After that, hell, I'd be lucky if she let him continue to fill out my Schedule C's.

I'll level with you, though. There was another thing bugging me, too. I'm pretty embarrassed talking about it, but the fact is, I looked forward to spending the night—I mean the *entire* night—with Stuart every so often. What's more, with the way my personal life was going, it would be a long time before I found someone else to burn off a few calories with.

I stopped at Jackie's desk on my way out. "See you tomorrow," I said.

She looked down at her watch. "But it's only five after four!"

"I know."

"Is anything wrong, Dez?"

"Oh, no. I just don't seem to be able to concentrate today, so I figured I might as well call it quits."

"You're *sure* nothing's wrong?"

"I'm positive. I've got a little headache, that's all."

"That's the truth?"

Okay. Let her have it her way. "Well, there *is* an outside chance it's a brain tumor, but they won't know until after the autopsy."

I got a perverse sense of pleasure out of seeing Jackie's face suddenly become an exact color match for her pink silk blouse. Her "Think you're pretty funny, don't you?" followed me into the hall.

Well, idiot, you might just as well have your fun now, I reminded myself. *She'll make you pay for that one tomorrow!*

I spent the rest of the afternoon at the movies. *Forrest Gump* was playing, and I'd heard all sorts of wonderful things about it. I walked into the theater with this "show me" attitude and walked out feeling totally let down. Of course, given my mood, I probably would have considered *Gone With the Wind* a B picture.

After the movie I stopped at a nearby Nathan's for two hot dogs, which were prepared to my exact specifications—with mustard and sauerkraut and almost burnt to a crisp. With the hot dogs I had the mandatory Coke and a huge order of fries. For the first time since last night I felt a little better. Not a lot. But a little.

Lucky for me, there are often times when I'm really upset that I'm able to escape into sleep. And this was one of those times.

I went to bed just before eleven, dropping off almost immediately. But then, when I was right in the middle of a halfway decent dream, the phone rang. Battling my way back to consciousness, I groped around on the table alongside the bed.

"Hello," I said groggily when I brought something that had a good shot at being a receiver up to my ear.

"Oh, I woke you, didn't I?" Ellen murmured. "I'm so *sorry.* But you never go to sleep *this* early."

"How early is 'this early'?"

"It's—oh! It's quarter past twelve. I didn't realize."

"That's okay. I even surprised myself by going to bed before midnight." Then it dawned on me. If Ellen doesn't have any plans, she's normally sound asleep at that hour. I sat up and switched on the lamp next to the phone. "What's up?" I asked anxiously.

"It can wait till tomorrow, Aunt Dez. Honestly. We'll talk in the morning."

"Not on your life."

"Well, if you're sure . . ."

"Will you *please* tell me why you called," I demanded.

"It's . . . about Mike. I just got off the phone with him a little while ago. He called to say that he's been thinking things over lately and that he, umm, decided things were moving too quickly. With us, that is. He feels it would probably be a good idea if we stopped seeing each other for a little while."

Et tu, Mike? My God, what was it with these men? It must be something in the drinking water! Ellen and I had both been dumped—okay, *more or less* dumped—at practically the same time! But of course, in Ellen's case it was a lot worse; she and Mike were really serious about each other. Or *she* was serious, at least.

I hardly knew what to say. This had to be extremely traumatic for my poor niece. I mean, Ellen's a very sensitive girl. I'd known her to lose it completely over something not nearly as important to her as her relationship with that overgrown quack. In fact, it was amazing to me that she hadn't dissolved into tears yet. "Don't worry, Ellen," I said very, very gently. "I'm sure—"

"Don't *you* worry, Aunt Dez. I'm fine. I really am. I don't even know why I felt compelled to call tonight. Probably so I wouldn't have to go through it with you tomorrow." Would you believe she actually giggled then?

"Oh, Ellen, I can't tell you how—"

"Go back to sleep, Aunt Dez," she interrupted in this calm, firm voice that I wasn't even aware she owned.

"And please, don't feel so bad. Everything's going to be fine. You wait and see."

Chapter 23

How could I possibly fall back to sleep again?

I was responsible for Ellen's pain. After all, who was the busybody that got her and Young Dr. Jekyll together in the first place?

Well, that valuable lesson about your nose and other people's business had at long last gotten through to me—but at poor Ellen's expense. In spite of her protests, she didn't fool me for a minute; she must be suffering terribly. (Although, I had to admit, it really wasn't like her to do it that silently.) I actually felt so rotten about my niece that I barely gave a thought to the sad state of my own personal life. At least for a while.

I couldn't have closed my eyes for more than an hour that night. And when the alarm rang, I was sorely tempted to defy it. But I don't know whether that was because I was so tired, so depressed, or because I lacked the moral fiber to face a militant Jackie—who undoubtedly would be lying in wait for me, thanks to my parting words to her the afternoon before. At any rate, at the last minute I decided to take the high road and obey the work ethic.

Jackie wasn't at her desk when I got to the office, and I made it to my own little cubbyhole without running into her. I couldn't figure out whether I was relieved or sorry. There's something to be said, you know, for meeting unpleasantness head on. In other words, coward that I am, I was anxious to get the thing over with.

I was just taking off my coat when I looked up to find guess-who in the doorway, hands on hips, head held high. "You have a message," she said tersely without meeting my eyes.

She entered the room and slapped a pink telephone slip on my desk, then immediately spun around and started to walk away. *Uh-oh, this could be a protracted estrangement we have here.* Gathering up my entire, but pathetically meager, quota of courage, I began to proffer my sincere apologies. I hurriedly addressed her retreating back. "Um, Jackie?" She stopped in the doorway. "I hope you're not angry about my being so, uh, uh . . ."

Turning to face me, she obligingly supplied the word. "Snotty."

"Yes, you're right; I was, wasn't I? And I'm really sorry, but I was very upset. I know I had no right to take it out on you, but, well, I guess that's just what I did."

"You won't get any argument from me," she snapped. But as she walked back toward me, her face took on a considerably softer expression than the one it had come in with. "Anything you want to talk about?" she asked, after which she immediately plunked her ample frame down on the chair next to my desk.

Now, the last thing I felt like going into just then was Stuart's "betrayal." (I was still dramatizing at this point.) But I knew that if I didn't explain, her nose would be out of joint again, and experience had taught me that the discomfort of baring my soul would be far preferable to facing Jackie's hostility.

So for about the next ten minutes I talked about Wednesday night's dinner, along with my earlier suspicions about Stuart's change in attitude. And when I was finished, Jackie said all the things I'd been saying to myself—in my more rational moments, that is. You know, that stuff about how there was no reason Stuart and I couldn't remain friends, and how we'd still see each other occasionally, and even how it was not beyond the realm of possibility that this Gretchen person and I could become chummy. But then she presented me with an entirely new take on the events. "This could be the best thing that's happened to you in years," she asserted.

"I'd love to know how you figure that one."

"Well, Dez, you do tend to get complacent; you have to admit it. And as long as you had Stuart to take you to dinner and the theater and act as your escort whenever you needed one and provide you with God knows what other little services"—she looked at me unblushingly when she said that—"you didn't even *try* to meet anyone else. A man you could get really serious with, I'm talking about."

"And *now* what do I do? Take out an ad in the newspapers?"

"People do, you know. It's not the worst way to meet someone."

"Well, if it isn't, you tell me what is," I retorted sourly.

"I'm not actually suggesting that's what you should do. What I am suggesting is that you put yourself in places where you're likely to meet eligible men. If I hadn't joined that bridge club, would I have met Derwin?" she wanted to know, said Derwin being the gentleman of advanced years and silver toupee who had been squiring her around of late. "And if Jeanette hadn't gone to that pre-Columbian art exhibit, would she have met Harry?" she demanded, this time referring to a divorced female attorney in the firm (the firm of Gilbert and Sullivan, that is) and her current beau. It wasn't easy to stifle a saracastic comment about what a lucky break that had been for Jeanette. She'd brought this joker Harry to the Fourth of July office picnic, where he immediately got himself crocked, fell in the lake and then, because he didn't know how to swim a stroke, had to be rescued by a ninety-five-pound secretary.

Anyhow, these were, apparently, not rhetorical questions. "Well?" Jackie was saying.

"I guess not."

"Of *course* not," she corrected. She got up then. "I imagine I should be getting back to my desk. Otherwise, Elliot Gilbert will have me reported as a missing person or something. But you think about what I've been telling you," she commanded.

I promised I would. And as soon as she left, I did. And promptly came to the conclusion that I'd certainly rather go out with a Stuart than a Harry or a Derwin. Limited though our relationship had been.

Now that I'd settled that, I reached for the telephone slip Jackie had deposited on my desk. The message was from poor Ellen. (Since last night's conversation I found that I rarely thought of my niece without this appellation in front of her name.) It said to call her back at the store.

I was really stunned that she was up to resuming her life so quickly.

"Ellen Kravitz speaking."

"Hi, how are you doing?" I said in what I hoped was a neutral voice—you know, not too gloomy (she was undoubtedly depressed enough by now) but not too cheerful, either (the circumstances hardly called for it).

"Oh, Aunt Dez. I'm glad you got back to me; I was worried about you." She *was worried about* me? "I know how upset you were when I told you about Mike."

I tore a page straight out of Jackie's book. "No, no, Ellen. I've been thinking about it, and I realize it could all be for the best. As long as Mike was around, you wouldn't have done a thing to try to meet other men. *Marriageable* men, I mean. But now that he's out of the picture, you'll—"

"But he isn't!" Ellen rejoined sharply. "Out of the picture, that is," she added a little less stridently. "He just wants some time to himself to make sure, that's all. But he'll be back. I know it."

Well, since the night before I had been entertaining the strong suspicion that my niece had been cloned and that I hadn't been talking to the real Ellen at all. I mean, she has slews of admirable qualities, but self-confidence has never been one of them. Yet just listen to her now! However, in the event science had nothing to do with the "new" Ellen, it stood to reason that her present attitude was a way of coping. So even though what I'd seen of similar situations caused me to have serious doubts about Mike's returning, I kept my mouth shut. Still, I can't say I wasn't concerned about how she'd deal with this thing down the road.

"I was going to call you, anyway," I said, moving on to a safer topic. "I thought maybe you'd want to come over for dinner tonight."

"Oh, that would have been nice, Aunt Dez, and

thanks for asking. But I promised to have dinner with one of the women at work—Claudette. You remember my mentioning her, don't you?"

"Sounds familiar," I answered absentmindedly.

She proceeded to give me a full description of Claudette, after which we talked for a couple of minutes more before ending the conversation.

Poor Ellen, I thought again as I put the receiver back in its cradle.

After a quick lunch with one of the paralegals who worked at Gilbert and Sullivan, I hurried back to the office for my one o'clock appointment with a potential client.

Now, I'd had only one other case since taking on the Corwin thing. And that one, which had arrived on my desk courtesy of Elliot Gilbert, turned out to be a real quickie. It involved locating a missing husband whose wife wanted to find him so she could serve him with divorce papers. It took only five or six phone calls and one skipped lunch (which I made up for later) to determine that the man was living in Utah, where he was cohabiting with a topless dancer.

Anyway, what I'm trying to bring out is that I could hardly afford to turn up my nose at some additional business. So I was really excited to hear from this man yesterday who had said he was interested in hiring me. In fact, I was even thinking that while I was still working for Evelyn Corwin, I'd get my old friend Harry Burgess, a semi-retired P.I. from Fort Lee, New Jersey, to give me a hand with this new investigation.

Unfortunately, however, things didn't exactly go as well as I'd hoped.

John Flannery was somewhere in his sixties, his late sixties most probably. A tall, burly man with bushy eyebrows and a ruddy complexion, his general build and thick stump of a neck, along with the bulging biceps so clearly outlined under his tight navy sweater, made me think of a longshoreman. I was surprised when he mentioned that he'd been a high school teacher for over thirty years.

He was, he told me, a widower, and he had a forty-two-year-old daughter. She was why he was here. It seems she'd gotten involved about a month ago with a much younger man, and Flannery wanted him investigated.

"Is that the only reason you want him investigated—because he's younger than your daughter?"

"Not just younger. *Thirteen years younger.*" Leaning forward in his chair, Flannery held my eyes with his own. "Look, Mrs. Shapiro," he said earnestly, "I'm worried about that girl. She's much too trusting."

I tried to reassure him. "I know a lot of women who are married to younger men," I told him, hurriedly amending that with "and happily." He was about to protest, so I bolstered my argument. "That sort of thing goes on all the time now. Let me ask you something, Mr. Flannery. If the age difference were reversed—with your daughter being so much younger than her boyfriend—would it still bother you?"

"Well . . . I guess not. No, I take that back. Let me show you something." Reaching into his back pocket, he removed a worn leather wallet, and after riffling through it for a moment, produced a photograph, which he placed on my desk, directly in front of me. It was a head shot of a woman. I picked it up and examined it. The subject in the photo wasn't what you'd consider pretty. Or even attractive. In fact, to be honest, she could have served as a flesh and blood definition of the term *plain*. I looked at him questioningly, silently asking what point he was trying to make.

"Irene—my daughter—took that picture for her passport last year." And after I handed the photo back to him: "She's not exactly a beauty, is she?"

I found myself squirming. "Well, uh, she has a *nice* face. And those passport things are always just awful. I wanted to burn mine," I said with a weak little laugh.

"This one's flattering."

I was beginning to get annoyed. "Look, Mr. Flannery, just because your daughter doesn't look like Heather Locklear doesn't mean—"

"You should see Carter. That's his name—Carter. Not anything simple like Bob, or Jim, or Bill." Flannery shook his head in disgust. "Carter," he said, spitting out the name as though he thought it would leave a bad taste in his mouth. "Big guy with blond hair and lotsa white teeth. He could pass for a movie star."

"What does he do for a living?" I asked, expecting to hear something like "He's in investments" or "He manages properties" or "He's an entrepreneur." You know, the kind of career that might be legitimate but, on the other hand, could also be a pretty good cover for a scam.

Instead, I was told: "He's a microbiologist."

It's not easy to talk with your jaw hanging open, but I came through. "Your daughter—what does she do?"

"Same thing. A microbiologist. They work together, the two of 'em."

I got up and quickly took the few steps required to cross the room. Then I removed John Flannery's black trench coat from the hanger on the back of the door. "Here," I said, thrusting it at him. Now he was the one with the dropped jaw. "Obviously this Carter is less superficial than you think," I told him, "and certainly a lot less than you are. It's time you took another look at your daughter, Mr. Flannery, starting with how intelligent she is. Maybe it'll help you figure out what *he* sees in her."

My visitor had a few not very kind words for me before he left. They only increased my satisfaction at having tossed him out. Even the distinct possibility that when the Corwin case was over there'd be nothing on my plate but bills on top of bills didn't seem to matter just then.

At that moment I felt as if I wasn't just standing up for Flannery's daughter Irene, but for Ellen and myself and all the rest of womankind. Well, those of us who aren't Heather Locklear, anyway.

Strangely, the encounter with Flannery also served to pacify my pit bull of a conscience. If I could give up *that* case, I reasoned, it was unlikely that at some subconscious level I was just prolonging the Corwin case to provide myself with an income. It was a thought that had begun troubling me lately. I guess it sprang up as a result of my complete lack of progress to date and was then nourished by the obvious opinions of some members of the Corwin household.

Now, however, thanks to John Flannery, I could stop worrying about my motive. The reason I hadn't concluded the investigation was because I wasn't yet one hundred percent convinced I'd done everything that could be done.

A few minutes later, I tackled my notes with renewed determination. I don't remember when I'd had more confidence in my ability. If there was even the smallest clue here, I'd find it, I knew. But when I shut the folder a couple of hours later, I had nothing to show for my efforts but eye strain.

It was possible I'd gone as far as I could go with this thing, after all. Still, I wasn't quite ready to throw in the towel. Maybe something would turn up. Or maybe I'd get a flash of inspiration. Well, I'd give it another day or two, at any rate.

Right before leaving for home, I called Evelyn Corwin—just to check in as I'd promised. I told her I hadn't made any real progress since I last spoke to her but that I'd continue to look into things.

But even as I said it, I wondered if there was any place left to look.

Chapter 24

Tomorrow was Saturday, so that night I decided to pamper myself a little by not setting the alarm. I slept until close to ten the next morning, at which time I opened one eye, peered at the clock, shut the eye and promptly fell back to sleep. When I woke up again, it was a little after eleven. I resisted the impulse to pull the covers up over my head—after all, enough was enough—and crawled out of bed.

When I was through with breakfast, I took a nice, long bubble bath. As soon as I finished covering myself and the bathroom floor with dusting powder, I got into my rattiest-looking and most comfortable bathrobe, poured myself a second cup of coffee, and sat down at the kitchen table to read through my notes again.

But then with the unopened folder in front of me, I wavered.

You're being compulsive, I informed myself. I mean, hadn't I been through this same fruitless exercise only the day before for maybe the hundredth time?

I countered that with: *But it won't be the first instance where you kept overlooking the obvious.* This was certainly true enough. Besides, I'd made up my mind yesterday to stick with the case for at least another couple of days. And since I didn't know who else to question or what else to do at this point, the notes seemed to be my only option.

I have to tell you, though. I think the real—the overriding—reason I gave it that one final shot was that the alternative would have been telling Evelyn Corwin I'd reached the end of the line. And right then I couldn't think of anything in the world that would have been tougher for me to do.

Which is why I always say that the true circumstances of little Catherine's death were uncovered as a result of my inimitable—and unquestionable—cowardice.

I proceeded at a snail's pace this time, paying close attention to every single word. And I did something else. Something I'd never tried before. As I finished going over each meeting or interview I'd had during the course of the investigation, I stopped and reviewed that particular section in my mind, making sure that it added up, that it fit with everything I'd read earlier.

I'd been at it for more than two hours when I suddenly came across something that jarred me. It was a small thing, really. But still . . .

Just to make sure I wasn't mistaken, I checked back to a previous page. I ran my finger quickly down the text. Aha! I was right. There *was* something out of whack here!

Now, don't ask me how I managed to miss it all those other times. Considering how many hours I'd spent with my nose buried in that damned file, I'm embarrassed to even think about that. But anyway, now that I *had* taken notice of what should have been obvious to me weeks ago, I didn't have any idea what it could possibly mean. But certainly it couldn't be very significant. The thing was, though, I had to come up with some kind of an explanation that would satisfy me.

It was when I was on my third cup of coffee—and practically ready to float out of there—that it struck me:

My God, you idiot! I think you may just have uncovered the murder weapon!

Chapter 25

Could it be? I wondered, close to bursting.

Of course it couldn't! I decided.

On the other hand, though . . .

Stop that, for heaven's sake. It's not even conceivable. You must be completely out of your mind!

Yeah? How can you be so sure? I demanded of myself.

Because it's ridiculous, that's how.

And finally: *But what other explanation is there?*

I picked up the phone.

Luisa answered on the fourth ring. "Corwin residence," she announced breathlessly.

"It's Desiree Shapiro, Luisa."

I didn't expect her to be delighted with this news. And from the sound of her voice, she wasn't. Nevertheless, she responded politely. "How are you, Mrs. Shapiro?"

"I'm fine. But I seem to have called at a bad time."

"Oh, no. That's all right. I just returned from the fish store, and I had my key in the lock when I heard the telephone. I didn't really think I was going to get to it in time."

"There's something I want to ask you," I said.

"Ye-e-s?" she responded uneasily.

"Do you remember saying to me that when Catherine came down for lunch that day, you were just about to clean the library and that you dropped everything and ran into the kitchen to fix something for her?"

"Yes, of course."

"Would you mind itemizing the cleaning things you were planning on using and telling me exactly where you left each one?"

The only indication that the housekeeper was surprised by this request was the silence that followed. "Well, let me see . . ." she mused after the brief hiatus. "I hadn't even gone into the room yet when Catherine came over to me and said she was hungry. I'm almost certain I left the vacuum cleaner right inside the door, to the left as you walk in. And the upholstery attachments—I put them . . ."

She went through the tools one by one, and a few minutes later, I hung up. Satisfied.

After that, I tried getting ahold of Catherine's pulmonary specialist. I phoned his office, reaching his answering service, as I'd anticipated.

"Will you please try to contact Dr. Pascal and tell him Desiree Shapiro called? I have to talk to him about little Catherine Corwin. Be sure to say it's urgent and that it won't take more than a minute or two."

His service assured me that every effort would be made to get in touch with the doctor.

Sergeant Jacobowitz was next on my list.

I expected a problem there; too. Jacobowitz was no doubt off for the weekend; if not, he was out on a case someplace. With my luck he might even be on vacation—a nice *long* vacation. By the time I finished dialing, I was almost convinced that he was on a year's leave in the South Seas or the Himalayas or God knows where and completely unreachable.

In fact, I did such a persuasive job on myself that I was momentarily stunned when I heard his voice.

"Sergeant Jacobowitz? This is Desiree Shapiro."

"Don't tell me you're still working on that Corwin case," he said.

"Yup. I'm still at it."

"No kidding? I woulda thought . . . But what can I do for you?"

"I'd like you to ask the M.E. if, when he conducted the autopsy, he checked Catherine for something. Something in particular."

"What did you have in mind?" And then when I told him: "You're kidding!"

"No, I'm not."

"I don't suppose you intend letting me know why you

want that information." He made that sound like a question.

"Of course I do. As soon as I get everything sorted out."

He laughed. "Why was I so sure you were going to say something like that?"

"Umm, any chance you could get back to me today?"

He laughed again. "You really *are* hot to find out, aren't you? Look, I don't know when I can get anyone to look into this for me. But as soon as *I* know, *you'll* know. Okay?"

I supposed it had to be.

Dr. Pascal called me at ten after six. He made no attempt to conceal his annoyance. "I understand you have this urgent need to speak to me," he said, his tone heavy with sarcasm.

"Yes. I'm sorry to bother you, Doctor. I know—"

"You can skip the amenities, Mrs. Shapiro. I'm speaking at a banquet tonight, and I'm late now. Whatever it is, please, just make it fast."

I hoped he choked on his creamed chicken! But being the consummate hypocrite when warranted, I covered it admirably. "Yes, of course, Doctor," I said sweetly, after which I set some kind of speed record in posing my question.

"Well, you have quite an imagination; I'll say that much for you. But I can't really see that at all," the doctor responded in this supercilious tone. Then just as I was entertaining the idea of placing my head in the oven, he cleared his elegant throat. "On the other hand, though," he amended grudgingly, "the Corwin child's health was extremely precarious. So I suppose it *is* possible that in a case like hers, something of that sort could lead to acute respiratory failure."

"Thank you, Doctor. Thanks very much."

"But I'm talking about only a very slight possibility. I hope you understand that."

"Oh, I do. I certainly do," I told him. But "possible" or even "a very slight possibility" was good enough for me.

*   *   *

For the rest of the weekend, I was glued to the phone, waiting to hear from Jacobowitz. Every time the damn thing rang, I came close to hyperventilating.

Ellen called on Sunday morning. "Just to say hello," she said. A friend of hers who had moved out to Tucson a few years ago was back in New York for a visit and would be spending the day with her, and Ellen was taking her to the theater and then to dinner at a very hot and pricy restaurant. "It'll be just great getting together with Roberta again after all this time," she enthused. "I can't wait to see her." She sounded really up. I hated to think of the letdown I feared was in store for her.

A short time afterward, I heard from my neighbor Barbara, who wanted to know if I'd be interested in going to a movie later. I claimed I was having dinner at Ellen's. (Well, it beat telling her that I was in no mood to put up with her pretentions or her fashion critiques, didn't it?)

Then right before noon, it was Jackie's turn. She wanted to know how I was feeling. It took awhile before I realized it was our conversation about Stuart that had prompted her concern. I said I was fine, sparing her and myself a rundown on my latest source of angst. I was really chafing to get off the phone, not because I was afraid I'd miss Frank Jacobowitz's call—I have call waiting—but because I was much too antsy to make small talk. Still, it *was* sweet of Jackie to check on me like that, and I didn't want to offend her (God *knows,* I didn't want to offend her), so I asked how Derwin was, and she was off and running.

She chirped on happily—and endlessly—about her silver-toupeed suitor, while I put in "that's nice" or "sounds great" or "how thoughtful" or whatever, whenever it was appropriate. Mercifully, there was a beep on the line after about fifteen minutes, and I explained to Jackie that I was expecting some information from the police.

"I have to hang up now, anyway," she told me. "I haven't even had my lunch yet." And she said it accusingly, too!

I greeted my waiting caller with a hello an instant

later, which was a little tricky to do, since I was holding my breath.

"Who *is* this?" demanded my wrong number.

Well, at least it had gotten Jackie off the line.

I didn't give up on hearing from Jacobowitz until after eleven Sunday night. And even then I took my bath with the door open—just in case.

On Monday I all but sat on my hands to keep from dialing *him.* I had to remind myself over and over not to be a pest, that I'd get my call as soon as Jacobowitz had something to tell me.

At twelve-fifteen I was having a sandwich at my desk (I couldn't even consider going out to lunch) when he finally got back to me. "I just talked to the M.E. And to answer your question, no, that's one thing they didn't look for. There didn't seem to be any reason to."

And with that, I knew with a certainty I can't even explain that Catherine Corwin had been murdered.

With a feather duster.

Chapter 26

It was one of the police photographs I'd examined in Sergeant Jacobowitz's office that had provided the essential clue.

In the close-up shot of the cherry table, I'd noticed a feather duster lying almost directly opposite the telephone system. And that table was smack in the middle of the library!

Do you see what I'm getting at? Luisa had made it clear the night I went over to talk to her that Catherine had intercepted her at the door, just as she was about to go in there to clean. She was so happy to learn the little girl was hungry, she said, that she "dropped everything"—all of her cleaning paraphernalia—and ran into the kitchen to prepare lunch.

I'd written the woman's words down myself; they were right there in my folder, in black and white. Yet I'd gone over my notes I don't know how many times and failed to see the contradiction between the housekeeper's statement and the police photo.

I still like to think I would have recognized that contradiction when I saw the photograph at the precinct if I hadn't been so distracted by the frame. (I'm talking about the frame with the collage of Catherine's pictures that appeared in the same close-up shot and which took me in another direction entirely.) But if I wanted to be completely honest with myself—which I often prefer not to be—I'd have to concede that while the frame might have given me a legitimate reason for the initial oversight, it was still a piss-poor excuse for not realizing the significance of the feather duster thing until now.

After all, the duster hadn't *walked* onto that table. Ergo, someone must have put it there.

But why?

It was the *why,* naturally, that was so all-important. It led to what even to me had at first seemed like an incredibly bizarre theory. But the more I thought about it, the more respectable it became. And my phone calls of the last few days had served to test the validity of this weird theory of mine—and then to reinforce it.

The conversation with Luisa confirmed that she'd left the feather duster near the door that Saturday, on a small square table just inside the room.

The brief exchange with Dr. Pascal (you could hardly call it a conversation) verified that given the severity of Catherine's condition, it was *possible*—if highly unlikely—that being tickled with a feather duster could have caused her death.

And, finally, Sergeant Jacobowitz established that the M.E. hadn't examined the little girl's lungs for dust particles.

Now, I'm not saying that what I learned *proved* that the feather duster was the weapon. What I'm saying is that it didn't *disprove* it.

And that was all I needed. Because there was just no other way to explain the why.

In bed that night and well into the morning, the same little scenario kept replaying itself over and over in my head.

I pictured Catherine sitting contentedly on the brown leather sofa, reading her book: *The Boy from Planet Pluto,* the title says. There's even a sweet smile on the child's face. Then I see a shadowy figure come into the room. Shadowy figure, noticing the feather duster on the small table next to the entrance, picks it up. Maybe merely absentmindedly at this juncture. Or maybe not so absentmindedly, but suddenly realizing how useful to him or her this innocuous household staple could be.

The intruder joins the trusting child on the sofa, disarming her with false pleasantries and an insidious grin (which is all my mind can see of the perpetrator's face). Almost immediately, he begins to tickle her—perhaps only playfully (better make that sadistically) at first, not yet realizing the full potential of the weapon being wielded. He runs the duster up and down her arm, her leg, and finally under her nose, backing her into a corner of the sofa. I visualize plainly—and with rising nausea—Catherine cringing in that corner, her small, frail body convulsed by terrible, uncontrollable laughter. I envision her tossing her head back and forth, the long blond hair falling across her face in her vain struggle to escape the now lethal duster. And I hear her manage a few desperate gasps for breath.

Then almost impossibly, Catherine has one final surge of strength. Breaking free of her assailant, she jumps up and staggers toward the cherry table, attempting to reach the intercom. She collapses only inches away from it.

Now the murderer—most likely after a quick check to make certain his victim is dead—realizes how essential it is to get out of that room. So throwing the improvised weapon down on the table, the triumphant killer—a grotesque smile completely filling the only visible portion of his/her face—rushes from the scene.

Chapter 27

I don't know just how many repetitions there were of my little playlet that night, but with each replay I added an embellishment or two, probably to give the scene a bit more dimension. Nothing critical, you understand: a whimper from the victim, a sneer or two from the villain. But these extra fillips in no way diminished the basic authenticity of the scenario.

I was, I knew, on the right track at last.

The only problem that remained—and it was a considerable one, I admit—was providing the killer with an identity.

As soon as I got to the office Tuesday morning, Ellen called.

She made it brief. "I'm off today, so how about coming over for dinner later when you're through with work?" she asked. "I haven't seen you in a while."

"Sure, I'd like that," I told her, trying my damnedest to keep the excitement over my recent discovery from seeping into my voice.

Apparently I succeeded, because "Good. See you tonight" was her only response.

The rest of that day I didn't get a single thing done. All I could think of was catching my killer. And exactly how did I intend to go about doing that?

It was, I thought, a very good question.

Just after six I arrived at Ellen's apartment building, a truly decrepit-looking structure that she'd chosen to call home solely because it had a working fireplace. Clutched firmly in my fist was a paper bag with two pint containers of Häagen-Dazs.

As always, I entered the building's only elevator with much trepidation, saying a small prayer that the antiquated contraption would not choose to break down before safely transporting me to the fourteenth floor. It was a very slow ride, with the car clanking a lot and creaking even more, giving me plenty of time to think. I repeated the promise I'd made to myself just after Ellen's phone call to keep my new theory to myself. For once I wouldn't use her as a sounding board for my investigation. And I certainly wouldn't burden her with the Stuart thing. She had troubles enough of her own.

When the car finally lurched to a stop on fourteen, Ellen was waiting in the open doorway of her apartment, right next to the elevator. After greeting me with a hug and pulling me inside, she relieved me of the ice cream. "I won't say thanks until I make sure one of these is Belgian Chocolate," I was told as she peered into the bag. She lifted the lid of one container—making a face at my Macadamia Brittle—then checked out the bottom container. "It is. So thanks," she said, smiling impishly at me.

"What would you say if I told you we weren't having Chinese for dinner," she posed when she was hanging up my coat.

"I'd probably pass out."

"That's what I was afraid of. That's why I'm ordering from Mandarin Joy," she giggled.

Well, Ellen was certainly in rare form tonight: giggly—even playful. I could have cried.

"What do you feel like tonight?" she asked.

"Oh, I don't know. You?"

She shrugged. "It doesn't matter to me. You choose."

"You must have some preference," I insisted.

Somehow, we arrived at a menu anyway. And after phoning in our order of assorted appetizers, sweet and pungent chicken and lobster with black bean sauce, Ellen took a bottle of anisette out of the small cabinet in the living room. "Mike brought it," she informed me, pouring the liqueur into two small glasses.

I didn't want to say what I was thinking about that lowlife, so I didn't say anything at all until she'd finished pouring. "Cheers," I murmured then, raising the glass she handed me.

"Cheers," she responded, raising her own glass and smiling at me.

Ellen had prepared some appetizers of her own—an eclectic collection if there ever was one. And we sat around talking about her Sunday with her Tucson friend, sipping our Italian liqueur and nibbling on French cheese and Swedish crackers along with some all-American pigs-in-blankets while awaiting our Chinese meal.

I recall looking around the room at some point and noticing—as I did almost every time I was here—how shabby Ellen's furniture was, virtually every stick of it having been a largesse from an aunt on her father's side who was about to remarry. Aunt Gertrude, it seemed, had intended to donate all of her furnishings to the Salvation Army, but this charitable inclination had been nicely quashed by the man who came to pick up the stuff. "We don't take anything in that condition," he'd announced with disdain, acting like Aunt Gertie was trying to pull a fast one.

Only a few days after that, the properly chastised bride-to-be attended a family dinner at Ellen's parents' home. (That was before they moved down to Florida, of course.) "Uh, you don't happen to know anyone who might be able to use any of my furniture, do you?" she inquired with some embarrassment during the soup course, immediately adding, "I'm afraid it isn't in very good condition, though."

"*I* would," said Ellen, who was a lot less fussy than the Salvation Army and who had signed the lease on her first apartment only a few days earlier.

And so now all of those chipped, scratched, torn, soiled and faded Salvation Army rejects graced my niece's living quarters, along with the only-used-once fireplace that had prompted her to move in here to begin with.

At any rate, just seeing everything again made me feel even more unhappy about Ellen than I'd been before. Oh, not that my own 3 Rms/no Vw are in any danger of gracing the pages of *Architectural Digest*. But they're comfortable, if not exactly breathtaking. This place, on the other hand, was downright depressing. I think I must have sighed or something, because Ellen glanced at me penetratingly. "What's wrong?"

"Nothing. Just a little tired I guess."

"You must be hungry, too. The food is taking forever tonight."

"Hungry? Are you kidding? I haven't stopped eating since I sat down."

"But there's *something* bothering you, isn't there?" she persisted.

"Absolutely not."

You could almost see her reminding herself just then. "Did you ever call Stuart?" she prodded gently.

"No." I felt myself coloring.

"Why not?"

"He called me."

"And?"

"And I was right. He's met someone."

"Ohhh, Aunt Dez," she wailed. "I'm so—"

And that's when the doorbell rang. Our food had arrived.

The discussion of Stuart was postponed so as not to interfere with our delicate appetites. At the table, conversation was relegated to movies Ellen had seen lately, a book I'd just finished and a new TV series we both loathed.

It was in the living room over Chinese tea, fortune cookies and Häagen-Dazs that Ellen got her update on what you could laughingly call my love life. And while I was telling her about Stuart's involvement with this Gretchen person, I found to my surprise that I was no longer angry or even particularly depressed. Just a little saddened by the possibility of losing a cherished friendship, or at the very least, having it greatly curtailed.

Ellen was at her most Pollyanna-ish. "I'm positive the two of you will continue to be friends," she assured me. "Stuart's always been just crazy about you—oh, I don't mean in *that way*—but he's always had very strong feelings for you. Maybe you won't see him quite as often anymore, but I'm sure you'll still be in close touch."

"Maybe."

"And who knows?" she offered brightly. "Maybe he and that Gretchen won't even last. You never can tell with these things."

Which led to my referring—however obliquely—to the subject I'd sworn to myself I'd avoid like the plague. "Enough about Stuart and me. How are *you* doing?" I asked pointedly.

Ellen frowned, then responded in this exasperated tone, "You refuse to believe me, but I'm fine." A moment later she reached over and patted my shoulder. "So please stop worrying," she ordered gently. And almost in the same breath, probably because she was so anxious to change the subject: "Hey, you haven't said. How's the investigation going? Anything new?"

"Uh, no, not really." I was turning telltale pink again.

"There *is* something new, isn't there?" she accused. "What's going on, anyway? You don't even confide in me anymore."

"That's not tr—"

"First Stuart, now this."

"Look, Ellen, I haven't wanted to bother you, that's all. You've got enough on your mind right now."

"Just stop that!" she commanded, eyes flashing. "You act like I'm in mourning or something."

So I wound up using her as a sounding board again, after all. But you tell me. What else could I do?'

Chapter 28

I laid everything out for Ellen. When I finished, she looked at me doubtfully.

"Are you saying the murderer went in to talk to the little girl, saw the feather duster lying there, and at that moment got the idea of using it to kill her?"

"Maybe. Maybe not. It's just as likely he wasn't actually thinking murder then. Possibly he—or she—just started fooling around and tickling her, and it wasn't until he saw Catherine's reaction that it occurred to him the duster could be used to get rid of her. I don't know. And maybe I never will know for sure. But this much I can tell you: The murder wasn't premeditated. The killer just saw his chance and took it."

"Wait. What if Catherine got terribly sick but didn't actually die? Wasn't the killer afraid that could happen and that she'd tell everyone what he did to her?"

"I doubt that he had time for any 'what ifs.' My guess is he just got caught up in the thing. But if he did consider that possibility, he probably decided it was worth the risk. After all, he could always claim he didn't realize how it would affect her and that he would never forgive himself for making her so ill, et cetera, et cetera."

"Brazen it out, you mean?"

"Why not? And if Catherine suggested to anyone that he'd been trying to kill her, well, keep in mind that when she said that car business was on purpose, nobody believed her."

But Ellen still wasn't ready to buy into my theory.

"Look," I told her, "I'd bet anything that little kid was murdered and the feather duster was the murder weapon. How else can you explain its ending up in the middle of the room like that?"

"Well, Catherine herself, maybe?" she put out tentatively.

"Do you think anyone growing up with lung problems like hers is going to play around with a feather duster?"

She mulled that one over. "I suppose not. But it's . . ." She shook her head in frustration. "It's so hard to even imagine."

"Remember what Catherine's health was like, Ellen. She had this severe congenital lung disease plus a bad case of asthma. And the killer tickled her without letting up. The poor little thing couldn't catch her breath. And whenever she *was* able to get a breath in, she wound up inhaling all that dust."

"I guess it *is* possible," Ellen conceded. "Has the feather duster been checked for prints yet?"

I managed to take offense at that. "No, but it will be," I responded tartly. The thought *had* occurred to me—honestly—but I'd kind of dismissed it. Quite a lot of time had elapsed since the murder, and I was certain the duster had been handled frequently since then. Still, it was worth a try.

Suddenly Ellen popped up with: "Say, what's that expression—'I almost died laughing'?"

"Sounds right."

"You know," she murmured as though to herself, "there might very well be something in that." Then she looked me full in the face. "Um, I have a confession to make, Aunt Dez."

"What's that?"

"A couple of minutes ago . . . well, I thought you were crazy, totally out of your gourd. But now I realize I should have known better, especially after so many years." My one-woman fan club smiled at me dotingly. "Honestly, you're really remarkable!"

It would have been more seemly, I suppose, if I'd uttered a mild protest right about then. But with a fan club of such limited membership, you take your accolades when you can get them. So I let her gush on.

"I'm positive that kind of thing would never occur to another living soul," she was saying. "I just can't figure out how you do it—always coming up with the answers like that, I mean."

And I could see that Ellen was beginning to embrace my theory with as much enthusiasm as I was.

A few minutes later, as we were sipping our second refills of tea, Ellen asked, "But who do you think would do something like that?"

"Damned if I know."

"You don't have any idea?"

"None. In fact, for one reason or another, I keep eliminating all of my suspects. Take Todd. He goes around telling everyone who'll listen how he felt about Catherine. But that's exactly what bothers me. Why would he make his feelings so obvious if he was the one who committed the murder?"

"Could be it's like a game to him," Ellen suggested.

"Yes, but then what about the car—the one that almost ran over her a couple of weeks earlier? Todd certainly couldn't have been the driver."

"That's true," Ellen agreed. "But maybe he was in cahoots with someone. Or maybe it *was* accidental that other time."

I didn't want to hurt Ellen's feelings, so I said, "It's possible." Which was meant to cover both these alternatives. But the truth was, I couldn't imagine anyone's being willing to enter into a partnership with that little creep for any reason, much less to commit murder. And I also couldn't accept that the car thing and the murder were two separate events. While I admit that coincidences do happen, it's been my experience that ninety-nine percent of the time incidents like that are tied together. And I intended going on that premise in this case. (I conveniently banished from my head that until very recently I'd been perfectly willing to accept as coincidence a little girl's narrowly escaping death and then dying of something else only fourteen days later.)

At any rate, it was apparent my response hadn't sounded all that convincing, because Ellen said, "You're pretty sure it wasn't an accident, though, aren't you?"

"Well, let's just say I'd be shocked if it turned out that way."

"How do you feel about Catherine's mother?" she put to me then.

"Stepmother, actually," I corrected. "She's not a very good suspect, either. In the first place, there's motive—or I should say *lack* of motive." I went on to explain about Donna's not even knowing that she'd be inheriting the $300,000-plus that was Catherine's share of her husband's estate. "According to my client, Donna was completely unaware there was a provision to that effect in the will. Besides, she'll be coming into a much more substantial amount on Mrs. Corwin's death. And Evelyn Corwin," I informed Ellen somberly, "is dying of cancer." It was hard for me to even say it.

"So you feel she can definitely be ruled out?"

Definitely was much too definite a word for me, if you know what I mean. "Well, I wouldn't say definitely," I replied. "There's always the possibility Catherine knew something that made it critical for Donna to silence her."

"Like?"

I shrugged. "Like say Donna had had a lover while her husband was alive. And say Catherine found out something along those lines. Well, there was always the chance she'd let her grandmother in on what she knew—maybe even inadvertently. And believe me, if Evelyn Corwin thought for a minute that Donna'd been cheating on her son, she wouldn't leave her a nickel. Incidentally, I tried looking into that angle and came up with zilch. But since Todd was the one who started me thinking Donna had something to hide to begin with, I probably shouldn't have bothered."

"And anyway," Ellen reasoned, "if Catherine was murdered because of something she found out about her stepmother and if Todd had the same information she did, how come he's still walking around?"

"You've got a point. Unless she really was aware of some secret of her stepmother's and he was just talking through his hat. Also, it's conceivable Mrs. Corwin might have put some stock in what Catherine told her. But no one in their right mind would take Todd seriously." Then I put in wryly, "Excluding a dummy like me, of course."

Ellen didn't bother to disagree. "Okay, let's talk about

Barrie—isn't that her name? How does she make out financially with Catherine dead?"

"Well, as I said before, her father's will stipulated that Catherine's entire share would go to Donna. But, of course, with Catherine gone, there'll be one less person to divvy up Mrs. Corwin's estate, which is where the real money is. Under *that* will Catherine's portion gets divided among the remaining heirs—Donna, Barrie, and Todd."

"So Barrie had a motive, then."

"Yeah. I guess," I had to acknowledge. It wasn't easy for me to contemplate the woman's killing her little sister. In fact, it bothered me a lot.

Almost immediately, though, Ellen threw someone else in the mix. "Wasn't Barrie's friend in the house that morning?"

"That's right. She was tutoring Todd."

"Well, maybe *she* killed Catherine so there'd be more money for Barrie when Mrs. Corwin dies."

I thought that was *really* far-fetched, and I told Ellen as much. Tactfully, of course.

She had another one for me. "Say, what about the husband?"

"*Whose* husband?"

"Barrie's, naturally."

"In the first place, he's an *ex*-husband. And in the second, why would he want Catherine dead?"

"Maybe because his ex would come into a bigger inheritance, and he's hoping to go back with her."

Now, I'd never actually considered Paul Lundquist a suspect. Plus it hadn't seemed to me that there was much likelihood of the couple's getting together again. And then I suddenly recalled how flushed Lundquist had gotten when I suggested there might have been some kind of hidden reason for the divorce. I hadn't paid that much attention to it at the time, but it was possible there was more to the breakup than I knew. "I don't imagine it would do any harm to have another talk with the man," I said.

"Good." Ellen grinned then. And you should have *seen* how smug she looked.

She's enjoying this, I thought. *And here I was, trying*

so hard to keep from bothering her. I'd actually been a good Samaritan, I decided, taking her mind off things this way.

I practically had myself prepped as a candidate for canonization when the telephone rang. Ellen shot out of her seat and raced to take it in the bedroom, bypassing the kitchen phone along the way. I heard the bedroom door bang shut behind her. When she came back after more than ten minutes, she was beaming. "A friend from work," she mumbled.

Her face put a lie to that one, but wisely—for a change—I didn't call her on it. A second later, though, she said softly, "Okay, I'm sorry. It was Mike. He wanted to know how I've been." And then she added hastily, "But that doesn't mean we're seeing each other again."

"Of course not," I agreed. But I was delighted. I took that phone call as a very positive sign.

And from her expression, it was apparent that Ellen did, too.

Not long afterward, I left for home. And en route in the cab I thought about what a good visit it had been.

Ellen had—hallelujah!—heard from Mike. Also, I realized I was now able to handle Stuart's involvement with Gretchen with a lot more equanimity (to say nothing of maturity). And finally, to top everything off, my dear niece's mention of Paul Lundquist had furnished me with a starting point, at least, for proceeding with the investigation.

But never—not even in my wildest dreams—could I have anticipated where that mention of hers would lead me.

Chapter 29

Evelyn Corwin called the next morning, just as I had my hand on the phone, poised to dial her. And even though I knew she'd never believe that, I thought I should mention it.

"I was just about to call *you*," I said.

"Really?" Her tone left no doubt as to her opinion of my veracity. "It's been over a week since I heard from you," she informed me dryly.

Actually, it had been only five days. But I could understand why it seemed a lot longer to her. And anyway, I knew I should have gotten in touch with her earlier—the very second, in fact, that I decided she'd been right all along, that Catherine *had* been murdered. But given the, well, let's call it "peculiar" nature of my theory, I had to get a little more comfortable with it myself before exposing anyone else to the concept. Discussing things with Ellen—I don't consider her just anyone—had helped a lot in that regard. But still, I wanted to postpone—at least for a little while—telling my client how the crime had been committed, anticipating the trouble she'd have in accepting it. (After all, who wouldn't?) Maybe before long I'd even have some actual facts to back me up. On the other hand, though, the woman was entitled to be told *something*; I'd made up my mind to that last night. "I have some news for you," I said cautiously.

There was silence on the other end of the line, so I continued. "I thought you'd like to know that I agree with you; your granddaughter *was* murdered, and I think I know how it was done."

I heard the sound of breath being expelled, followed by a whispered "Thank you." A moment later, Mrs. Corwin asked hesitantly, "Do you . . . have you any idea yet who did it?"

"Not yet. But I'm working on it."

"I can't thank you enough, you know," she murmured. "I was beginning to think I was as crazy as everyone else thought I was."

"I'm sure no one thought—"

"Oh, yes, they did. And I guess I can't blame them. After all, when it comes right down to it, I didn't exactly have much of a basis for how I felt. But anyway, we're finally getting somewhere." A few moments later this was followed by the question I'd been readying myself for. "Tell me," she said timidly, "how did it happen?"

"It's a complicated story and kind of weird. Please give me a little time on this. I'll explain the whole thing to you as soon as I get everything sorted out in my mind. Maybe by then I'll have a line on the murderer, too."

"Don't be silly, Desiree," my client snapped, no longer the least bit diffident. "I've been waiting a long time for this. A *very* long time. Tell me whatever it is you do know."

"Well, uh, it would be better if we did this in person. Why don't I stop by to see you in a day or so?"

"Why don't I stop by to see *you* in an hour?"

She hung up just as I was opening my mouth to protest.

Evelyn Corwin walked into my office almost briskly— and without appearing to rely too much on her cane. She looked so chic that for a minute or two I forgot how ill she actually was.

She was wearing a striking ensemble—a simple three-quarter-length coat and matching wool skirt in a deep, deep red with a coordinating red-and-white-striped silk blouse. The clothes fit as if they were made for her (which they probably were), and the color was extremely flattering to her hair and skin tones. I was about to say as much, but something in the determined way she headed for the chair told me to save my breath. Just then she wouldn't have cared if she'd gotten a rave from Mr. Blackwell himself.

"Well?" she said, sitting down and waving off my offer to take her coat.

"You see, there was this police photo . . ." I began.

Mrs. Corwin didn't utter a single syllable until I was through. Then she looked at me and nodded slowly. "So *that's* how it was done."

No "You should be committed." No "I never heard of anything so ridiculous in my life." Not even an "Are you sure?"

What I got from my client was complete acceptance. And I was so surprised by it you could have knocked me over with a—*Oh, God! I don't believe I almost said that!*

Anyway, for a brief time she sat there silently, head bowed. Then she looked up and met my eyes. "What's next?" she asked.

"I haven't worked out a definite plan yet," I responded. "Knowing what I do now, though, it should be easier to find out who the killer is." But even as I said the words, I worried that I might just be engaging in some very wishful thinking.

I telephoned Luisa as soon as Evelyn Corwin left.

"You know the feather duster you were using the day Catherine died?"

"Of course."

"Now, this could be very important. I don't want you to use it again. Or even touch it. Just leave it wherever—"

"Oh, Mrs. Shapiro, I'm sorry," the housekeeper interrupted, "but I threw it away last week. The feathers were starting to come out, and so I picked up a new one. I hope you don't really need it for anything. . . ."

"No, no," I said, "it probably wouldn't have made any difference anyway."

Which was the only thing that kept me from bawling like a baby.

That night I contacted Paul Lundquist.

He was so friendly and pleasant that it was practically impossible to conceive of his being involved in a murder. Nevertheless, I'd called him for a reason, so I quickly got down to business. "I wonder if I could talk to you again—just for a few minutes."

"You're still investigating little Catherine's death?"

"That's right."

"*More* questions?" Then he chuckled. "I expected you to cross me off your list once you saw what a poor source of information I was the last time."

"Well, something's come up that I think you might be able to clarify for me. It won't take more than five or ten minutes," I promised, even though I suspected this was nowhere near the truth.

"All right. Be glad to, if it's important."

I said it was, and it was agreed he'd stop by my office at five o'clock the next afternoon.

To be honest, though, after getting Lundquist to meet with me, I wasn't at all sure why I wanted him to.

Chapter 30

It was five after five. Paul Lundquist had just arrived and was hanging his tan Burberry trench coat in back of the door. He lowered his slightly paunchy six feet—give or take an inch—onto the chair. "So what is it that's come up?" he asked with an ingratiating grin.

For a second or two I couldn't remember how I'd phrased my reason for asking to see him again, so I stared at him blankly. Then it came to me. "Oh, yes," I said after what seemed to me like an interminable time. "I've gotten some information—and I know this is an intrusion on your personal life, but I really do have to check everything out even though I myself don't know at this point what bearing this could possibly have on the case—"

He spared us both any more of this rambling attempt at an explanation. "Why don't you just come out and ask me what it is that's on your mind?" he suggested affably.

"All right. I've been told that you're anxious to get together again with your wife—your ex-wife, I mean."

"With *Barrie*? I assure you there's no question of that."

"Well, it's what I heard," I maintained, feeling defensive, which was pretty stupid considering I hadn't heard any such thing.

"It's just not true," Lundquist responded simply.

"I'm afraid I can't tell you who said it, but I assure you the party was very reliable," I persisted.

"I'd have to disagree. Whoever it was gave you a bum steer."

There really wasn't anything I could say to that. "Okay, you should know," I conceded. "But there was something else I wanted to talk to you about, too."

"I'm ready," he told me lightly.

"The last time we met, you seemed pretty disturbed when I asked if there was another reason—besides your involvement with someone else, I mean—that you and your wife divorced."

He frowned as if in concentration. "I don't remember being particularly disturbed by that question. If it seemed that way, maybe it was because I was beginning to resent all that digging around in my personal life." Then he added quickly, "Oh, not that I'm blaming you. I know it's your job. But it *can* get a little irritating."

"I suppose it can. But Todd was really insistent about there being something else that caused the breakup."

"My son is not exactly an unimpeachable source," Lundquist countered with a faint smile. "If I remember correctly, I warned you about placing any stock in the things he has to say."

"Yes, you did. But it's still necessary for me to double-check. And he does tell the truth sometimes. You said so yourself."

"Well, of course he does; everyone does. But believe me, this wasn't one of those times."

I was obviously not getting anywhere, which is really exactly what I'd expected. Still, I felt I had to give it one final push before managing what I hoped would be a graceful retreat. "That's too bad. I was counting on finding *something,* at least, that Todd had leveled with me about."

"Why is that important?"

"Because recently I learned something very troubling." I told him about the collage of Catherine and the big red X's. "Your son could be in a lot of trouble about that," I said.

"Why? He never made any secret about his feelings for Catherine."

"I know. But this was pretty extreme. It seems—and please forgive me—as if his hatred of that poor little kid was almost pathological."

"Just what did Todd say about those X's?" Lundquist demanded.

"Oh, he claims his actions had nothing to do with her

death and that it was healthy to get his feelings out in the open."

"He happens to be right. It *is* better to air your feelings. Listen, his marking up the pictures like that is certainly upsetting—believe me, I'm disturbed by it—but why would that put him in trouble? It's not as if anyone *killed* Catherine."

"That's where you're wrong, Mr. Lundquist," I told him evenly. "The murder weapon has just been uncovered. I'm sure the official report will come out any day now." Well, it was true. Kind of. The first part, at any rate. After all, I didn't actually say it was the police who'd uncovered the weapon.

Lundquist gasped. He stared at me in disbelief, then muttered in a voice filled with horror, "Oh, my God, my *God.*" There was a pause before he said, "But you can't really think that Todd . . . You do know he's only twelve years old, don't you?"

"Yes, I know. But children have been known to murder before."

"Just look at this thing logically. Why would Todd admit to defacing the pictures if he'd harmed Catherine herself? No one caught him at it, did they?"

"No. But your son seems to think he can get away with anything, and maybe that includes murder. I promised Donna I wouldn't mention the incident to the police if it didn't impact on Catherine's death, but now that it's been definitely established she was murdered, I'm a lot more concerned. Could be his obliterating her features was symbolic—his way of getting Catherine out of the picture a second time." I thought this observation worthy of a high-priced shrink.

Lundquist immediately put me in my place. "That's ridiculous; you're not a psychiatrist, you know," he responded angrily, the last vestige of his good nature having fled to places unknown some time earlier. "Todd may be screwed up, but he isn't homicidal. And anyway, maybe I'm thick, but I can't see what all this has to do with the breakup of my marriage."

"Nothing, really. Not directly, that is. But the point I've been trying to make is that so far Todd hasn't given me even one reason to believe him about *anything.*"

And then I played my trump card, such as it was. "Listen, Mr. Lundquist, I don't want to think that a twelve-year-old boy would be capable of a thing like this. I'd like to believe Todd when he tells me his hatred for Catherine never went any further than that obscene thing with the collage. But frankly, I just don't know. As you yourself said, I'm no psychiatrist. And when he even makes up lies about his own parents' divorce, I can't afford to ignore the possibility that he's ... I'm sorry ... that he's unstable. And for all I know, maybe even dangerously unstable."

Lundquist turned beet red, opened his mouth, then promptly snapped it shut. Finally he said, almost matter-of-factly. "Why do I have the strong feeling you're manipulating me?"

"Oh, I—"

He put up his hand to silence me. "Todd told you the truth. I didn't leave Barrie for another woman; there *was* no other woman. But I really can't say anything more. All I can tell you is that the reason Barrie and I split up couldn't possibly have had anything to do with what happened to Catherine."

I was totally floored. But I managed not to let it show. "That's probably so," I argued, "but there's also an outside chance you don't recognize the significance of whatever it was that prompted the breakup. That's why I need for you to level with me. If it turns out to have no connection with Catherine's death, I promise you, it'll be our secret."

Lundquist began shaking his head.

The man was *forcing* me to resort to blackmail (but of the most benign variety, naturally). "I don't want to go to the police, believe me. But now that we have a murder here, the authorities will expect me to tell them whatever I know about the case. *Everything* I know."

He didn't so much as bat an eyelash. He just sat there, and I had absolutely no idea what he was thinking. So in desperation I offered up this gem: "Is there really anything that could be more important than keeping your son out of trouble?"

And then, accompanied by the blackest look that had ever, I was sure, crossed Paul Lundquist's normally genial face, I got the response I'd been hoping for. "All right," he muttered—and I swear his lip curled—"you win."

"I loved Barrie very much when we broke up," Lundquist said, making a point of looking everywhere but at me. "She was a good wife and she's a good person. She couldn't control what happened any more than I could. It took me awhile to accept that, but now I know it's true."

"Barrie, met another man?"

"No. Saundra King."

"I don't understand."

"She fell in love."

"She fell in love with Saundra King," he all but snarled (and I really couldn't blame him). But then, nice guy that he was, he followed up with a mumbled "I'm sorry."

I felt really stupid. The plain truth, though, is that a contingency of that sort had never even occurred to me. But, hey, I was still a woman of the nineties, wasn't I? "I can see why you might not have wanted to broadcast a thing like that, but on the other hand, I don't understand why it has to be such a deep, dark secret," I told him, sounding, I thought, very sophisticated and "with it." But then I had to go and continue. "After all, relationships between, um . . . what I mean is, relationships of that . . . nature aren't even so unusual anymore." Well, so much for the sophisticated "with it" image I'd so recently conjured up for myself. And it wasn't even that I had a problem accepting the women's homosexuality; it was only the discussing of it that made me uncomfortable. Just like I'm uncomfortable talking about anyone else's sex life—including my own. (Okay, okay. So I'm repressed or something.)

Lundquist seemed to thaw a little. "I agree with you," he said, a fleeting grin, no doubt prompted by my obvious embarrassment, momentarily relaxing his features.

"Then why—"

"Just try convincing your client of that, though. If she ever found out the truth about the breakup, she'd disinherit Barrie in a minute. That's why you can't let this go any further."

"It won't, I swear. Like I said, not unless it turns out to have a direct bearing on the murder." From what I knew of Evelyn Corwin, Lundquist had cause for concern. Mrs. Corwin had practically bragged to me about disinheriting her son for a while after he married his second wife—Catherine's mother—because she considered her an unsuitable choice. And hadn't she made some reference to being old-fashioned and not rewarding things that weren't right? As I recalled, those were almost her exact words.

"She's the reason Barrie and Saundra haven't set up house together, I'm sure," Lundquist asserted. "But anyway, Barrie was worried sick her grandmother would find out about the thing with Saundra and cut her out of the will. And she wants that money for Todd—to make a nice home for him. I'd like him to have that, too. Even if it *is* with King—although God knows, I'd prefer that it wasn't." He sighed before going on. "I wish I was in a position to do more for him financially myself but, well, I'm just not." He sighed again, more deeply this time. "It's also extremely important to Barrie—to both of us—that Todd gets the help he needs, which is another thing that takes money. Plenty of it. He *is* seeing a therapist, but not as frequently as he should, probably. Besides, I don't even know how much good this guy is doing him. But he's all I can afford right now. At any rate, that's why they—she and Saundra, although I don't doubt it was mostly Saundra—dreamed up that business about the other woman."

"And they made you go along with it."

"Not *made* me; pleaded with me. Barrie did, anyway. And I felt I should, for Todd's sake."

"It must have been a pretty tough situation to accept—your wife and Mrs. King," I said at that point.

"It was—very. You should've seen me when Barrie first told me what was going on. I went nuts. I think I called her every name in the book. I was bitter for a long time, too. And not just because of what it was doing to my life, but for what I was afraid it would do to Todd's." He looked directly at me for the first time then. "And the thing is, it came out of the blue. I had no idea she was a . . . a—Christ, it's even hard for me to say—a lesbian. You know when I got my first clue?"

I shook my head.

"When she said she was. Can you believe it? That must make me about the biggest schmuck in the world, I guess." He punctuated this indictment with a short, self-deprecating laugh.

I hurt for the man. "They say that very often something like that isn't at all obvious," I responded, not having any idea whether this was true or not but hoping it might help a little.

"Well, all I can say is that it sure as hell wasn't obvious to me."

"What about Todd? When do you think he became aware of the situation?"

"I had no idea he even suspected anything. Barrie and I have both been extremely careful, but Todd's very astute—almost intuitive."

Oh, is that what they call it?

Lundquist leaned forward, looking very earnest. And very sad. All the hostility he felt toward me seemed to have dissipated with the unburdening. "You know, Mrs. Shapiro," he confided, "it took me until fairly recently to come to grips with the fact that Barrie was in love with Saundra King and to fully appreciate that she's no more in control of her sexual orientation than I am of mine. The thing I still can't figure out, though, is how she could have picked someone as overbearing as *Miz* King.

"That woman's some piece of work," he went on, a small crooked smile (or was it a grimace?) turning up a corner of his mouth. "Every other day she adds some embellishment to the basic cover story I agreed to with Barrie. I hear that now she claims Barrie started wearing those wild outfits and all that junk on her face as a result of my being an inattentive husband or some such bullshit. The truth is, my ex was walking around decked out like a Day-Glo color chart before I even met her. But leave it to King to play loose with the facts."

And then Paul Lundquist said something that brought me to the brink of tears.

"I want you to understand something, though. It isn't that I have anything against Saundra; she's okay, I suppose. It's just that my Barrie was—is—a really special lady. She could have done better."

Chapter 31

I can't say I have all that much confidence in my own assessment of people; by and large, I'm a lousy judge of character. But every so often I do hit it right, at which time I become inordinately proud of myself.

Like today.

I mean, I had a favorable impression of Paul Lundquist right from the start. Which is kind of strange when you think about it, given that I'd been led to believe he ditched his wife for another, younger woman—in my book a crime right up there next to murder. So I had to have some kind of intuition going for me to respond so positively toward him, didn't I? In fact, I think the real reason I met with him again was not to verify Ellen's theory so much as to prove it wrong. Which I had. No matter how much he still dug her, Lundquist couldn't possibly be entertaining any hope that he and Barrie would get back together again. Not under the circumstances.

At any rate, I was kind of knocked out by what I'd just learned from the man. So instead of stopping off for a bite after my meeting with him, which is what I'd intended to do, I went straight home.

By the time I arrived at the apartment, I was really hungry. But I had no idea what I could possibly fix for supper, the larder being unusually barren just then. I opened the refrigerator for inspiration, and fortunately, I found it on every shelf.

I'd make myself a "refrigerator omelet;" that's what I'd do. (This concoction having been so named by Ellen because I throw in just about everything I happen to have in the refrigerator at the moment.) Tonight's version featured a bit of Swiss cheese that was probably only hours away from turning moldy, a little parmesan, some small pieces of red pepper, onions, the last vestiges of an Italian salami, and a few peas and green beans.

I ate in the living room watching TV, mostly because I wasn't quite ready to deal with the implications of my conversation with Lundquist.

Once I'd done justice to the omelet—which, believe me, tasted a lot better than it sounds—I put up some coffee. And because who can drink that horrendous stuff I make without something to take your mind off it, I got out the Häagen-Dazs. It was only after I'd polished off my second plateful of Macadamia Brittle and washed up the dishes that I gave myself permission to do some serious thinking about the relationship between Barrie Lundquist and Saundra King—and how that relationship might be connected to little Catherine's death.

I was resigned to this being a time-consuming project. So first I made myself comfortable, kicking off my shoes and getting out of my dress and into a robe. Then I took out a yellow pad and a couple of ballpoints and sat down at the kitchen table, poised to take volumes of notes.

I gave Barrie and Saundra over three hours' and four pages' worth of intense scrutiny. And almost simultaneously, some important points about my other suspects finally occurred to me—and don't ask what took me so long, either. Finally, though, everything clicked into place.

Barrie Lundquist had killed her sister.

How did I know?

Simply because she was the only one who could have done it.

Let's talk about the others first.

The second I settled on the murder weapon—and therefore, was able to definitely rule out in my own mind anything like an untraceable poison (which might have been administered at any time before the little girl died)—I should have scratched Todd as a suspect. He just didn't have the opportunity to commit the crime. He'd been with Saundra King all morning, except for about five minutes when she left the room to go to the bathroom, and that was hours before Luisa went out for the carton of milk—and Catherine was alone downstairs in the library. I realized I was assuming that King hadn't lied for the kid. But I couldn't see her doing that. Particularly since it was really to her advantage that he get nailed for the murder; otherwise, it looked like she'd eventually have to live with the little bastard.

And Donna flunked the opportunity test, too. Oh, she could easily have sneaked back home from her shopping expedition, killed her stepdaughter, and then returned to Saks so Nicholas could pick her up at the store. But there was something Donna hadn't considered when, if you recall, she'd so kindly—and unnecessarily—brought all this to my attention (and for that matter, neither had I until a few minutes earlier): She had no way of anticipating that Luisa would be going to the market for milk that day. Even if, let's say, Donna herself had disposed of the remainder of the milk, thereby creating the necessity for the housekeeper to leave the house to replace it, how could she have determined just when Luisa would get around to it?

Besides, now that I'd zeroed in on the murder weapon, there was still another reason I could be certain Donna hadn't made those plans to kill her stepdaughter. Nobody—not Donna and not anyone else, for that matter—could possibly have foreseen that the feather duster would be left where it was and that it could be utilized to do the job.

No. It was obvious that Catherine had died on that day and in that place because circumstances had made it possible.

And no one but Barrie would have been able to take advantage of those circumstances.

Who was to say what time she actually quit work on the afternoon of the murder? It could certainly have been much earlier than the one-thirty she claimed. And then once she got home and found Catherine alone . . .

Of course, I could only guess at what drove her to commit such a heinous crime. But you didn't exactly have to be an Einstein to come up with a motive that was both strong and totally plausible.

It was absolutely vital to Barrie that the true nature of her friendship with King remain a secret. Right? Well, suppose Catherine—who was so often confined to the house—had seen or heard something that could expose that friendship for what it really was. And then suppose Barrie was aware of this. Could the woman take the chance of Catherine's mentioning—perhaps even inadvertently—whatever she'd learned to her grandmother? Not unless she didn't mind losing a few million dollars, she couldn't.

Now, you know how difficult it had been all along for me to so much as consider the possibility that Barrie might have murdered her young sibling. Particularly since she did seem to have genuinely loved her. But in light of what Paul Lundquist revealed about his ex's determination to get the money for Todd's sake, I could see where Barrie's feelings for her son had taken precedence over everything else, provoking her into sacrificing (that was the only way to put it) her little sister.

Lundquist couldn't have been more right, I decided, when he told me his Barrie was a special lady. She certainly was!

Okay. So at long last I'd arrived at a solution where everything added up. But how on earth was I going to get anybody to believe me? I mean, I finally had my killer, but when it came to evidence, I had exactly zip.

I don't remember how much longer I sat at the kitchen table, drinking one cup of vile coffee after another—and taking it without a chaser now, too—as I tried to decide how to proceed. But at some time in the early hours of the morning, it got to the point where I could barely remember my own name, so I called it quits and dragged myself off to bed. I fell asleep immediately.

On Friday I woke up exhausted and with the certain knowledge that if I had even one more sip of that coffee of mine, I'd choke on the stuff. So I put on the teakettle, then popped a couple of slices of rye bread in the toaster and sat down to mull things over some more.

It was between the third and fourth bites of my second piece of toast that I settled on a plan of action. To be honest, it was really formulated out of desperation; I just didn't know what else to do. And even as I firmed the thing up in my mind, I recognized it for being the flimsy little scheme it was.

*   *   *

As soon as I got to work, I steeled myself to calling Barrie. I knew I had to seem at least marginally friendly so as not to put her on her guard. But I was terrified I wouldn't be able to pull it off, considering the bitter taste I had in my mouth just thinking about the woman.

I gave myself a pep talk before dialing—one of those brief "You *can* do this" psych jobs. But by the time she picked up the phone, I was shaking in my rust leather boots. "I have a couple of things I want to go over with you," I said, wondering how I was coming across, and then realizing my voice was quivering too much to sound hostile. "I'd really appreciate it if we could get together for a few minutes later."

"Well, I can't take any time off today," she replied, not seeming to notice anything out of the ordinary in my tone. "We're in the middle of a presentation here," she explained, quickly adding "for a change" with a fair facsimile of an Ellen giggle. "In fact," she went on, "you have great timing. I've been in a meeting since eight o'clock. I just came back to my office this second to pick up a folder, and I have to run right out to the conference room again."

"Oh, I didn't mean this afternoon; I know how busy your job is," I told her. "I was thinking of later on—tonight. Any time you say."

"Gee, I'm sorry, Mrs. Shapiro, but I won't be in town tonight. Todd and I are spending the weekend in Vermont with this friend of mine. I think you spoke to her a couple of weeks ago: Saundra King?" She didn't wait for confirmation. "Can we do it Monday evening? Say around nine?"

Damn! I was practically ready to chew nails. "Sure, that'll be fine," I answered pleasantly, phony that I am. "And enjoy your weekend."

As I believe I told you, I've never been what you could call patient, not even by the most liberal definition of the world. But I was practically off the wall after my conversation with Barrie. As far as I was concerned, Monday's appointment might as well have been slated for the year 2000. I tried my best to put it out of my mind, but no matter what I did to occupy myself, the thought of finally being able to confront Catherine Corwin's murderer barreled its way back into my head.

At around four o'clock Ellen called to find out if I had an update for her. I filled her in on my meeting with Paul Lundquist.

She gasped more than once during the short narration. And then when I was finished, she asked if I believed him.

"Absolutely," I told her.

"So I guess that means he didn't figure on getting back with his ex."

"Right."

"So he wouldn't have had any reason to murder Catherine?"

"None."

"Oh." She sounded so disappointed that I felt I had to console her.

"Don't feel bad. I can't even count the number of dumb ideas about this case that I've come up with. Not that *your* idea was dumb, Ellen, but—"

"That's okay, Aunt Dez, I didn't take offense. Wanna try again?" She giggled before saying resignedly an instant later, "Okay. Where do we go from here?"

I smiled at the "we." Then I announced—giving the words the dramatic reading I felt they called for—"We go straight to Barrie Lundquist. *She's* the killer."

"You're kidding! Oh, my God! How do you know?"

I explained the thought processes that had brought me to this conclusion. And afterward Ellen questioned me timidly. "Uh, I suppose you're positive it was Barrie?"

"It all fits; don't you see? Why? What do *you* think?"

"I think you're probably right; you always are. And it does make sense. . . ." Her voice faded away.

"Then what's bothering you?"

"It's only that I feel just awful for Mrs. Corwin—one granddaughter murdering the other one. Have you told her yet?"

"No. I won't do that until I see what happens with Barrie on Monday."

And then I realized that since last night I'd been focusing all my energy on ways to trap the killer. But pretty soon I'd have to wrestle with the *really* tough job that lay ahead of me: figuring out how to break the terrible news to my client.

I was at the front door of my apartment at a few minutes past seven, after making an absolutely crucial stop at D'Agostino's on my way home from work. The telephone started to ring just as I was turning the key in the lock. I plunked my bundles on the floor and raced inside, managing to grab the receiver right before the answering machine kicked in.

"What kept you?" my neighbor Barbara Gleason asked curtly. "I was about to hang up."

"Hold on a sec, okay? I have some groceries out in the hall."

I went back to her question as soon as I'd retrieved the bags. "I only got home just now," I explained. "Anyway, you could have left a message on the machine."

"I hate those things, you know that." Actually, I didn't know that. It's hard to keep up with Barbara's likes and dislikes. The only thing I was sure of was that she had a definite opinion on everything. "I was wondering if you felt like grabbing a bite and going to a movie tonight," she said.

I thought it over quickly. It might be a good thing to get out of the apartment; I'd only make myself crazy if I didn't. And besides, I'd turned Barbara down the last couple of times she called about getting together, and I didn't want to give the impression I was avoiding her. "Sounds good to me," I told her.

"This *is* a nice surprise," she observed, a trace of acidity in her voice. "I thought maybe you'd made plans with your niece again."

"Oh, no. I—"

"Forget it. I suppose I sounded truculent, didn't I?" She went on without waiting for an answer (which was fortunate since I wasn't exactly sure what *truculent* meant, and when I looked it up in the dictionary later, it didn't mean what I thought it did). "What do you think you'd like to see?" she asked.

"Well ..." I was hesitant about making any suggestions. Barbara and I definitely do not have the same taste in movies.

"Well, what?" she responded impatiently.

Okay. She asked for it. "I understand that *Four Weddings and a Funeral* is just terrific."

"That figures."

"Why? What did you have in mind?"

"There's this wonderful foreign—" She stopped herself. "No. Let's make it *Four Weddings and a Funeral*," she told me magnanimously.

I insisted she choose the restaurant. A sensible decision, since I have no doubt it's what she planned on doing anyway.

We had dinner at a place in the sixties, not far from the theater. Barbara didn't even bother picking up the menu in front of her, immediately making up her mind to the cobb salad. "It's very good here," she said pointedly, in a not too subtle attempt to get me to follow her lead.

I nodded and continued to seriously study the options on my menu. A couple of minutes later, the waitress put in an appearance at our table. "I'll have the fried shrimp with French fried potatoes," I told her, laying down the menu.

Barbara almost had apoplexy. She didn't even wait until the woman was out of earshot before starting in on me. "Desiree, Desiree," she moaned, shaking her head and making this infuriating clucking sound. "I don't know *where* you get your eating habits. Do you have any idea what fried food does to your arteries?" I didn't answer; I prefer not to think about things like that. "Well, do you?" she persisted. (Barbara teaches third grade, and I really think she sometimes has a tendency to forget just which of us are her students.)

Naturally, I'd been well aware I would be treated to a lecture the minute she heard the word *fried* or any variation thereof. And I'd planned to ignore it as I usually do, by reminding myself of my friend's many admirable qualities, including her being a remarkably quiet next-door neighbor (no small attribute when you consider that I live in a building that has tissue paper for walls). But anyway, I really don't know what got into me that night—or maybe I do. At any rate, I just kind of boiled over. "Look, Barbara," I practically hissed, "I'm sure you mean well, but I *hate* cobb salad. In fact, the only thing I hate more than cobb salad is being told I should *eat* cobb salad. Or anything else, for that matter. I ordered the fried shrimp because I feel like *having* the fried shrimp. Maybe tomorrow night I'll have a sensible dinner, but if I do, it will be my choice."

Barbara looked stunned. "All right," she muttered, coloring. "I'm sorry if I upset you, but I did mean it for your own good."

"I know you did. And I'm sorry if I upset *you*. It's just that I'm—"

"From here on in, I won't say a thing, no matter what kind of garbage you put into your stomach," she informed me. "I promise I'll just sit there and mind my own business, even . . . even if your menu's prepared by Dr. Kevorkian!"

"Listen, Barbara, I—"

"That's what I get for worrying about you, I suppose," she said with a little catch in her voice.

Wouldn't you know I'd wind up feeling guilty?

I enjoyed the movie a lot. As I'd suspected, however, it was far too pedestrian for Barbara. Plus, the little set-to we'd had at dinner had left her in a less than agreeable mood. I didn't have to prod to get her opinion of the picture.

"That was a dumb plot, and I can't stand Hugh Grant," she announced as we were walking out of the theater.

"Really? I think he's very attractive—for a good-looking guy, that is." Now, considering my taste for undersized, pathetic-looking men, that comment not only made sense, but it was also—or so I thought—sort of humorous in a way. And I laughed a little when I made it. Barbara's lips didn't even twitch.

"Do you want to know who's attractive?" she demanded. She mentioned some French actor I'd never heard of with a name I couldn't pronounce.

But I wanted to apply a little balm to her bruised

feelings. So I told her, "I'd be the last one to argue with that." Then just for good measure, I threw in, "I can't wait for his next picture."

"It should be out in a couple of weeks," Barbara let me know. "We'll go see it then." And she smiled at me. We were friends again.

Chapter 32

Dinner and a movie with Barbara Gleason turned out to be my favorite part of the weekend.

I spent Saturday afternoon on all the messy jobs that Charmaine—my every-other-week cleaning lady who hadn't shown up in so many weeks I'm not sure I'd recognize her anymore—would have done if she'd bothered to put in an appearance. In the evening I sewed on a couple of missing buttons, polished my nails and ironed a permanent press blouse that was anything but permanently pressed—all of these chores disposed of not more than a few yards from a blaring television set.

Now, although I admit I've never been ecstatic about scrubbing the toilet bowl, I'm glad I occasionally get a chance to take care of all the other stuff—the personal stuff, I mean. There are even times when I actually look forward to devoting a few quality hours to myself. But with the upcoming meeting with Barrie being such a gigantic and nerve-wracking presence in my mind, it would have been a godsend just then if I'd had something a little more stimulating to focus on than buttons. And the thing was, if I somehow managed to avoid driving myself crazy on Saturday, there'd still be the rest of the weekend to get through.

Around noon on Sunday I heard from Stuart. "Hi, Dez," he said, "I've been meaning to call you. Just wanted to see how you are." I told him I was fine. And then he told me *he* was fine. Also everything with Gretchen was fine. Also his nephew (the one who loves the Rangers) was fine. There was an awkward silence once we were finished with all of that, and finally Stuart said, "Well, take care. I'll be in touch. Maybe we can have lunch one day soon." And I said swell. And that it was nice hearing from him.

But of course, it wasn't nice at all. I don't have so many good friends that I can lose them with equanimity. And it was apparent from our stilted conversation that Stuart and I were no longer *comfortable* with each other. Worse yet, I was very much afraid that we never would be again.

I felt incredibly sad after that phone call.

I stopped at a newsstand on my way to work Monday morning and bought a small supply of magazines: *People, New York, Vogue, Redbook*. And for most of the day I kept nervously thumbing through them—whenever I wasn't occupied in checking the clock, that is. At around four, though, I realized I'd had it; I was too tense to sit still any longer. So I grabbed my coat and my attaché case and—after informing Jackie of my intentions, naturally—just took off.

As soon as I got downstairs, I was assaulted by a blast of frigid air. I drew my beige wool coat closer to my body and turned up the collar, burying my face in the cloth. The temperature couldn't have been over thirty degrees that day, and the biting wind made it seem a lot colder. My appointment with Barrie wasn't until nine, which meant I had five hours to kill. And I had to come up with a merciful way to kill them. But it was too bone-chilling to just stand there trying to provide myself with an itinerary. So I started to walk, hoping something would occur to me before long.

I didn't have to cover much ground—which was fortunate. And not only because my teeth were chattering at the rate of about a thousand clacks per minute, but also because, as I may have mentioned before, I'm not exactly into exercise (I loathe it). Yes, I know how good for you it's supposed to be. But they say the same thing about cauliflower, and I wouldn't be caught dead eating it. Anyway, when I came to the Murray Hill, a movie theater blessedly close to my office, I decided that was as good a place as any to wile away a couple of hours.

The theater was showing four movies, so I checked the schedule posted on the cashier's window and bought a ticket to the one that had gone on most recently. It turned out to be a comedy, and I'd missed only eight minutes of it. The name of the thing escapes me and the plot was equally forgettable, but it did make me laugh two or three times.

When the picture ended, I realized that in spite of the knot in my stomach, I was hungry—not surprising, since I'd had a very early and pathetically skimpy lunch at my desk. I remembered this little Italian restaurant in the neighborhood that I'd been to a month or two before. It was nice and quiet, and the food was pretty good.

I opened the meal with a glass of Chianti (I had to try to loosen the knot, didn't I?), following which I began filling the empty space inside me with house salad, a formidable portion of spaghetti puttanesca and three pieces of garlic bread. Then I had a couple of cups of coffee that tasted the way coffee was meant to taste. Still, you could tell my appetite wasn't what it should have been; I passed on dessert.

When I left the restaurant, it wasn't quite eight o'clock, still too early to head uptown. So I stopped off at a luncheonette and had another cup of coffee, one I didn't really want, before grabbing a cab to Park Avenue and Sixty-eighth Street.

Barrie Lundquist was at the kitchen table, drinking out of a large mug when I arrived. She had on stretch, ankle-length, leopard print pants that clung to her like Saran Wrap, a tight, ribbed turtleneck sweater in a kind of chartreuse-y color, and the sky-high beige platform sandals she was wearing the last time I saw her. Poking out of the shoes were toenails painted in that garish shade of fuschia I also recalled from my previous visit (at least it looked the same to me). And once again she was decorated with enough jewelry to open a decent-size boutique. But she seemed to have acquired a lighter hand with her makeup. Or maybe it just hadn't been applied in the last few hours. At any rate, she looked almost like ordinary people that night. Very flashy ordinary people, that is.

"You must be freezing; it's so bitter cold out now," she commented when I sat down. Turning around, she

indicated the white Krupps coffeemaker on the counter.
"I made a fresh pot about five minutes ago. I hope regu-
lar's okay with you; I don't think we even have any
decaffeinated in the house." And before I had a chance
to say forget the coffee—and try to keep from snarling
when I said it—she jumped up to pour a cup for me.

Well, of course, I couldn't just sit and stare at it, so I
took a few sips.

"Is that better?" she wanted to know.

"Oh, yes. Thank you." Actually, it did serve the purpose of giving me a little time to collect myself and keep
my hostility in check.

She smiled, looking pleased. "There's nothing like
having something hot to drink to get your circulation
going again, is there?"

It was almost impossible at that moment to imagine
this genial, smiling young woman doing what she'd
done—and to her own flesh and blood, too.

"Have you learned anything new about Catherine's
death?" she asked, suddenly turning somber.

"As a matter of fact, I have," I informed her evenly.
"I've learned that she was murdered."

Barrie's mouth opened as if she was about to speak.
But no words came. Finally, she managed a hushed
"Catherine?"

"Catherine," I echoed.

"You must . . . you have to be . . . is there a possibility
you're mistaken?" she said, the dark eyes misting.

She is good. I'll give her that. "No," I stated flatly.
"I'm not mistaken."

"But . . . but how? I don't understand."

And so it was time to recite the latest and most complete version of my feather duster scenario. And frankly,
I thought that in my presentation of it, I'd struck the
perfect balance between reality and theater.

But apparently, I wasn't quite the actress that Barrie
had just shown herself to be, because afterward she
looked at me skeptically. I cut off the protest I knew to
be a split second away. "Look, I won't go into how I
found out about this. Not this minute. But the evidence
is overwhelming." (Maybe just a slight exaggeration.)
"And Dr. Pascal, Catherine's pulmonary specialist,

agrees that it's very likely it happened that way." (Another slight exaggeration.)

"Who was it that ... that did it? Do you have any idea?" she asked fearfully.

"That's something I'd like *you* to tell *me*."

"Me?" she said numbly. "But how could I pos—" She broke off then, a horrified expression on her face. "Oh no! You couldn't possibly think *I* killed Catherine. I *loved* her. She was my baby sister!"

"I think you did love her. But you love your son more."

"What does Todd have to do with it?"

"You want your share of your grandmother's money for his sake, don't you?"

"Yes, but—" She stopped abruptly, and there was a sudden understanding in the eyes that looked at me now. "I get it," she retorted contemptuously. "You think I murdered Catherine for a bigger piece of the inheritance."

You had to admire the performance. I mean, this woman could give Meryl Streep acting lessons.

"No," I told her, "I don't think that at all. You *are* the only one with both motive and opportunity, though."

"Maybe nobody's informed you of this, but my grandmother's will is more than generous to Todd and me. We certainly didn't need Catherine's share."

"When I said motive, that isn't what I was referring to. But a case *could* be made that you killed Catherine because of the, umm, special nature of your relationship with Mrs. King."

"I don't know what you mean by 'special nature,' " Barrie said in a shaky voice.

She was forcing me to come right out with it. "I mean that the two of you were lovers."

There was a long pause before the low, tense whisper: "How do you know about *that*?"

"That's not important, is it?"

"I guess not," she conceded. "But just how does my sexual orientation come into this?"

"You're aware that your grandmother would write you out of the will if she ever found out about you and Mrs. King. Isn't that true?"

"Yes, but—"

"The authorities could conclude that you were afraid Catherine might spill the beans about the two of you. And that in order to prevent her doing that . . ." I spread my arms to signify that no more needed to be said.

"But I doubt if she even knew what a lesbian *is*," Barrie protested. "Catherine led a very insulated life."

"Catherine watched television all the time, didn't she? Besides, she didn't have to know exactly what was going on to say something to your grandmother—like maybe that she saw you and Ms. King kissing."

There was no doubt about it: The color on Barrie Lundquist's cheeks—which even though toned down was still about twice what most women would rub into their faces—suddenly became more intense.

So that was it!

"This is ridiculous! Even if Catherine did see something, and even if I was *positive* she'd tell my grandmother about it, I would never have harmed her," Barrie declared passionately. "Not for anything in the world."

Now, I told you I'd worked out a little plan. And while I didn't have all that much confidence in it at first, I was starting to think it might just do the trick.

"Look, Mrs. Lundquist," I began in a voice practically overflowing with compassion, "I don't believe you killed your sister on purpose. I think you were kidding around with her that day and that you went a little too far. It was an accident—a tragic accident. Only you were so distraught by what you'd . . . by what had happened, you couldn't bring yourself to tell anyone about it."

Of course, that wasn't anything remotely like what I really wanted to say to her. I wanted to shout that she was rotten, miserable scum who'd done away with her poor little sister for a few lousy bucks—okay, a few million lousy bucks—and for that weird son of hers who was also rotten, miserable scum, no doubt thanks to his mother's crappy genes. But I was pragmatic enough to recognize that I had no actual proof a crime had even been committed. To say nothing of any evidence to bear out my contention that this woman was the perp. So getting her to confess to something less than intentional murder was really the best I could hope for.

There was, however, no confession. The response I got was "It didn't happen like that. For the simple reason that I had nothing to do with Catherine's death."

"I think you should be aware," I proclaimed, "that I've come across a witness who saw you entering the house just after the housekeeper left for the market." I didn't even have the decency to flush.

"You're lying!" Barrie accused hotly.

"I don't lie!" I retorted almost as hotly. After all, this bitch was maligning my character.

"Well, then, whoever claims to have seen me lied. Or was mistaken."

"Think about this carefully, Ms. Lundquist," I urged. "If I go to the police with what I have, there's a chance that you could end up being locked away for a long, long time. Maybe for twenty or thirty years. And naturally, I'm also going to have to report the results of my investigation to my client. So even if, for some reason, the police don't act on my information, you can bet a few million bucks your grandmother will. Which means you'd be depriving Todd of the financial help you wanted for him."

Barrie seemed about to say something at this juncture, something I didn't want to hear. I saw to it she didn't get the chance.

"On the other hand, though, if you admit that Catherine's death was an accident, you won't get more than a couple of years, I'm sure." She gave me a really withering look, so I immediately amended this with "It's even possible you won't get any jail time at all." *God forbid!* "Plus, it wouldn't be necessary for me to mention your relationship with Saundra King to my client."

Listening to myself, I decided my argument had some real teeth to it, particularly with this final assurance: "And if you convinced your grandmother—and I'd help you do it—that you were desperately sorry about what happened and that you regretted not going to the police about it in the very beginning, well, I doubt that you'd have to worry about losing out on the money."

Now, don't get me wrong. I wasn't at all happy about this bargain I was attempting to strike. In fact, if I could have had my way, Barrie Lundquist would get the chair and be fried to a crisp! (I know that sounds ghoulish and it's far from PC, but it's exactly how I felt.) As things stood, though, this looked to be my only hope of seeing to it that she got at least a taste of the retribution she'd earned for herself in spades.

Of course, if we reached any sort of agreement, it also meant that I couldn't be a hundred percent honest with the person who'd hired me. And in a perfect world I'm sure that would have bothered me a lot. But then again, in a perfect world there aren't any people who go around murdering other people, especially innocent little kids. And besides, this version of the events would certainly be a lot easier for an elderly and ailing Mrs. Corwin to live with than the truth.

So I was willing to forgo the ideal for the possible—and without beating up on myself too much for doing it, too.

Barrie's reaction to my proposal wasn't exactly unexpected. "Are you finally finished?" she demanded shrilly.

"Oh, I almost forgot. Naturally, you'll have to deny making that earlier attempt on Catherine's life; otherwise, no one'll buy that this was an accident."

"Yes, I see what you mean. But *you* think the two things are tied together, don't you?"

I wasn't about to admit it. "Well, uh, I thought they could be. But, uh, of course I wasn't absolutely sure, so I just considered it a possibility."

She treated the waffling reply as if I hadn't spoken at all, challenging me with "And if that's the case, you can't actually believe I killed her by accident, can you?"

"That isn't—"

"There's something I should probably mention, Ms. Shapiro," she said. And there was this smug little smile on her face as she got to her feet. "I was in Milwaukee the day of the car incident. On business. And you can check that out with my boss, the client, and the three other people who made the trip with me."

Then walking purposefully to the kitchen counter, she tore a sheet from the small pad hanging directly underneath the wall telephone.

"Here," she said. "Let me give you their phone numbers."

Chapter 33

Of course, one of my first orders of business when I took on the case should have been to check out everyone's whereabouts during that automobile incident. I mean, it didn't make sense not to. So okay. Call me an idiot. And tell me how careless I was and what a piss-poor investigation I'd conducted. You wouldn't be saying anything I didn't very quickly point out to myself. And in much stronger language. Believe me, if it had been anatomically possible, I'd have kicked my multi-dimpled rump from here to L.A.

And all I can say in my own defense—and I feel compelled to offer one, however meager it may be—is that some of the mistakes I'd committed on my first two murder cases were a lot worse. (Depending on how you look at it, though, this could be more of an indictment of my investigating skills than any mitigation for my latest completely inexcusable failing.)

I must have apologized to Barrie Lundquist about a hundred and fifty times that night before slinking almost tearfully out of her house, the picture of total humiliation.

I continued to berate myself right up until I was standing in the lobby of my building. Then, while I was fishing for the damn key—which as usual, had worked its way down to the very bottom of my enormous and crammed-to-bulging hangbag—it dawned on me that I'd been a little too quick to exonerate the woman.

Suppose, I inquired of myself, *Barrie Lundquist had had an accomplice?*

Well, from there it was only a short hop to the most likely possibility: her lover, Saundra King. The more I thought about it, the more plausible it became that the two had conspired to murder Catherine. And by the time I finally laid hands on the errant key, I was thinking things like *Yes, that's it! Definitely. I should have seen it right away!*

Of course, I'd first have to look into King's whereabouts during the aborted hit-and-run. But I was pretty confident she wouldn't be able to account for her time. Not to my satisfaction, anyway. And then after that I'd have another talk with Barrie Lundquist. What I'd say to her under these new circumstances, I had no idea. But I'd think of *something*. For now it was a relief just to realize I hadn't been such a complete ass after all in accusing her of the crime.

Still, I couldn't help feeling foolish about my glaring oversight. And I had a really urgent need to talk about it. So since it was only 10:52 when I walked into my apartment and Ellen is almost always up until eleven, I gave her a call. She was more than willing to take my confession.

"You have no idea how stupid I've been," I told her after establishing that I hadn't wrested her away from a sound sleep.

"Why, what happened?"

I briefed her on my disastrous meeting with Barrie Lundquist, coming down pretty heavily on myself in the telling. "It was just so incompetent of me not to check out where everyone was that other time. I can't even *believe* that I didn't."

"Don't do that to yourself, Aunt Dez," Ellen pleaded. "I didn't think of it, either." Which didn't console me at all.

"Uh," she suggested then, "I don't suppose Barrie could have been lying?"

"Not with the fistful of phone numbers she shoved in my face. Oh, I'll give a couple of them a call tomorrow, but I can tell you right now that they'll corroborate her story."

"I guess you're right."

"But anyway, what I started to say was that as soon as I got home, the truth hit me."

"Which is . . . ?"

"That the two of them—Barrie and Mrs. King—were in this together."

"That *would* make sense—Mrs King's being involved," Ellen agreed. "Especially since they'll probably be living with each other one of these days, so if Barrie inherits a bundle, her friend also benefits."

"That's where I come out, too," I responded, gratified. I realized then that I was feeling much more tolerant of my considerable failings; getting all of this off my chest had been very helpful. "Well, I'd better hang up now and let you go to sleep," I said. "Thanks for listening."

"Oh, you know how interested I am in your cases. I'd be really upset if you *didn't* talk to me about them." A pause. "Uh, Aunt Dez?"

"What?"

"I was going to tell you about this in the morning. Honest."

"Tell me about what?"

"Mike. He called just a few minutes before you did."

"And?" I prodded excitedly.

"He said he just wanted to make sure everything was okay, and we talked for a while. And then he asked to see me Wednesday night—he's off Wednesday. I don't think he really intended to do that when he called—ask me out, that is. But once we started talking, well, I guess it was kind of a spur of the moment thing."

"However it was, I'm glad he—"

"I said I was busy."

"You *what*?"

"See? I knew you'd react like that. I just thought I'd let him cool his heels for a while. I think it'll do him good."

I really had to hand it to that niece of mine. In her place, I'd have considered doing the same thing—but chances are, I'd have chickened out and made the lousy date. "I think it'll do him good, too," I let her know. "And I'm proud of you."

"Really?"

"You'd better believe it. And I'll bet he calls again next week."

"Oh, no," Ellen protested, "you're wrong, Aunt Dez."

"You want to—"

"I'm sure I'll hear from him before then."

* * *

It was almost midnight when the phone rang. "Oh, Desiree," Pat Martucci said, "you weren't in bed yet, were you?" Apparently, this wasn't really a major concern, because she went right on to say she'd been meaning to get in touch with me, and after that she politely inquired as to how I'd been, following which she asked if there was anything new in my life. I gave her the short, stock answers I knew she was hoping for, while noting that she sounded incredibly cheerful for a woman who not that long ago had lost the one true love of her life.

Anyway, it didn't take too long before she got around to clueing me in on the reason for her call. "I was wondering if you had any plans for Wednesday night."

Now, dinner and a movie with Pat is normally much easier to take than when you're pursuing the same itinerary with Barbara Gleason. It's really very pleasant, actually. What's more, I hadn't seen my old friend in quite a while, and it would have been nice to get together again. But I was feeling too pressured about the case to even consider it right now. "Well, I don't have any actual plans, but—"

There was no way she was going to make it easy for me to decline. "Oh, I'm *so* glad. I just met the most wonderful man. An archaeologist. He keeps saying he digs me. Isn't that cute?" she gushed.

Yeah. Adorable, I refrained from responding—and in *that tone,* too. "I'm really sorry, Pat, but—"

"I've known a lot of men," Pat Martucci formerly Altmann formerly Green formerly Anderson gushed on, "but I've never felt this way about anyone before. You'll just love him," she added. Which is when the warning light finally went on.

"What's this about?" I asked suspiciously.

"Well, Burton has this cousin—Mel or Moe, something with an M, anyway. And he's terrific. He lives in Chicago, I think it is, and his company is transferring him to New York. He doesn't start working here until next month, but he's going to be in town on Wednesday to attend some kind of meeting, and he and Burton made plans a long time ago to spend the evening together. That was before Burton and I met, of course," she tittered. "Well, I told Burton not to worry, that I knew the perfect woman for whatever-his-name-is."

I didn't bother trying to conceal my exasperation. "My God, Pat! How could you say that?" I exploded. "You've never even met this person!"

"That's true," she conceded without missing a beat. "But Burton has."

"Forgive me. Of course, that makes all the difference, considering how intimately Burton and *I* are acquainted." She was so outrageous that I almost forgot what I'd been trying to tell her. "But that isn't even the point—and don't interrupt," I said, getting back on track. "The main thing is that I'm in the middle of a very demanding investigation, and that consumes pretty much all of my time right now."

"But it's not even healthy to deny yourself a social life," Pat protested.

"And anyway, I hate blind dates."

"Oh, don't be like that, Dez. If you're not willing to take a chance, you could be passing up a really great— a really *terrific*—person."

Now, I'd used that same argument myself any number of times. Particularly on all those occasions I'd tried to induce a kicking and screaming Ellen to meet the "terrific" man *I* had lined up for her. But while it had made sense to me for Ellen to take a flyer like that, I had a little difficulty in applying the same logic to myself.

Then too, what I said about how pleasant it was going out with Pat? This does not hold true for going out with Pat in company with her current significant other. My friend can be nauseatingly demonstrative when smitten. Also, she becomes painfully coy. I've even heard her dribbling baby talk, for God's sake! And although I consider that kind of behavior inappropriate for any grown woman, I find it absolutely ludicrous for a middle-aged type with a body like a Mack truck. (While I'm on the wide side myself, Pat's dimensions are impressive in *both* directions!)

"Come on, Dez," she said in this wheedling tone she sometimes affects, " 'all work and no play' and all that kind of stuff." And then: "You won't be sorry. Burton mentioned Le Cirque for dinner."

Sure he did. In her attempts to be persuasive, Pat has, on occasion, been known to veer away from the truth. "Oh, then he's made reservations there?" I inquired; all innocence. I couldn't help it. She practically begged for that.

"Um, I don't know if he's actually *called* yet, but, uh, he will. He likes to go to nice places, and he's a real sport. You'll see."

"I'd like to help you out Pat, I really would. But with the investigation—"

"If you don't come, I won't be able to see Burton. I told you he's already committed himself to this what-ever-his-name-is," she whined. And to point up the urgency of the situation: "Burton and I have been spending every night together since we met, you know."

This last bit of intelligence did not have the effect she'd intended. I was very tempted to say, "Okay, then Wednesday would be a good time to stay home and clean out your closets or write in your diary or read a book or something." But I didn't. I heard my own grudging "All right, all right, I'll go" before I'd even made the decision consciously.

I can be such a wimp!

It happened maybe a half hour later, as I was removing my makeup.

I swear I wasn't even thinking about the case at the time. Not consciously, anyhow. But suddenly I remembered a comment Paul Lundquist had made the first time I met with him. Which immediately brought to mind something Todd had mentioned to me very early on, too—something that not even he would have had any reason to lie about.

And that's when I knew for sure—and this time there was no mistake—who had murdered little Catherine Corwin.

And it wasn't her sister Barrie.

Chapter 34

Once I stumbled on the truth (and that's really the most accurate way to describe it), I realized that my so-called "evidence" against Barrie Lundquist had relied on her being the only person involved in the case who appeared to have both motive and opportunity. (Which, when you think about it, isn't evidence at all.) But now I was aware that there was someone else....

The real killer's motive was a lot less obvious than Barrie's. So much less obvious that I'd completely overlooked it. And then there'd been that alibi—which it took until this instant for me to see was worthless garbage—to stand in the way of my recognizing opportunity. But I had an overriding reason to be certain that I was now on firm ground:

At long last, I had facts.

I set the clock for the completely unreal hour of 5:45 and fell asleep almost instantly.

When the alarm went off, my body felt as if I'd just put it to bed. But I *willed* it to get up. Following which I hurriedly slapped on my makeup and dressed. (Hurriedly for me, that is.) After I'd whipped my appearance into more or less passable condition, I had a cup of my incomparable brew to chase some of the fuzziness out of my brain. And then I dialed. It was 6:43.

"Corwin residence," Luisa announced.

"This is Desiree Shapiro, Luisa. It's urgent that I talk to Mrs. Lundquist."

"Hold on, please" was the cool, noncommittal response.

A minute or two later, the housekeeper was back on the line. "Ms. Lundquist said it will have to wait until this evening. She has to be at work at eight-fifteen today."

"Can you give her a message, please? Tell her I know who the killer is now—the *real* killer—and that I *must* speak to her *right away*. It could be a matter of life or death."

"I'll tell her," Luisa agreed, with what I thought was remarkable indifference.

"What is it this time?" Barrie asked curtly a few moments later.

I began by repeating practically verbatim what I'd just requested that the housekeeper relay to her. "I know who the killer is—the real killer—and I have to see you. It's a matter of—"

"Yes, I know. Life or death."

I overlooked the sarcasm. (After all, considering how I'd acquitted myself last night, the woman was entitled.) "You're the only one who can help bring your sister's murderer to justice," I announced.

"How can you be certain you've got the right person *this* time?" Barrie put to me, a nasty little edge to her voice. (But like I said, she was entitled.)

"If you'll let me stop in for a couple of minutes, I'll tell you."

There was this total silence, followed by an enormous sigh, followed by a resigned "I'll meet you at lunchtime." And then: "But we'll have to make it someplace very close to my office."

"You don't understand. This can't wait. Suppose I come over now—before you leave for work. I won't detain you for very long, I promise."

Another enormous sigh. "All right. How soon can you get here?"

"Just give me about twenty minutes."

"Make it fifteen."

"I'll be there. And Ms. Lundquist? Please don't say a word to anyone else about this phone call."

"What's there to say? And by the way, Ms. Shapiro, don't think for a minute I'm convinced that you haven't jumped to another lame-brained conclusion that'll only be good for wasting a lot more of my time."

And with that, she slammed down the receiver.

*   *   *

When I arrived, Luisa led me into the breakfast room, a striking hexagonal-shaped area with green-and-white-checked tile flooring (marble, probably) and a lovely floral wallpaper that had huge pink peonies with dark green leaves spaced at wide intervals on a pure white background. Barrie was sitting at the rectangular glass-topped table, drinking coffee. There were crumbs on the starched white linen place mat in front of her, indicating that she'd already eaten.

She gestured for me to take the seat across from hers, where a place had been set with a small white and gold plate on another starched linen mat. Then without a word she got up and walked over to the sideboard directly behind her. A large coffee urn stood there, along with a half dozen cups and saucers. She filled a cup from the urn and handed it to me. And after that she sat back down again, motioning at the same time toward the basket of toast and pastries in the center of the table. "Help yourself," she invited tersely.

"No, thanks. The coffee is all I can manage right now," I told her as she passed me the cream and sugar.

Her shrug conveyed that she wouldn't have cared if I starved.

Now, remember my observation the night before about Barrie's applying her makeup with a lighter touch? Well, forget it. You had to see her first thing in the morning when all that glop was nice and fresh to get its full impact. I mean, she had me regretting I hadn't worn my sunglasses.

"Okay, go ahead," she ordered.

Well, at least I couldn't accuse her of chewing my ear off.

"Look, I really don't blame you for feeling like this. I'm terribly sorry for the things I said to you last night; I wish I could take them back." Then I offered this lame excuse (true, I'm afraid, but lame, nonetheless). "I guess that having finally established that Catherine was murdered, I was just so anxious to wrap things up that I pounced on the only person I thought had both motive and opportunity. I found out I was wrong. There was someone else and—"

"How do you know you're not barking up the wrong tree again?"

"Because there was a dead giveaway to the killer's identity—something I totally overlooked until about one o'clock this morning."

"Which is?" She was drumming her fingers impatiently on the table now.

"Which is that Saundra King had allergies."

"What is *that* supposed to mean?" Barrie asked testily, her fingers still curled on the tabletop as the motion stopped abruptly.

"Follow me on this, okay? Weeks ago your ex-husband mentioned to me in passing that that one time Mrs.—Ms.—King visited the two of you on Long Island her allergies started acting up. Well, it didn't even make a dent at the time—about the allergies, I mean—but then this morning it suddenly popped into my head."

"So?" she broke in.

"So thinking about it triggered my remembering something Todd told me. Todd said—practically at the start of my investigation—that when Ms. King came back from the bathroom that day, he wouldn't let her come near him. He complained about her having a cold."

"I don't see—"

"She'd been tutoring him right up until then, hadn't she?"

"Listen, I don't know what you're getting at," Barrie retorted, "but if you're trying to make a case against Saundra now, I'd forget it if I were you. Because it won't wash. She was only gone from Todd's room for five minutes, and that was long before Luisa went out to the store."

"That's according to *her*."

"Did Todd tell you something different? Because you can't bel—"

"No, he didn't. But Ms. King could have claimed almost anything without worrying about Todd's disputing her. After all, it wouldn't matter if he did. Weren't you just about to tell me yourself that you can't believe him?"

"I guess so," she conceded. And then she shot out—

and in a tone that practically dared me to say yes—"So are you suggesting she lied?"

I figured it would be best to kind of ease into my answer, hoping she wouldn't find it quite so hard to accept that way. I chose the words carefully. "Let's say that Ms. King wanted to ... confuse things," I put to her. "Well, it seems that wouldn't have presented a problem even if Todd wasn't quite so ... even if he were a more credible witness. In fact, she could probably have been gone from that room for as long as fifteen or twenty minutes without his being any the wiser. As you undoubtedly know, he started listening to a CD as soon as she walked out, and most likely he got all caught up in it. As to just *when* she left, he really had no idea. But of course, Todd's being ... the way he is made it that much easier. If he *had* contradicted her on either of these two points, it would have been his word against hers. And like I said, she was certainly aware of just what his word is worth."

"This is ridiculous!" Barrie asserted, her voice rising. "Saundra wouldn't kill Catherine; she *didn't* kill Catherine. And anyway, what would she have had to gain?"

"Money."

"But she didn't stand to benefit financially."

"Sure, she did. Indirectly, at any rate. The two of you are lovers; you're planning to live together. Anything that affects your lifestyle is bound to affect hers, too." And then as an afterthought, really: "And how is Ms. King's p.r. business, anyway?"

"It's—it's ... What does *that* matter?"

Bingo! It seemed I'd hit pay dirt! But before I had a chance to even think of pursuing that angle, Barrie lashed out at me.

"You're driving me absolutely crazy! You start out by talking about Saundra's allergies, and then you go off on some tangent. I *still* don't see what her being allergic has to do with a damn thing!"

She was right, of course. I'd gotten myself derailed before demonstrating how Saundra King's allergies were the clue I'd been searching for all this time: the clue that identified Catherine's killer.

"Sorry," I responded. "What I started to say was that

Ms. King's sniffles and sneezes or whatever didn't manifest themselves until after she returned to your son's room. That's right, isn't it?"

"It could be; I'm not sure. But what makes you so positive it wasn't a cold? And even if it *was* her allergies, would you mind telling me how that makes her guilty of murder?"

"I know this is painful for you," I said gently. "It must be practically impossible to even imagine that someone you care for like that might have murdered your little sister. But just hear me out for a couple of minutes longer, okay?" I chose to interpret Barrie's hostile stare as a signal of consent. "Catherine died because she was tickled with a feather duster," I went on. "And that same day Ms. King suddenly develops some symptoms that she passes off as a cold. But these symptoms are also consistent with an allergic reaction, and we know she has allergies. What's more, you can be sure those symptoms of hers weren't evident even a second before she walked out of Todd's bedroom, because he was just waiting for an excuse not to let her near him."

"This isn't even worth listening to!" an obviously agitated Barrie interjected angrily. But for the first time there was fear in her eyes. And I knew then that I was reaching her—on some level, at least.

I honed in on motive. "Look, Saundra was aware that Catherine had seen something she shouldn't have, correct?"

The response was none too swift in coming. "Yes, that part, at least, is true," Barrie finally acknowledged.

"How did she feel about that?"

"She was very upset, but it was for *my* sake—and Todd's. She didn't want us to lose out on anything."

I couldn't see Catherine's murderer as being quite that selfless. "Don't forget that her business wasn't doing all that well and that you'd be in a much better position to help her financially if you got that inheritance of your grandmother's."

"But Saundra would never—" She stopped. "Wait a minute," she said, opening her eyes wider and straightening her spine. There was even the hint of a smile hovering at the corners of her mouth. Suddenly, the woman was wearing the expression of someone about to pull off the coup of the century. "How could Saundra possibly have known when Luisa would be going to the store?" she challenged. "Or, for that matter, that she'd be going to the store at all?"

"Oh, she couldn't. Do you want me to tell you what happened?" I didn't risk the reply. "I think your friend Ms. King left Todd's room to go to the bathroom," I went on quickly. "Just as she said. Only a lot later than she claimed. But when she was in the upstairs hall, she heard Luisa calling out to Catherine that she was leaving for the market. Well, this was her chance—although to do what, I'm not really certain. Maybe all she had in mind at this point was to quiz Catherine about what she'd witnessed. But at any rate, she went downstairs and found her sitting by herself in the library, reading. And then she spotted the feather duster near the door. Now, in Ms. King's case, it's likely she appreciated the potential of that feather duster right from the beginning. After all, she knows what dust does to *her,* and—"

"No! You're wrong!" Barrie exclaimed, her voice high and shrill. "Something like that would never even cross Saundra's mind!"

"Just answer one question for me, okay? Where was she the Saturday Catherine was almost struck by a car?"

(Yes, here I was again, pointing my finger at yet another suspect before checking into that. So of course, you're probably thinking right now that I'm hopeless, that I *still* hadn't learned my lesson. And I guess I can't really argue. But you see, this time I just *knew.*)

I got the kind of answer I would have predicted. "She was at home that entire day. She had a business proposal to write."

"I don't suppose anyone was with her."

"No, she was by herself, I believe," Barrie responded haughtily, managing to stare me down.

"What color car does Ms. King drive?"

"It's black. But then so are millions of other cars in the city, aren't they? Listen, Ms. Shapiro, what you had to say is very interesting. And maybe even possible. The only trouble is, it's not true. And it's certainly not *proof*

of anything. Do you think a jury would convict Saundra
of murder just because she sneezed a few times?"

"No, I don't. That's one reason I came here to talk
to you."

"Well, we've talked, and I have to go to work now,"
Barrie informed me, getting up and towering over me in
a pair of three-inch-plus red pumps. "That means you're
being asked to leave." She said it lightly but firmly.

I made no effort to be accommodating. "Do you remember my telling you that this was a matter of life
or death?"

"Well, that's one way to get your foot in the door,
isn't it?" she remarked dryly.

"I meant it."

"All right." She sat back down again, plainly exasperated. "But just say whatever else you've got to say in a
hurry, so I still have a job by the time I get to the
office." With that, she glanced at her watch.

"It won't take long. I just want to ask you one last
question. Are you willing to bet your son's life that
Saundra isn't a killer?"

"Why ... why ... what do you mean?" she stammered, all that vivid color of hers rushing from her
cheeks.

"I mean that there's no doubt he's aware of what goes
on between you and Ms. King—he hinted as much to
me a long time ago. And as big a—a prevaricator [Well,
it does sound better than *liar*] as everyone knows Todd
to be, Ms. King could still perceive him as a threat. After
all, he could decide to open his mouth about the two of
you at any moment, and there's always the chance someone might take him seriously."

Barrie's reaction was as close to a guffaw as you can
get. "This is really rich! You've been sitting here for half
the morning telling me nobody would believe anything
Todd says. And now when it suits you, you're trying to
convince me Saundra's afraid he'll give our relationship
away. Come *on*, Ms. Shapiro! You can't have it both
ways."

"I grant you that ordinarily nobody places any stock
in Todd's little stories. But this is different. You and
King have evidently not been overly circumspect about

your love affair; that's why Catherine and Todd observed whatever they did in the first place. And that being the case, it's plausible other people—maybe including your grandmother—have at least had their suspicions concerning the two of you, suspicions that until now they chose to ignore. But a few words from Todd could very well make that a lot harder to do."

"Oh, please," Barrie protested, dismissing the idea with a wave of her hand.

"Remember, Saundra King's already killed once to prevent information about your affection for each other from reaching your grandmother. Are you really so certain that at some point she won't decide it's necessary to do it again?"

"You're all wet—about everything. I'd trust Saundra with my life." But Barrie Lundquist's tone didn't quite match the conviction of her words.

"You haven't been listening," I said bluntly. "I'm not talking about *your* life; I'm talking about Todd's."

"Oh, but Saundra would never hurt Todd." And then so softly that for a moment I wasn't exactly sure what I'd heard: "Would she?"

Chapter 35

"I just can't deal with this," Barrie stated evenly. And right after that she covered her face with her hands and began to cry. Now, while I'd also managed to put her in a state of saturation during our first meeting, it was completely different. I mean, you couldn't hear a thing this time. Only her body, heaving with silent sobs, revealed her terrible pain.

When she finally lifted her head up, she looked like nothing you've ever seen. All the beauty aids she'd shoveled onto her face earlier that morning had merged with the tears, and her cheeks were now exploding with color: black and red and purple and green. . . . She grabbed the crumpled linen napkin in front of her (believe me, this was not a paper napkin kind of house) and wiped her eyes. Then she dug into the side pocket of her thigh-high yellow skirt and extracted a bunch of tissues.

"Since Catherine died, I never know when I'm going to need these," she told me after a few hearty honks.

"I'm really sorry I had to put you through this."

Barrie smiled wanly. "You play dirty, Mrs. S., you know? Using Todd like that, I'm talking about. The one thing that would finish me off for sure is for something to happen to him, too."

"I felt that I—" was as far as I got in defending my tactics. She continued as though she hadn't even heard me.

"What you told me wasn't exactly a revelation. Oh, I don't mean I actually *knew* anything; I didn't. But the thing with the car? The truth is, almost as soon as it happened, it flashed through my mind that Saundra might have been . . . well, that she might have had something to do with it. You see, after Catherine caught us kissing, Saundra was terribly upset. She was afraid Catherine might mention something to my grandmother unless we did something about it. That's the way she put it: 'did something about it.' It made me kind of uncomfortable her saying that, so I asked what she had in mind. She said—and I don't remember the exact words, but this is more or less the gist of it—'I wasn't taking about anything dire, so don't look so worried.' She claimed that all she meant was that maybe she'd have a little chat with her."

"And did she—have that chat?"

"Not that I know of."

"Tell me, how long before she was almost run over did Catherine witness the kiss?"

"Only a few days. That's what bothered me."

"And did you ever question Saundra about being responsible?"

"I never got the chance. When she came over the next morning, I told her what had happened. But I didn't really know how to handle it from there. I mean, nobody believed the thing was actually deliberate, and in a way, I didn't either. But in *another* way, well, the timing was just too . . . too perfect. Do you see what I mean?"

"Yes, of course."

"At any rate, I was trying to broach the subject—you know, find out if she could possibly have been involved. It isn't easy, though, coming up with a tactful way of accusing the person you want to spend your life with of attempted murder. But then Saundra brought it up herself. She said she hoped I didn't think *she* had anything to do with that car business. And I said of course not and that, anyway, we were all sure that Catherine only imagined that the car was aiming at her. I suppose Saundra was still concerned about my believing her because she took my hand then and looked at me in this piercing way she has. She told me she really loved me and that she could never harm anyone who was important to me."

"And did you feel she was telling the truth?"

"Sure, I did. Probably because I wanted to. Besides, with the family so convinced it was an accident, well, they convinced me, too. Or maybe I convinced myself."

"And when Catherine died? Did you think Saundra had anything to do with *that*?"

"Oh, no! I had no idea it was *murder*," Barrie exclaimed, her voice rising. "Why would I when she'd been so sick, and everything pointed to her dying of her illness?"

"What do you think now?"

"That you're right—about her being murdered, about Saundra, about everything. I wish to God you weren't, but I know you are."

"Look," I said then, "I'll need your help if we're ever going to make Saundra pay for killing Catherine."

"But . . . but what can *I* do?" she asked timidly.

"There's a chance I might be able to convince the police to put a wire on you," I proposed. "If I can, would you be willing to wear it and try getting Saundra to incriminate herself?"

A look of fear leapt into Barrie's eyes. "Oh, I'd never be able to pull it off," she protested. And then after nervously licking her lips: "I'm really a lousy actress, honestly."

My response—motivated by desperation—was none too kind. "Don't you care what happened to your little sister?"

"You know I care! But even if I . . . even if I agreed to wear the wire, do you really think that knowing how I felt about Catherine, there's the slightest chance Saundra would admit to me that she killed her?"

She had me there.

"Well, then I'll have to come up with another way to get the job done, won't I?" I responded, giving my voice a confidence that my mind didn't share.

"You'll keep me informed?"

"Don't worry about that; of course I will," I answered extra-gently. This suddenly solicitous attitude of mine was supposed to make me feel like less of a louse for the way I'd just lashed out at this poor, stricken woman. But it didn't quite make it; I still wasn't overly fond of myself right then. "In the meantime, though," I advised, "I'd have as little contact with King as possible if I were you. Only try hard not to give her any cause for suspicion."

"That won't exactly be easy."

"You can always say you're busy with work or something. And I'd keep a watchful eye on Todd, too. Make sure you never leave him alone with her," I cautioned. "Not even for a second."

Barrie shivered. "You really think he's in danger, then?"

"I honestly don't know," I answered.

Chapter 36

When I left Barrie a couple of minutes later, she looked completely miserable. And assuring her once again that I'd figure out some way of nailing King didn't do a thing to lift the gloom.

"I know I should be glad to hear that, but to be honest, all I feel right now is this terrible depression," she confided. "In a funny kind of a way, it's almost like Catherine died all over again."

Luisa was just showing me out when Todd came bounding down the stairs. He stopped short when he saw me.

The housekeeper shot him a warning look. "Your breakfast is in the kitchen," she said. "Better hurry up, or you'll be late for school."

"Well, look who's here," he snickered, ignoring her. "Still trying to figure out who killed the 'little princess'? Geez, you don't know how to do *anything*, do you?" And then came the really heart-warming part: "Except gain weight, o' course."

Hey, if Saundra King decided to waste this kid, I guess I could manage to live with it, I said to myself. And only half in jest.

In the taxi on my way to the office, I thought about the call I'd soon be making to my client. I gave mental thanks that I hadn't jumped the gun and phoned her before this—when I had her granddaughter pegged as the killer. And then I realized that Evelyn Corwin hadn't called me, either. Not in almost a week. Which kind of surprised me. Well, it was really all to the good. At least now I wouldn't be telling her the perp was somebody she cared about.

I dialed her number the minute I sat down at my desk.

"Mrs. Corwin isn't in," her housekeeper informed me in this perfunctory tone.

"Do you have any idea when she's expected?"

There was silence for maybe two or three seconds before the woman said, "I'm not too sure. I'll, uh, tell Mrs. Corwin you phoned."

"Would you ask her to get back to me?"

This time there was a briefer delay before the reply, but still the hesitation was apparent. "Yes ... I'll do that."

If my antenna had been working right that morning, I might have been alerted by the tentativeness in the woman's responses.

But it wasn't, and so I wasn't, either.

For the remainder of the day and most of the evening, I tried to devise a scheme for getting Saundra King to admit to the murder. I considered using the same approach I'd tried on Barrie, but I abandoned the idea almost at once. In this instance it didn't make any sense. King was smart enough to realize that when you're coughing and sneezing like that yourself, you can forget about convincing anyone that you didn't know what you were doing.

Okay, so if I couldn't convince the woman to confess to a lesser crime, it meant I had to work out another plan. But right there's where I went blank. Completely, totally, one hundred percent blank. I tried to think positively, assuring myself that it was only a matter of time before I came up with something absolutely foolproof. But I had a strong suspicion I was lying to myself. And I was just a little panicky.

At a quarter to ten the next morning, the phone rang. I was relieved to hear Evelyn Corwin on the other end of the line. For some reason, I'd begun to feel uneasy about her.

"I hope you have news for me," she said. You couldn't miss the fatigue in her voice.

"Listen, is everything okay? You sound tired." And then I added with a small chuckle, "Besides, it's not like you to wait so long to bug me."

"Everything's fine, Desiree," she replied, ignoring the attempt at levity. "I was in Sloan-Kettering for a couple of days. Nothing serious; they just wanted to run some tests. But it seems to have knocked me out a little."

"I was with Barrie yesterday morning," I complained, "and she didn't say a word to me about your being in the hospital."

"That's probably because she didn't know about it. I told Frances—my housekeeper—to just tell everyone who called that I was out. I didn't have any idea you tried to reach me until I got home this morning. Frances sees herself as my protector. Says she didn't want anything to upset me."

"She must be very fond—"

"It's what happens when you have people working for you for over thirty-five years. They start to think *they're* running things. But anyway, as I *started* to say"—and there was more than a hint of reproach in her tone—"do you or don't you have something to tell me?"

I couldn't have held out another second, anyway. The words came out in a rush. "I know who the killer is now," I said triumphantly, after which I paused for congratulations.

I didn't get them. "Don't *do* that!" Mrs. Corwin admonished, her voice remarkably strong now. "Who is it, for heaven's sake?"

"I thought it might be better if we talked in person."

"It would certainly *not* be better. Will you please tell me who it is before I come over there and strangle you?"

Her frustration was, of course, understandable. And she was entitled to her answer. "It was Saundra King. She's the one who mur—"

"I *told* you it couldn't have been a member of my family!" Evelyn cried exultantly. And then after a moment: "But why on earth would *she* want to kill my Catherine?"

Well, here it was: the question I'd been dreading. Also, the reason I'd tried for a face-to-face meeting. I mean, there was no way to explain King's motive without going into her relationship with Barrie. And the very thought of apprising my client of that turned me to jelly. And to do it over the phone—well, that was almost unthinkable.

"Why don't you let me stop by?" I urged. "I could be at your apartment in—"

"I want to hear this second why that woman murdered my granddaughter!" Evelyn Corwin snapped.

"But—"

"Now."

There was no room to argue.

"You're positive Barrie knew nothing about the murder?" Evelyn asked a short while later.

"Not until I talked to her yesterday."

"Well, that's something, anyway," she murmured. "But wait a minute. Wasn't Mrs. King with Todd, in his room, at the time Catherine was killed?"

"That's only what she says. She did leave him to go to the bathroom, remember. And he doesn't really know when that was or even how long she was gone."

"I see. That does make a difference."

"Uh, listen, about Barrie ..." I put in tentatively, "this thing with Mrs. King—their relationship, I mean—well, it must be difficult for you to accept. But it's—"

It was obvious I couldn't count on finishing a sentence this morning. "Listen, Desiree, if I'd learned about this ... this unnatural attachment between Barrie and that vile, murdering witch even a couple of months ago, I might have taken some kind of drastic action. But now ... well, I've already lost one granddaughter; I don't intend to lose a second."

"I'm glad to hear that, Mrs. Corwin. Very glad."

"And by the way, I want to thank you for all you've done on this case. You've given an old woman peace of mind. No. More than that. You've actually saved my sanity." Evelyn choked up at this point, and it was a moment before she was able to continue. "You're quite a detective, Desiree; you did a remarkable job. And I'm very, very grateful."

Now, this probably would have been the time to confess that I wasn't all that deserving of her praise—that in fact, only a few days ago I'd leeched onto her blameless granddaughter as a vicious killer. But if the thought crossed my mind, it was so fleeting I wasn't even aware of it. "I'm just happy I was able to help," I told her in my most self-effacing manner.

"Have you spoken to the police about this?" she asked then.

"No. I really don't have any hard evidence to take to them yet."

"And how do you propose to to go about getting it?"

"I don't know—not yet, anyway. But I'm sure I'll come up with something." *My God! I'd better!*

"You have no doubt, though, about Mrs. King being the killer?"

"No, I don't."

"I don't, either," she responded with satisfaction. "But you have to make me a promise."

"Of course, Mrs. Corwin. Whatev—"

"Promise me you won't do a thing until you hear from me. I need a little time to digest all of this."

"I'll wait for you to contact me."

"Thank you. I'll be in touch soon. And remember, you're not to do a thing in the meantime—nothing. Oh, and Desiree?"

"Yes?"

"Call me Evelyn," said my client. And for the very first time.

Chapter 37

Almost immediately after my conversation with Evelyn Corwin, I tried reaching Ellen at Macy's. I was told she had the day off, so I dialed her apartment, only to find that the line was busy. When I dialed again a few minutes later, she answered so fast, the first ring never got the chance to finish its ringing.

"I just this second hung up the phone," she said in this strange voice. I couldn't even attempt to identify the emotion behind it.

"I know. I called a little while ago. What's up? Are you okay?"

"I'm fine. Why do you ask?" She went on without even taking a breath. "I was talking to Mike!" she squealed into the receiver. "I'm seeing him Friday night!" *Suppressed excitement—that's what I'd heard a moment ago.*

I squealed, too. "Ohhh, I'm *so* glad!"

"See? I told you he wouldn't wait a week to call again!"

"You certainly did," I happily concurred.

"I'm not surprised or anything; I was expecting to hear from him. But now that I'll actually be seeing him, I'm so hyper I can hardly stand it. In fact, I'm a basket case just talking about it. So let's not, okay? What's happening with the case? Anything new?"

"You might say that," I told her dryly. "Since our last conversation I found out I was wrong about the killer— again. Well, half wrong, anyway."

"What do you mean?"

"It wasn't Barrie and Saundra who killed Catherine. Barrie didn't even know her little sister had been murdered. The whole thing was Saundra's doing."

"How did you find out?"

"I'll explain when I see you. My intention was to ask if you'd like to come over for dinner Friday night. Under the circumstances, though, I guess Friday's out."

"I guess so," Ellen agreed with a giggle. "How about tonight? Or Thursday if you don't mind doing it after I get through with work."

"Of course I don't mind. So let's make it Thursday." I didn't want to mention tonight's blind date; I didn't even want to *think* about tonight's blind date. I'd been regretting my commitment to Pat with increasing intensity since the second I made it.

"Fine," she said, sounding a little disappointed. "Oh, and I'll bring over my new dress to show you. Did I mention that I finally found something last weekend?"

"What new dress are we talking about?"

"You know, the one for Mike's cousin's wedding."

Well, how do you like that!

"But tell me one thing now, will you?" she said then, acting as though it wasn't the least bit strange to outfit herself for an affair to which everyone else on God's green earth would have—with excellent reason—assumed they'd been disinvited.

"Shoot," I responded absently, still shaking my head over this astonishing optimism of hers.

"What did the police have to say about your outsmarting them like that—the way you always do?" Ellen has no compunction at all about dissing New York's finest if it will make me look good.

"I haven't talked to the police about it yet. While I know she did it and even Barrie knows she did it, I have no idea what I can use for proof."

"Oh, you'll think of something," Ellen assured me. "*That* I'm sure of."

"The main reason I called, though," I told her, "was to thank you. I'd never have come up with the killer if it hadn't been for you."

"*Me*? What did I do?"

"You got me to finally begin investigating the case the right way, remember? The way I should have the minute I took it on."

"Oh, for heaven's sake! Sooner or later you would

have done that on your own." But she sounded extremely pleased, nonetheless. "I'll see you tomorrow night, then, and you'll tell me everything, okay?"

"You bet. And Ellen?"

"What?"

"I'm really thrilled about Mike."

"Thanks, Aunt Dez," she said softly. "I am, too."

I can't tell you how ecstatic I was over Ellen's happiness. I realized I was jumping the gun a little, but I couldn't control myself. As soon as I put the receiver down, daydreams about her wedding took command of my head, pushing everything else straight out of it.

I immediately got this image of her in full bridal regalia, her large, dark eyes dewy, and her smile, well, radiant would be an understatement. She was an absolute vision, decked out in exquisite white lace from her mantilla-like veil right down to her mile-long train.

Naturally, I gave myself a featured role in the proceedings. I was wearing this floor-length cream chiffon number, which was not only the most elegant dress I've ever owned but which practically made my hips disappear. (It's ridiculously easy to achieve miracles of this sort in a daydream.) I had on matching cream silk shoes, of course, and I was carrying this lovely bouquet of soft pink camellias as befits the bride's only attendant. (She wouldn't *not* have me as her attendant would she? After all, I'd introduced her to the groom.) Oh, and I didn't waddle down the aisle; I floated!

It was a dazzling affair, held in the grand ballroom of the Plaza—or whatever name their largest and most impressive room goes by. Or maybe it wasn't the Plaza at all; maybe it was the Waldorf or the St. Regis. At any rate, between the astonishing number of magnificent floral arrangements and the I-don't-know-how-many guests, I managed to fill up practically every inch of available space. As for the menu, while I didn't get around to actually working it out, I don't have to tell you, do I, that everyone raved for months afterward about the incredible delicacies they were served that night.

Uh-oh.

Suppose Ellen and Mike played me dirty. I mean, what if they decided to flaunt their independence and insist on paying for these nuptials of theirs themselves? I knew Ellen's parents could afford to go overboard for their only daughter, but I doubted the bride and groom would be able to foot the bill for anything so lavish.

Well, never mind. I could adapt.

I quickly moved the wedding party to a smaller hall, trimmed the guest list, cut the hors d'oeuvre selection from twenty items to ten, replaced the Dom Perignon with a very agreeable domestic vintage and dumped about three-quarters of the flowers. All this accomplished, I turned my attention to getting rid of Ellen's train—or at least some of it. Then I put myself in silk instead of chiffon and chopped a few inches off the hemline (soon finding, I might add, that this new choice was equally kind to the hips.)

You know, it was working out just fine. A nice, intimate little affair was really in so much better taste than one of those garish extravaganzas, don't you think? And hey, maybe we could somehow get the mayor of New York City to perform the interfaith ceremony. Wouldn't *that* be a nice touch!

It was at this point that I wrenched myself away— with much difficulty—from Ellen's wedding. There was, after all, another, more immediate matter to attend to.

I spent what was left of the morning closeted in my office, trying again to devise some sort of scheme for trapping Saundra King. But one idea was worse than the other, and after an hour or so of totally fruitless contemplation, I began to get really tense. Maybe my client had given me a reprieve, but sooner or later I'd still have to come up with a decent plan—or face the unthinkable: that little Catherine's killer would get off scot free.

I gave my poor overextended brain a short break. Picking up the phone, I dialed Barrie Lundquist's office. A secretary or somebody answered her extension. She didn't put Barrie on until I'd identified myself.

"I just wanted to know how things are going," I told

her as soon as we'd dispensed with the hello, how are yous.

"Okay, I guess," she responded dejectedly. "I still can't believe Saundra actually did what she did. I thought she was . . . well, I loved her a lot."

"Yes, I know. And I'm sorry," I murmured. "Have you been managing to steer clear of her?"

"So far. She called me Tuesday afternoon. She thought we might meet for dinner that night, but I said I was leaving for L.A. on business after work that day and wouldn't be back for a week at the earliest. She wanted to know what hotel I'd be staying at, but I told her my secretary made the reservations and that I wasn't sure of the name of the place. I said I'd be getting in touch with her from there as soon as I could."

"Good. I see you're screening your calls."

"Yeah. At home, too. Just in case she calls there for some reason—like to find out if anyone's heard from me. I've alerted everyone about what to say, but I only hope Todd doesn't pick up and decide it would be a kick to tell her I didn't go anywhere, that I've just been avoiding her. You know how he can be sometimes."

My "yes" was in conjunction with the reflexive shudder that normally accompanies the mere mention of Barrie Lundquist's only child.

"But don't worry," she continued. "I don't think there's much chance of that. Luisa almost always answers the phone." There was a slight pause before she asked me cautiously, "Umm, have you figured out yet how you're going to get her to confess?"

"No, not yet."

"You'll let me know what happens, though?"

"Yes, of course." *Assuming, that is, that something does happen.*

Lunch was spent at my desk, where I partook of a cold, really greasy burger and cold, just as greasy and also undercooked French fries, adding a stomach ache to the monstrous headache I'd already inflicted on myself that day. Then I went back to my thinking.

It was just past three o'clock when—hallelujah!—I finally devised a plan.

Saundra King, you diabolical, despicable bitch, I thought, *you have had it!* I was positively elated for all of about three minutes. Then I had to concede that there was very little chance I could pull the thing off. I won't bother you with the details; all I'll say is that it required Todd's cooperation. So you know what an iffy proposition *that* made it.

At about five-fifteen I left for home, still plagued by both a pounding headache—which four Extra-Strength Tylenols had done little to relieve—and the legacy of that miserable lunch in the pit of my stomach.

Chapter 38

I walked in the door at a few minutes before six, which meant I hadn't allowed myself all that much time to get ready for my date that evening. Pat's latest whatever-you-want-to-call-him had made reservations for seven-thirty at a Chinese restaurant about six blocks from my apartment. (From everything I'd heard, the food there was supposed to be pretty good, too, although no way it was in the Le Cirque category.) Now, while close to an hour and a half may be sufficient for most women to get themselves together, that's really pushing it for me—either because I require an unusual amount of work or because I'm unusually disorganized. Probably a little of both.

If you're familiar with Murphy's Law, you may have some idea about how things progressed during my preparations that night. I mean, *everything* went wrong. First off, in the middle of my shower the hot water turned ice-cold. Then I wound up breaking the point of my eyeliner and didn't have a clue as to the whereabouts of the pencil sharpener. After that, probably because I was a little edgy by this time, I didn't manage to get my lipstick on straight until the third try. I won't even *mention* the run in my brand-new panty hose. Or the fact that when I was fully dressed I noticed that my hem was sagging, and I had to change every stitch of clothing— right down to my underwear.

In spite of all of these dire mishaps, however, my in-domitable spirit prevailed, and I somehow made it down-stairs by seven-thirty. If things had gone the way they should have from then on, I wouldn't have arrived at the restaurant more than ten minutes late. But the Fates double-crossed me.

It was rough getting a cab that night. And I'd been jockeying for one for close to ten minutes—and losing out repeatedly to my speedier and/or more aggressive neighbors—when it started to drizzle. So naturally, faster than you can say *oh, shit*! there didn't seem to be a vacant taxi in this entire city. I did think of heading back upstairs for an umbrella and then letting my beautiful only-worn-once navy leather pumps transport me the six blocks to the restaurant—a thought that actually curdled my blood. Fortunately, however, I was able to quickly convince myself that walking would take much too long. Besides, who could say that any second now an available cab with my name on it wouldn't come barreling around the corner?

A few minutes later, it began to rain for real. I couldn't hide in the doorway—not if I had any hope of nailing a taxi, that is. So I remained at the curb and allowed the water to beat down unmercifully on my unprotected head, doing unspeakable things to my glorious hennaed hair. It didn't take long for those beautiful navy leather pumps of mine to become seriously waterlogged. And even without looking, I knew that my mascara had joined the raindrops that were working their way down to my chin. The weather plus Saundra King plus the headache that wouldn't go away plus the stomach ache that still hadn't completely disappeared really started to get to me. I yearned to return to my nice dry apartment and just call Pat at the restaurant and tell her I'd suddenly gotten sick and wouldn't be able to join them. (With the aches in my head and stomach that wasn't exactly a lie, was it?) But of course, the saintlier side of me had to put its two cents in; after all, I *had* made a promise to a friend, and it wasn't like I was at death's door or anything. On the other hand though, tears were beginning to sting my eyes, and ...

The cab seemed to materialize out of nowhere, screeching to a stop directly in front of me and splashing dirty water all the way up to my eyebrows. I was furious. Also a mess. But I didn't dare complain. When the young woman occupant got out, I meekly took her place and was soon careening down the street for the most nerve-wracking six-block ride I've ever endured.

It goes without saying that I was not at my most irresistible by the time I sloshed into Chung Fu's. I deposited my soiled and dripping coat with the cloakroom attendant—who held it in front of her with two fingers as though she feared contamination—and made a bee-line for the ladies' room.

Doing my best to ignore the image that stared back at me from the mirror—a sight that could easily prostrate the fainthearted—I proceeded to mop up as much moisture from my person as more than a dozen paper towels could hold. Then I made some emergency repairs to my face, following which I tried running a comb through the flat, sticky mess occupying a major portion of my head. Two of the comb's teeth broke immediately, leaving the remaining six to do what they could. Which wasn't nearly enough.

When I finally worked up the courage to show myself in the dining room, I spotted Pat immediately. She was totally engrossed in doing exotic things to somebody's ear. The recipient of her attentions was a tall, thin man with an almost all-white handlebar mustache and long salt and pepper hair, which he wore tied back in a pony-tail. I got the impression he was at once both terribly embarrassed and having the time of his life. Facing the two and with his back to me was my guy—"Mel or Moe, something with an M, anyway."

Pat was so intent on her work that she didn't look up until I was almost in her lap. "Oh, Dez," she said, "I was so *worried* about you. What happened? You look just *terrible*!" (Pat never has been much on tact.)

"It's a long story," I responded, "and I'm sorry I'm late, but it was really unavoidable."

"This is Burton Wizniak," she said proudly, after which Burton Wizniak disengaged himself—but not too swiftly—from the arms encircling his neck and got to his feet. "And *this*," she announced as if she were awarding me an emerald necklace or at the very least a brand-new Porsche, "is Bruce Simon." (I didn't even wonder about that Mel or Moe business; Pat's never been much on names, either.) Bruce glanced up at me disinterestedly, then half rose—drink in hand—and pulled out my chair with obvious reluctance. He sat back down again before I was even seated.

Well, the guy wasn't my type, anyway.

Bruce Simon wasn't too tall, maybe five-six or seven, I'd estimated during those pitifully few seconds he'd almost taken the trouble to stand up. The height part was okay with me, though. So was the fact that his dark brown hair was pretty sparse and very obviously arranged to conceal that fact. What *wasn't* okay with me was how solidly the man was built and the overly confident, supercilious look he was wearing on his face. I mean, when you're drawn to men who make Woody Allen seem macho, a Bruce Simon isn't even a possibility.

"So what kept you?" he was asking.

"It's raining," I pointed out without expression, "and I couldn't get a cab."

"It didn't start to rain until well after seven-thirty," he observed with a similar lack of expression.

"Listen," I said testily, hating myself for even bothering with an explanation, "I was a little late coming home from work, and then I had a few phone calls while I was getting dressed—business calls—so it took me longer to get ready than I'd planned." (I *had* to improvise. I didn't think he'd be impressed by the eyeliner thing. Or even the ripped panty hose.)

"You hotshot business tycoons should allow yourselves more time," he advised with a totally humorless grin.

I made a fast decision not to knock his gin and tonic into his lap. Mostly for Pat's sake. (If it had been hot coffee, however, I just might not have been able to resist.) "I'll have to keep that in mind," I muttered. "Thanks for the advice."

That awful grin of his—it was a smirk, really—got wider. "Any time."

Right about then Pat finally desisted from nibbling on Burton's ear in favor of something more substantial, and we agreed we'd order some appetizers along with four main dishes that we'd all share.

"What would you like, hon?" Burton asked his goddess of passion.

"Oh, anything you would, hon," the passion goddess responded predictably.

"Desiree?"

"How about some spare ribs to start with?" I suggested.

"I'm not crazy about spare ribs," said Bruce. *Figures!* He picked up the menu at his elbow, scanning it quickly. "Everybody like shrimp toast?"

"It's fine with me." That from Burton.

"Whatever everyone else wants." This from a sickeningly agreeable Pat.

"I don't care," I grumbled, pouting because I could practically *taste* the ribs.

"Well, then, shrimp toast it is," Bruce stated cheerily. "And how about some egg roll? Is that okay with you, Desiree?" He fastened these innocent-looking hazel eyes on me, feigning solicitude.

"Peachy," I growled.

"We'd better get some egg rolls, then. We wouldn't want to disappoint Desiree, would we, guys?"

It went on like that through the entire ordering process. I couldn't remember when I'd met anyone quite so obnoxious. Even Pat, who is normally completely oblivious to her surroundings when she's in her amorous mode, couldn't help noticing the hostility between us. "Uh, Bruce was really worried about you, Desiree," she offered, trying to put that impossible snot in a more sympathetic light. "He was afraid you might have had an accident or something."

"I couldn't think of any other reason for someone to keep three other people waiting for close to an hour without taking the trouble to call," he said matter-of-factly.

"It so happens that I practically *drowned* trying to get here," I fumed.

"Yes, I realize that. But there *are* phone booths on almost every corner, aren't there?"

I wracked my brain for a nasty comeback that was truly inspired, but Burton spared me the pain of failure. "Go outside and try to find yourself a puppy to kick, Bruce," he told his cousin good-naturedly. And to me: "Bruce had a terrible day. He just found out the guy he was supposed to be working for up here is leaving next week. And there's a good chance his replacement will be the son of a bitch he used to work for years ago in Chicago."

"That's pretty lousy," I said, sounding almost like I actually gave a damn.

"Yeah. Tell me about it," Bruce groused. And then unexpectedly, he smiled. And it was a halfway decent smile, too. "Okay, maybe I did overreact. But that still doesn't mean you couldn't have called."

"Or that you couldn't be a little more pleasant to somebody you don't even know," I shot back.

"Touché."

I was a little more kindly disposed toward the man after that. Just a little, though. While it was understandable he would be upset after what he'd just learned, I couldn't bring myself to forgive him for taking his frustrations out on me. And I certainly had no intention of rewarding his disgraceful behavior with any of my witty and sophisticated repartee. So while we were waiting for our dinner I concentrated on the white wine I'd ordered, not even looking at Bruce. Which seemed to be okay with him, since he was now attempting to make his latest gin and tonic disappear.

I expended every effort to avoid glancing at Pat and Burton, too, but sometimes my eyes, almost of their own volition, shifted in their direction. (As, for that matter, did almost every other pair of eyes in the room.) I mean, Pat was putting on quite a show. She was all over the guy—not that he was objecting or anything—alternating between the ear, neck, and mouth areas, all of which she explored with genuine dedication. And she seemed to have sprouted a half dozen more hands, besides. When they weren't caressing Burton's neck or paying homage to his almost nonexistent biceps, they'd drop out of sight and she'd rest them on his knee (At least I kept telling myself it was his knee.) But then when she cooed, "Oo *are* gonna give oor baby a widdle kiss, aren't oo?" I'd had enough. Really enough.

"So," I said turning in desperation to my escort, "is this your first trip to New York?"

* * *

I wouldn't say we chatted warmly for the rest of the evening. All I really learned about the man was that he'd been divorced for years and that he worked for one of the largest brokerage firms in the country. Practically everything else we touched on—whether we were talking books or plays or movies or politics—evolved into a source of disagreement. But now the tension between us was almost exhilarating. The game of one-upmanship we appeared to be engaged in was really keeping me on my toes. I'd give him this: Bruce Simon certainly had a quick mind.

The dinner, when it finally arrived, was delicious. My stomach ache vanished somewhere between the shrimp toast, egg roll and dim sum. While the pineapple duck, moo shoo pork, scallops in black bean sauce and Hong Kong steak succeeded with my head where all of that Extra-Strength Tylenol had failed.

Following the meal, Bruce suggested an after-dinner drink.

"Uh, do you mind if Pat and I cut out now?" a red-faced Burton asked sheepishly. "I have an early meeting tomorrow morning."

Before either of us could reply, Pat said, "Is that okay with you, Dez?"

There was no doubt as to what my answer was supposed to be. And I was extremely relieved at being able to oblige. Now that we were through eating, she'd started to inventory Burton again, and I couldn't bear to watch them anymore. In fact, I couldn't even bear to *not* watch them anymore. "Oh, yes. Absolutely," I assured her wholeheartedly.

Bruce echoed my sentiments. (It seemed we did agree on something.) "You guys take off," he said hastily. "We'll be just fine. Particularly now that they've removed all the sharp knives from the table."

We sat there sipping our liqueurs for about a half hour, during which time I had to admit to myself that there was something attractive about the man. In a way, anyhow. Although he didn't appeal to me, personally.

When we left the restaurant it was no longer raining, so there were available cabs all over the place. Bruce stunned me by insisting on seeing me to my building and then upstairs.

"Well, it was an interesting evening," he remarked at my door. "Maybe if I really crave female companionship when I get settled up here, I'll give you a call," he kidded.

"And maybe if I lose my memory—or my mind—I'll go out with you again," I retorted. Not quite sure if I was kidding or not.

Chapter 39

The next morning, I'd just finished brushing my teeth and was thinking—and not altogether unpleasant thoughts, either—about last night when the downstairs buzzer sounded. Startled, I ran to the intercom. "Yes?" I said into the white wall phone.

"Mrs. Shapiro?" a deep voice inquired.

A second "Yes?"

"This is Mrs. Corwin's chauffeur."

"Nicholas?"

"No, it's Karl, Mrs. *Evelyn* Corwin's chauffeur. She asked me to deliver something to you."

Now, what could this be about? Pressing the button to admit him to the building, I peered over my shoulder at the living room clock. It was ten after seven.

A few minutes later, a uniformed chauffeur was on my threshold, a small cream-colored envelope in his outstretched hand The man was vaguely familiar. Then I remembered. He'd brought Mrs. Corwin to my office that very first day. God! It seemed like a century ago!

I was so curious about the envelope that as soon as Karl turned away, I ripped it open, unfolding five or six cream-colored sheets of paper. When I did, a check fluttered to the floor. I picked it up; I'd have a look at it in a second. Then closing the door behind me, I began to read.

It was a letter written on Mrs. Corwin's personal stationery. There was a date in the upper right-hand corner: "Wednesday, 3:00 P.M." It took only two sentences for my knees to buckle. I made for the nearest chair and sank into it, heart pounding.

"Dear Desiree," I had read, "I've asked Karl to deliver this to you at seven a.m. on Thursday. And since

I always come in to breakfast about eight, you will undoubtedly be the first to learn of my death."

I sat there stunned. It seemed like a very long while
before I could bear to look down at those cream-colored
sheets again. But eventually, mouth dry and hands moist
and shaking, I forced myself to get back to them—and
to Evelyn Corwin's staggering words.

This morning, after our talk, I invited Saundra
King to have dinner at my home tonight—ostensi-
bly to discuss her relationship with Barrie. She very
graciously accepted. And so in just a few hours I
will be putting into motion a plan that, hopefully,
will lead to her conviction for murder—albeit *my*
murder.

I want you to understand just how I expect to
do this, because it's possible I may need your help.
I pray, Desiree, that I can rely on you again, this
one final time.

Here is how I've worked it out.

Mrs. King and I will be having a fairly amicable
discussion over our meal. But once the main
course is over, I will complain of feeling chilly and
ask if she would mind getting a sweater for me
from my bedroom—which is on the second floor.
The moment she leaves the table, I'll ring for Frances to come in and clear away the dishes, and I'll
mention that Mrs. King went to the powder room
and has been gone for quite some time. I'll say
that I wonder what could possibly be keeping her.
(This is important, as you'll soon see.)

Now, I've already informed the household—
Frances, Stella, my cook, and Karl—that after dinner they have the rest of the evening off. I'll wait
until they've left the apartment, then claim that
I'm not feeling very well and that I'd appreciate
Mrs. King's helping me to my room. I can't conceive of any reason she'd refuse, can you?

Once upstairs, I'll lie down on the bed and have
her bring me my medication, following which I will
"accidentally" spill all six of the capsules. She—

being the kind and thoughtful person we both know her to be—will, naturally, retrieve them for me. I'll pretend to check my watch then, and I'll say that it's not quite time for me to take them but that she can just leave the bottle on the bed table. At this point I will also tell her that I'm really not up to talking anymore and, apologizing profusely, will request that she let herself out.

As you may have guessed by now, I've done a little substituting here, replacing the medication prescribed for me with something a bit more lethal—cyanide, to be specific. So after making certain that Mrs. King is out of the house, I will wipe her fingerprints from the pill bottle just as she would have done if she actually *had* tampered with the medication. And then I'll remove two of the capsules, get myself a glass of water, and swallow the damn things. According to my research, death will come in a matter of minutes.

Desiree, I understand that there are often—but not always—telltale signs with cyanide poisoning. I would expect there to be an autopsy, but if the medical examiner—or whoever it is who decides these things—should rush to the judgment that this is unnecessary and that I died a natural death, I am counting on you to see to it some member of my family insists an autopsy be performed. In that case, the cyanide will easily be detected. Moreover, suspicion should fall on Mrs. King, known to be the last person to see me alive. And you can help matters along by suggesting the police check the remaining capsules for fingerprints—assuming they fail to do so on their own (which would hardly surprise me). This, of course, would also derail any question of suicide. And here's where that business with Frances comes in. She'll attest to my dinner guest's having been gone from the table for an extended period, providing ample time to doctor the capsules.

Regarding motive, I believe that Barrie will enlighten the authorities as to Mrs. King's concerns about my discovering the true nature of their relationship. But if for some reason my granddaughter neglects to supply this information, I trust I can leave that, too, to you.

I suppose that's about it. I really think I've done a pretty professional job in plotting all of this out, don't you? In fact, I think I'd probably have made a very good P.I. myself—or maybe a master criminal. I'm not quite sure which.

Oh, just a couple of other things.

I don't want you to think I'm taking this action because I don't trust you to find a way to bring Catherine's killer to justice. On the contrary, I have the greatest faith that you would have eventually seen to it that Mrs. King paid for the terrible thing she did. But this gives me the opportunity to bring her down myself. And that's a tremendously satisfying feeling.

And please don't view this as heroic on my part. I am suffering from a terminal illness that would soon have become both very painful and extremely debilitating. By swallowing these two small capsules, I am sparing myself that pain and leaving the world under my own steam—and with dignity.

Again, Desiree, I beg you to help if the need should arise. But in any event, I am confident you will not betray this confidence.

With my best wishes always,

Evelyn Corwin

P.S. I have enclosed what I hope you will consider a generous check. Please know that it has nothing to do with this request. Consider it a thank-you for the incalculable service you have already rendered to me and to my poor sweet Catherine.

Chapter 40

At this mention of the check, I became aware that I was still gripping it in my fist. Without so much as a glance, I placed it on the table next to my chair.

I can't really explain how I felt just then. It was as if I were in a daze. I was even too numb to cry.

Mrs. Corwin—*Call me Evelyn, she'd instructed the last time I ever spoke to her*—didn't have to worry; I'd see to that.

Clutching the letter to my chest, I got to my feet and walked into the kitchen. I emptied this huge, ugly ashtray I keep on the counter as a receptacle for odds and ends like paper clips and rubber bands and quarters for the washing machine. I replaced these things with the cream-colored sheets. Then rummaging around in the drawer, I located my box of safety matches.

Seconds later, I put a flame to the only evidence that stood between Saundra King and what I fervently hoped would be a lifetime behind bars.

With a terrible sadness I watched Evelyn Corwin's words turn to ashes. And then for a long time I just stared, unseeing, at the charred black residue.

I knew—as Evelyn had known, in spite of her protestations to the contrary—that she'd taken the only course possible to assure that her granddaughter's killer did not go unpunished. And I knew that with her suicide she had escaped weeks, maybe months, of suffering. Still, that didn't prevent the lump from forming in my throat or keep my eyes from burning with the tears that were not yet prepared to flow.

I looked at the clock. Eight-twenty. *I always come in to breakfast about eight,* she had written. *But not today,* I said silently, *and not ever again.*

But I couldn't be sure of that, could I? Something might have gone wrong.

I went to the phone, not even able to complete the call on my first try, my fingers were trembling so. I dialed again. When the ringing began, I held my breath. Did I want her to be there—alive and as feisty as ever?

I didn't know. I still don't.

At the sound of Frances's voice, the lump in my throat seemed to grow to epic proportions, and my lips felt as if they'd been glued together. Somehow, though, I managed to say the words: "Mrs. Corwin, please. Desiree Shapiro calling."

"I was just on my way to wake her, Mrs. Shapiro. She must have overslept this morning. . . ."

Here's a preview
of the next exciting
Desiree Shapiro novel,
*Murder Can Wreck
Your Reunion*

"A *what*?"

"A *divorce* party," my niece repeated. "Sybil's divorce became final a few weeks ago—you remember Sybil, my friend from college, don't you?"

"I never met her, but she sounds familiar. I think I remember hearing about her."

"That's what I meant. Anyhow, she's throwing this big bash over the weekend to celebrate her divorce."

"How very nineties of her," I remarked sarcastically.

"Oh, come on, Aunt Dez," the voice on the other end of the wire coaxed. While not exactly accusing me of getting stuck in some kind of time warp or even—God forbid—of not being "with it," Ellen's patronizing tone made it fairly obvious she was thinking along those lines.

Of course, some divorces really are cause for celebration. But as for actually serving as a reason to throw a party, well, that's a bit too *now* for my taste. I told Ellen as much.

"It's a lot better than sitting around and feeling sorry for yourself," she countered.

I conceded that maybe it was. But grudgingly.

"Anyway, I mentioned the party to you before."

"Not a word," I contradicted.

"Oh, I thought I did. Four of us have been invited for the weekend," she chirped. "We'll all go out on Friday and stay over until Sunday. The real festivities aren't until Saturday night, but Sybil lives in this wonderful house in Clear Cove—you know, out on Long Island—"

"I *know* where Clear Cove is," I broke in, just to remind her that I wasn't born yesterday (although, come to think of it, she'd certainly made it clear she was aware of that fact).

Ellen went on unperturbed. "Yes, well, she has this charming old house with a swimming pool and tennis courts and everything—it's really gracious living, Aunt Dez. A bunch of us used to spend weekends there during summer vacation. You remember that, don't you?"

"I'm not senile!" I shot back mean-spiritedly.

I guess I should explain that I was in a lousy mood before Ellen even called. And it wasn't because I'd had a bad day at work—which I hadn't. Or because I'd just gotten my period—which I had. The reason I was behaving like such a class A witch was that I'd returned home only minutes earlier from a Bloomingdale's white sale. And let me tell you, if you're in the market for a truly unnerving experience, I can recommend a Bloomingdale's white sale. What made things even worse, though, was that after doing battle with practically every ambulatory female in Manhattan, all I had to show for my considerable efforts was one crummy fingertip towel, one broken fingernail, and two very sore feet. But of course I had no business taking things out on Ellen.

"You were even getting together out in Clear Cove after you graduated—you and your friends—weren't you?" I asked in a more cordial tone.

"Only once. Sybil got married after her junior year in college, so then we started meeting for lunch in the city every so often instead—you know, whoever could make it. I'm really looking forward to going out there again; I used to absolutely adore that place."

"Can Mike get away for the weekend?" I asked,

Mike being Ellen's (the way I liked to look at it) almost-husband—or at the very least, almost-fiancé. He was doing his residency at one of the local hospitals, and I didn't remember him ever having the luxury of an entire weekend off. (Of course, in the not too distant future they'd have to let him take a lot more time than a weekend. Two weeks would be just right for a honeymoon in Paris or maybe for a romantic Caribbean cruise—I was flexible.)

"No, Mike's on duty," Ellen informed me. "But men—even husbands—aren't included, anyway. Not to spend the weekend, that is. They've just been invited to the party on Saturday night. I think the whole town's been invited to *that*."

"But you're going out on Friday?"

"Uh-huh, I'm leaving the store early, so I can catch the five-thirty train" ("the store" being Macy's, where only recently they'd acquired the good sense to promote Ellen from an assistant buyer to a full-fledged buyer). "Sybil said she'd have someone pick me up at the station. I'm just *thrilled* about seeing everyone again, Aunt Dez." Then abruptly, the animation left her voice and she murmured, "I wish Mike could get away and come to the party, though. I feel a little funny about going off like that while he's so hard at work."

"It's only for a couple of days, for heaven's sake. And it's not as if he'd be able to spend any time with you if you stayed in the city. So don't be silly; just go and enjoy your friends." And then I gushed, "I'm sure you'll have a wonderful time."

Of all the dumb platitudes! I wasn't sure of any such thing, and I had no business saying I was.

But in my own defense, there was no way I could have anticipated that thanks to this harmless little get-together, my one niece would wind up a murder suspect.

And a premier suspect, at that.